undeniably yours

Heather Webber

This is a work of fiction. All of the names, characters, locations, organizations, and events portrayed in this novel are either the products of the author's imagination or are used fictitiously and are not construed to be real.

Copyright © 2014 Heather Webber
All rights reserved.
ISBN: 1500235830
ISBN-13: 978-1500235833
www.heatherwebber.com

Cover art: Nausika Georgakopoulou [BlackCatDesign]

All rights reserved. No part of this book may be reproduced or transmitted in any form whatsoever, except for brief quotations used in articles or reviews, without permission from the publisher.

DEDICATION

For my family with much love.

ACKNOWLEDGMENTS

It's an amazing feeling when friends and family take time out of their very busy schedules to *volunteer* to read a manuscript, offer comments, corrections, and encouragement. Thank you, Dad (Charlie), Lori, Shelly, and Meredith for all your help whipping this book into shape.

Thanks, copyeditor Cyndy, for your eagle eyes. Any lingering mistakes are all mine.

A shout-out to Nausika at BlackCatDesign for her wonderful cover design.

And a very big thank you to my readers for continuing to inspire me to write more of Lucy's stories.

1

It took a lot to shock the hell out of me.

Over the years I'd developed a high tolerance to life's little surprises thanks to my big dysfunctional (yet loving) family, well-meaning friends, and hot as hell (ha!—recently almost literally *on fire*) boyfriend whose heart tended to give out on a moment's notice. And, of course, there was my work as a psychic. It was my job at Lost Loves, a division of my family's matchmaking business Valentine, Inc., to use my supernatural abilities to reunite couples who'd been separated by time or distance and everything in between. I also helped find missing persons as a consultant for the Massachusetts State Police. Those both tended to be served with a side of eyebrow-raising bizarro, especially the latter.

I'd become accustomed to dealing with crazy people, both the harmless kind and the psychotic variety. I associated with looney tunes on a regular basis. I'd fought off sociopaths. I thought I'd heard it all, seen it all, and experienced more than my fair share of life's sneak attacks (some good, some bad).

But as I stood in the doorway of my cottage on that Sunday morning in early June, the birds chirping as though nothing earth-shattering had just been revealed, I stared at the man standing before me. I'd been stunned silent by the words Detective Lieutenant Aiden Holliday had spoken.

"Can we come in, Lucy?" he finally asked.

He didn't wait for my answer. Brushing past me, he carried inside the little girl he'd just declared to be his daughter.

His *daughter*.

It felt like I'd been pitched into a blind drop on a steep rollercoaster and was now suspended mid-air, gripping the safety bar for dear life, my mouth open in a silent scream.

"I—" Snapping my mouth closed, I stared and shook my head.

Sure, there were many times in my life I'd been rendered completely speechless. My parents, for example, had the ability to quiet me with only a glance. PI Sean Donahue's kisses could shut me up fairly quickly. My grandmother Dovie's nutty behavior often made me bite my tongue. I supposed speechlessness was simply a byproduct of my crazy life, but Aiden's bombshell had me really struggling for something to say.

There just weren't words.

Thoreau, Sean's Yorkie, danced around Aiden's feet as he headed for the sofa, and Ebbie, a fluffy black cat with vibrant green eyes, ran for the bedroom, squeezing her small body through the narrow opening created by the slightly ajar door. I figured she assumed there was safety in numbers. Sean and Grendel, my three-legged Maine coon, were in there sleeping. She was learning fast. As a new addition to the household, she was still adjusting to things around here.

Using a pair of crutches, I hobbled over to a chair, my big orthopedic boot unwieldy and heavy. I'd recently broken my foot chasing after a purse snatcher (long complicated story). As I passed a mirror, I nearly did a double take at my humorous reflection. My long dark-blond hair could currently be described as finger-in-a-light-socket frizzy rather than curly. My golden-brown eyes were wide and unblinking like some sort of fixated owl. Overall, the surprised look on my face could spark a viral Internet meme it was so comical.

Tugging down the hem of my summer robe, I set my crutches aside, and sat in my favorite swivel rocking chair. I couldn't stop staring at Aiden and the little girl in his arms.

As surprises went, this was a particularly adorable one. Appearing to be about eighteen months old, she had big blue eyes and short light-blond hair so fine that it looked like silk. Something dried stuck to her plump rosy cheek (cookie residue maybe?), and salty grit had gathered at the corner of her eyelid. Stubby, chubby legs were clad in a pair of denim shorts. A pink tank top and a pair of tiny white sandals completed her outfit. Itty bitty toenails had been painted with a bright pink polish, the color chipped along the edges.

Blinking at me, she clung to Aiden's neck even tighter, like a koala to a tree. She appeared completely bewildered. Shell-shocked. It was no wonder.

Apparently, the little girl's mother was missing. And Aiden had just asked for my help in finding her.

I'd met Aiden Holliday last year on a search for a missing little boy. He'd become my boss at the state police not long after, and now he was engaged to one of my best friends, Em Baumbach.

I thought I'd known everything about him.

But I hadn't known this, and I didn't think Em had any idea either.

A daughter. Holy shitballs.

"I—you..." Nope. Still couldn't form a sentence.

"I know," he said. "I know. I'm still thrown myself, Lucy. I...I didn't know she existed until a few days ago when her mother dropped her off at my place."

Dropped her off? Why?

Pressing my hands to my face, my thoughts raced. Aiden had been MIA for the past few days, causing more stress to Em than he could ever imagine. She'd even resorted to spying on him to see if he'd been cheating.

He hadn't been.

But he had been keeping a secret. A tiny, beautiful one.

"Who?" I managed to say.

"Her mother?"

I nodded.

Dropping the backpack he had slung over one shoulder onto the floor, he let out a deep breath. "Kira Fitzpatrick."

Was he serious? "The TV reporter Kira Fitzpatrick?"

Ah. There. That was better. A full sentence at last. Kind of.

Thoreau's little tail wiggled as he happily sniffed the pack, top to bottom as Aiden said, "We dated for a while a couple of years ago. Met while she was doing an investigative piece on one of my cases." He tried to extricate the little girl's arms from around his neck, but she resisted, and he didn't force it. She blinked up at him, and he smoothed a hand over her hair, soothing her.

My heart melted right then and there, pooling into a sentimental puddle near my booted foot.

"Our relationship was nothing terribly serious. We were both so busy." Looking troubled, he studied his daughter's face. "Kira didn't tell me..."

"What happened?" I asked. "I mean...why do you have her now?"

Summer sunlight streamed through the bank of windows facing the ocean, scattering sunbeams across my wooden floors. Temperatures would skyrocket later, but for now, the windows were open, letting in the breeze and the salty sea air. The crashing symphony of waves played against the cliffs.

My little house was located on Dovie's expansive estate in Cohasset, on the south shore of Massachusetts, atop a high bluff overlooking the Atlantic. Her place, named Aerie, was a sprawling stunning home full of classic New England charm and her eclectic whimsy. My place started out as an artist's cottage, then was renovated into a guest house, and now was…mine. It was a fraction of the size of Dovie's, but I loved every inch of it.

Curtain sheers fluttered as Aiden said, "She knocked on my door Thursday night just after dark."

Thursday night. Three nights ago.

He went on, his pale blue eyes widening as he spoke. "There was a wild look in her eyes as she handed me a car seat with the baby still strapped in and then went about tossing a couple of duffel bags into the foyer."

"Wild as in drugs or alcohol?"

"No, Lucy. Wild as in…pissed as hell, but I saw a little bit of fear there, too."

Kira Fitzpatrick was well-known for being fearless. She was relentless when pursuing a story, and wasn't above breaking a few rules. "What did she say?"

"She said that she had something to do and would be back as soon as she could. She also told me to keep the baby safe at all costs."

"That's it?"

"That's it. She kissed the baby, turned, and ran. I didn't

even know the baby's name until I found her birth certificate in a packet of paperwork in one of the bags. Ava Holliday Fitzpatrick."

"Pretty," I said.

Numbly, he bobbed his head in agreement.

Ava, I noticed, had loosened her grip on his neck and was watching Thoreau with curiosity.

"I don't even know if she's really mine," he said softly. "I mean, I'm listed as her father on the birth certificate, but..."

"Oh, she's undeniably yours. Look at those eyes and that chin. Hell, I'm surprised she's not holding a Tic Tac box," I said, referring to his addiction to the little mints. I held out my hands. "Give her to me."

Suspicion clouded his features. "Why?"

"Because," I said, "you look like you need a stiff drink or a really long nap. When's the last time you slept?"

The corners of his eyes wrinkled as he squinted, trying to recall. "Two, no, three days ago."

"Hand her over."

He didn't.

"What?" I asked, insulted. "I'm inoculated."

"What do you know about babies?"

"I know babies," I insisted. "Remember I once worked in a daycare?" I'd been fired from that job, but this probably wasn't the best time to regale him with that particular story. Again, I reached over the coffee table and held out my hands.

Reluctantly, he unhooked the girl's arms from around his neck and handed her over. Ava stared at me as though I had ten heads, but she settled against my chest fairly quickly. She was warm and soft and cozy in my arms. I held on tight as Aiden went into the kitchen and took the bottle of whiskey from the cabinet. It was only a little past seven in the morning, but I wasn't one to judge him right now. He found a glass and poured.

"We should call Em," I said.

"Not yet."

"Right now."

"No. She'll freak the hell out."

It was true. She would. "We still need to tell her. She's been worried sick about you." I left out the part where she'd stalked him out of concern. He probably wouldn't find it too amusing.

He downed the whiskey in one neat shot, then poured another, capped the bottle, and put it away. He was never one to do anything in excess—even therapeutically.

"Plus, she has exams this week," he said. "She needs to focus on studying."

She did have exams for her summer classes, but... "I think she'd agree this takes precedence."

"I don't know, Lucy."

Thoreau put his paws on the edge of my chair, and Ava giggled at him, reaching for his head. His tail wiggled as he licked her hand.

"*Scow, scow, scow,*" she said, suddenly leaning so far forward that she almost toppled off my lap.

I quickly grabbed her, holding tightly. I was glad Aiden hadn't seen that little display or else I'd be banned from holding her ever again. "You have to tell Em. Let her decide what's most important to her."

"Give me a day. Two." Coming back to the sofa, he rubbed bloodshot eyes and took a sip of his drink. "I can't deal right now."

I'd seen him like this a time or two before while working on cases, when he was so involved in his investigation that he lost himself and forgot simple human basics like showering.

His usual blond crew-cut had grown out a bit and now stuck up every-which-way. Slightly reddish stubble covered his strong jaw. His clothes were stained and wrinkled.

Normally Aiden was in complete control. This man…was spiraling out of it.

"I understand not being able to deal," I said. "I've had my fair share of curveballs lately, but this is Em we're talking about."

The scent of Johnson's baby shampoo wafted up, and I greedily sucked it in. There was little I loved more than babies—my grandmother would be beside herself if she knew exactly how much. She'd been nagging Sean and me to get busy having kids so she'd have a great-grandchild, but now that my brother had that situation covered, I was hopefully off the hook for a while. Sean and I had a lot to work out before we moved on to the baby phase. Marriage first would be nice. Hell, an engagement even.

Dragging a hand down his face, Aiden said, "I heard how you were almost roasted like a campfire marshmallow."

"Thanks for bringing that up." The scent of smoke still lingered in my nostrils. It had been only two days since the fiery showdown.

The tiniest of smiles quirked the corner of his mouth. "How's Sean?"

"Lucky. A concussion. Lots of stitches. He's been ordered to bed rest for the week."

"I'm sorry I wasn't around," he said darkly.

We'd been through a lot, Aiden and I. There had been more sad endings than happy with the cases we investigated. And there had been many times he'd protected me from the evil that seemed to permeate our line of work. It *had* been unusual not having him around.

"It's okay," I said. "You taught me well, and I found help in the strangest places." I explained about the Diviner Whiners, the group of misfit psychics I belonged to. The name had been coined by reporter Preston Bailey, who'd once been my nemesis but was now a friend...and would soon be family. She was engaged to my brother and expecting their baby. So far, the pregnancy had been extremely dangerous. She and the baby had almost died, but both were holding steady now.

"I missed a lot," he said.

"You were busy." I fluffed a ruffle on Ava's shirt.

"I'm glad you and Sean are both okay."

"Thanks," I said quickly, not wanting to talk about my recent brush with death thanks to a demented arsonist. The wounds, the ones below the surface, were still too fresh. After all, it had only been a couple of days since the terror had ended. "Yeah, well, I'm getting used to playing with fire. You, however, are going to get burned badly if you don't talk to Em. If she finds out about Ava from someone else..."

"Lucy," he warned.

He didn't scare me. "Aiden."

"I need some time to focus on finding Kira for a few days."

"You're being a stubborn ass."

Pain flashed in his eyes, making him wince. "Ouch."

"Sorry, but you are. Either you love Em enough to tell her about this right now, or you shouldn't be engaged to her. It's really that simple."

He leaned forward, placing his elbows on his knees and his head in his hands. "I'll tell her."

"Good. Now, what do you know about Kira's disappearance?"

"Not much, honestly. The night she dropped Ava off, I expected her to come back in a few hours. When she didn't I figured she meant she'd be back the next day. No show. I made a few calls. In the last couple days, I've done a little digging, using up some old favors. Kira isn't at home, hasn't been to work, and as of Saturday morning no one had officially filed a missing persons report."

"Why don't you do it?"

His jaw clenched. "Ava."

Realization dawned, and I wrapped the girl's hand around my fingers. "You're scared."

"Kira was worried about Ava's safety the night she dropped her off. I need to be careful. I don't want to put Ava in any more danger than she may already be in."

I closed my arms around the girl, hugging her even closer to my body. Who on earth could hurt such a sweet little thing? But I didn't really have to ask the question. I knew all about the monsters that roamed around, looking like perfectly normal people on the surface, but who hid their evil with phony smiles and false pretenses.

"It's been too long," he said. "Kira should have returned by now. It's time I turned my full attention to figuring out what's going on. And, as I said, I'd like your help."

I didn't hesitate. "You have it." I'd have to postpone a reading I scheduled later today, but other than that, I was free.

Aiden was right—Kira should have resurfaced by now.

Something was wrong.

Very wrong.

In missing persons cases, the first forty-eight hours were critical for recovery. We were already past that by ten hours.

As I glanced down at Ava, I hoped that time hadn't already run out for Kira.

2

"I have two leads to start with." Finishing off the rest of his drink, Aiden set the tumbler on the coffee table. He drew his right ankle up to rest on his left knee, leaned back against the plump cushion, and dragged a hand down his face as though that could erase the tension etched around his eyes, his mouth.

It couldn't.

Ava wiggled in my arms, and I slowly lowered her to the ground. With one hand she held on to the coffee table, and with the other she reached stubby, eager fingers toward Thoreau, who was more than happy to play.

"*Scow!*" she squealed, her voice high and filled with utter delight.

I loved the natural happiness and curiosity of babies. True innocence. And I absolutely hated with every fiber of my being the people who stole that purity from them.

"What's she saying?" I asked. Amused, I wondered if she thought Thoreau was a cow.

"I don't know." He fought off a yawn, barely winning the battle. "She only talks a little bit. Basic words like mama, juice, up, down. But she's always jabbering, stringing syllables together. The only time she really cries is at bedtime. Missing Kira, I imagine, and missing normal routines."

"It's been quite an upheaval for her." I didn't say it, but he had been a stranger to this little girl. She had to be completely confused.

"I know, Lucy. I know."

Birdsong floated through the open windows as I struggled to recall all I knew about Kira. I could easily picture what she looked like with her chin-length auburn hair that she always styled in loose curls, her inquisitive no-nonsense hazel eyes, her high cheekbones, and full lips slicked with nothing but sheer gloss. Mid-thirties, medium height, nice teeth, and a go-get-'em attitude. But other than appearances, I didn't know much. "What are your leads?"

"One is Kira's producer at Channel 3, and the other is a neighbor she was reportedly close with, Morgan Creighton." He kept a watchful gaze on Ava as she tentatively investigated her new surroundings. Her steps were wobbly but taken with wild abandon.

I stretched my aching leg, adjusted my robe, and tried to figure out what direction to take with this case. "Do you know if Kira was currently working on a story?"

"No idea," he answered, "but it's a good place to start.

She was serious about her job and not exactly known for fluff pieces."

Kira Fitzpatrick was one of the best investigative reporters around. Having burned more than one bridge, it was possible she was hiding from one of her many enemies. It was easier to hide one person than two, which might explain dropping Ava with Aiden.

"I need to report her missing," Aiden said softly. "It's the only way I can truly get this case rolling. I'll be able to get the subpoenas I need to access her bank accounts, her phone records."

It would be nice to know if she'd withdrawn any large amounts of money recently, or used her credit or debit cards. Phone records would be invaluable, not only to pinpoint whom she'd last spoken to, but to also build a timeline. Both were excellent places to start and would tell us a lot, including possible locations to search.

"But I have to keep Ava safe. Kira was extremely worried for Ava's safety. I can't help but conclude that Ava is at risk from whatever—or whomever—had Kira agitated."

I watched the little girl wander over to the bassinet Dovie had dropped off a week ago, another one of her strong-armed hints for Sean and me to procreate as soon as humanly possible. Ebbie and Grendel had taken a liking to the bed and were going to be sorely upset when Dovie repossessed it to give to Preston and my brother Cutter.

The sea breeze tussled Ava's hair, making the short fine strands stand on end as she continued to explore. "What do you plan on doing with Ava while we investigate?" She couldn't possibly go with us.

Clasping his hands, he leaned forward. "I don't know what to do. I thought about taking her up to my parents' house in Maine, but I don't know who's aware that I'm her father. If someone is desperate to get to her, they might come looking for me, and as an extension...my family. I need a safe house. Somewhere no one would think to look. And I need someone to watch her who I trust. Someone who's good with kids." Looking hopeful, he added, "I was thinking Dovie. She has a condo in New York City, doesn't she? She could take Ava down there..."

She did. And Dovie would probably jump at the chance, but there were two big problems with that. One was Em and the fact that she'd kill him for not picking her. The other was that Dovie was already out of town. "She's gone. Last night, she spirited Preston and Cutter down to her house on Martha's Vineyard for a couple of weeks while Preston recuperates." Dovie had taken away Preston's phone and disconnected the Internet at the summer cottage. "No distractions or worries."

At first, Preston hadn't wanted to go. She didn't know how to unplug, and certainly wasn't used to not operating at full speed. But all it had taken was some gentle prodding by Cutter, and the full effect of his puppy-dog eyes, and she was packing her bags.

She'd taken some time off from her job as a columnist at the *Mad Blotter*, and fortunately, she wasn't taking summer classes as she worked to earn a degree in journalism. Knowing Preston, though, she was probably itching to get back to writing. She had enough material on the recent arsonist case to fill several stories.

I was glad they were out of town. If Preston knew about Ava and Kira... She wouldn't be able to keep out of the investigation. That was the last thing she needed right now. She needed to focus on healing.

I had to make sure she didn't find out. Dovie, too, because she couldn't keep this secret—it was too big. I was going to have to call Cutter and enlist him in my efforts.

Aiden shook his head in dismay.

I shifted on my seat, drawing my good leg up beneath me. "What about Em? She fits all your criteria. And she has the added perk of being a pediatrician." Well, a former pediatrician. Taking care of sick children all day had taken an emotional toll on her, so after much deliberation she left her job to go back to school to get her teaching degree. "And, she's still living with Dovie, who has plenty of room for a little one to run around. She even has a nursery done up in anticipation of all the great-grandchildren I'm supposed to produce."

He closed his eyes for a long second. When he reopened them, I saw nothing but anguish. "I...I can't," he whispered.

"Why not?" I was honestly surprised. Em seemed the perfect solution.

"Dovie's house is too close. I can't put Em in danger. It's too risky."

Ah. I should have connected those dots. Aiden was nothing if not protective of those he cared for.

Trying to come up with a solution, I rocked as I watched Ava stomp toward the fluttering curtain sheers. She had a stiff gait, and was top heavy, but she was a speedy little thing. Much faster than I was these days thanks to my broken foot. My gaze settled on my orthopedic boot, and a solution to Aiden's problem popped into my head. It wasn't that long ago that I'd needed a safe house of my own...and had received a little help from an unlikely source. "What if Dovie's house became a safe house?"

"It's not possible," he said.

"Oh, but it is." I smiled. "I know people."

Humor flashed across his features before being chased off by his anxiety. "Who do you know?"

"Rent-a-ninjas."

"Rent-a-what?"

"You don't have to use that disgusted tone. They're not really ninjas, but are a group of highly-trained protection experts who are basically invisible when they're on duty. They spent a good chunk of time here last week while that arsonist was on the loose, so they already know the lay of the land."

One of his eyebrows lifted in skepticism. "Did you find them in the Yellow Pages?"

"No," I said, insulted again. "They came to me through Jeremy Cross."

Aiden stared at his empty tumbler with undisguised longing. "Who?"

Ava giggled as Thoreau ran circles around her legs. "*Scow! Woof, woof!*"

I couldn't help but smile at her. "Jeremy is part of the Diviner Whiners," I explained to Aiden as I watched Ava plop to the floor to play with Thoreau. "Kind of. It's a long story." Jeremy, a former FBI profiler, was an animal communicator with a devastating history of dealing with psychos. He was a man of many secrets, few words, and much angst.

He was also a perfect match for my other best friend, Marisol. They'd had a coffee date yesterday, and I wondered how it had gone—she hadn't called with an update yet. Although her first impression of him hadn't been favorable, auras didn't lie. If both could let down their walls, I knew they would be happy together.

It was a big if.

Be that as it may, Jeremy was a security expert. In fact, Sean and I both owed him our lives—a debt I wasn't sure I could ever repay. Standing, I tightened the sash on my robe and reached for my crutches. "No one is going to make it on this property who doesn't belong here." I slowly made my way to the kitchen, where earlier I'd abandoned my coffee when he rang the doorbell. "It's the perfect solution."

"I don't know, Lucy. I don't know these guys. How am I supposed to trust them with...my daughter?"

The anxiety in his voice nearly broke my heart. He was being torn apart by what he knew he had to do, and what his heart was telling him.

"I do know them," I said, trying to reassure him. I stuck my mug in the microwave. "I trusted them with my life, with Sean's, with Dovie's, with Em's... They didn't let me down. They won't let you down."

He held my gaze. "Highly-trained security experts, you say?"

"Yes."

"They carry weapons?"

"An arsenal."

"All right," he finally said, though he didn't sound happy about it. "Can you make the arrangements?"

He hated turning control over to someone else, but there really wasn't another option. We needed help. The microwave dinged. "Absolutely."

Ava laughed as the curtains billowed into her face. Joyous little shrieks that filled my heart with happiness. Then suddenly, I found myself blinking back tears.

The thought of losing my own mother—not only losing, but not knowing what happened to her—made my chest tighten so much it hurt to breathe. As flighty as my mother might be, she was...my heart.

I'd had a complicated upbringing. My father was a world-renowned matchmaker, the King of Love, thanks to his secret psychic ability to read auras. It was a gift that reportedly came from Cupid himself and had been passed down through the Valentine bloodlines. When I was fourteen a lightning strike zapped my ability right out of me and zapped in the gift of finding lost objects...and also other abilities I was still learning about.

Cupid, reportedly, had also given my family a curse. We couldn't see our own auras, and therefore, our matches were left to chance. So far, not a single Valentine marriage had survived the curse. My parents remained married but in name only. They'd led separate lives for most of my life...and in fact, during that time, my father went and had himself a love child no one knew about until six months ago. Cutter. The general public didn't know about his parentage—at least not yet, but I was sure it would come out eventually.

Recently, my parents had started dating again. I didn't expect it to last much longer, though I had to admit, it was cute seeing them together.

Despite my crazy life with my nutty family, my *psychicness*, and my independent streak, my mother had always been there for me. Through thick and thin, breakups, denouncing my trust fund, and even dead bodies.

I could only imagine the pain of what it would be like if she abruptly disappeared, and I could only hope that other than the obvious upheaval of being dropped off with Aiden, Ava was oblivious to all the grim questions surrounding the disappearance of her mother.

She seemed to be as she giggled while trying to catch the fluttering curtain.

Suddenly, the bedroom door whipped open, and Sean's body filled the opening, peering out with his eyes narrowed. Bare-chested and sleep rumpled, he wore only a pair of drawstring pajama pants and a perplexed expression. Dark stubble covered both his superhero jaw and his cheeks as his milky gray gaze darted from me to Ava to Aiden.

He blinked then refocused on the little girl, who watched him with the curiosity of someone viewing a carnival sideshow freak.

I couldn't exactly blame her. Bruising discolored his face, his head was wrapped in white gauze to cover dozens of stitches, thanks to an unfortunate run-in with a baseball bat. He looked like a cross between a ghoul and a mummy. My gaze went to an old scar on his upper left chest. Beneath it was an implanted defibrillator that kept his heart from stopping any time it pleased.

The man was a mess.

A gorgeous mess.

My gorgeous mess.

In the grand scheme of things, we hadn't been dating that long—only since November. But there had been an instant, undeniable connection. Love at first sight—as sappy as that sounded. It was only with him that I could see visions of the future. When our palms touched it was electric. Literally. Little zaps that revealed what was in store for us. Some good. Some bad. He couldn't see the visions, but he could *feel* them, the emotion. It was unusual. Magic.

His searching gaze finally settled on me. "Where'd she come from? Dovie didn't get her as a housewarming gift, did she?"

I smiled above the rim of my mug. Even though Sean had also recently moved in, unlike Ebbie, he already knew how things worked around here just fine. "Don't go giving her ideas," I said. "That's Ava, Aiden's daughter."

Sean's dark eyebrows snapped downward in confusion. "His what?"

I poured him a mug of coffee and slid it across the breakfast bar. "Daughter."

My Maine coon, Grendel, came striding out of the bedroom. The big orange and white furball was inordinately graceful for a cat with only three legs. Lazily blinking golden eyes he headed toward his food bowl. He was perpetually hungry.

"*Meow! Meow!*" Ava cried, lurching to her feet. She ran full-tilt toward the cat.

The fur rose on Grendel's back. He hissed and practically did a flip to dart back into the bedroom. Ebbie was probably laughing her ass off at him from her spot under the bed.

"*Meow!*" Ava chased after him so quickly that her feet tangled up with each other. With a surprised cry, she pitched forward.

Before I could even squeak out a warning, Sean reached out, caught the girl, and hefted her easily into his arms.

I let out a relieved breath. Aiden, who'd leapt off the couch in those scary seconds, slowly lowered back down. Again, he mournfully eyed his empty glass.

Sean looked between us. "I think my concussion is messing with my hearing." He carried Ava to the breakfast bar. "Because I thought I heard you say this little one was Aiden's daughter."

"Your hearing is fine," I said. "Granted it's the only thing that is right now. Ava belongs to Aiden."

The corner of his mouth lifted in a smug grin. "Ms. Valentine, I thought I proved to you last night that there are other things that work just fine on me."

I drew my lower lip into my mouth to keep from smiling too broadly. "There was that… Slipped my mind."

"Maybe you need a reminder," he said with a hint of promise in his voice.

Warmth swept over me. "Maybe so."

"Hello?" Aiden interrupted. "I'm sitting right here. And don't talk that way in front of my daughter."

Sean's gaze lingered on me for a moment more before Ava captured his full attention. She pointed to his head. "Boo-boo?"

"Yes, pretty girl," he cooed. "Boo-boo."

She made kissy noises, and the smile he gave her stole my heart straight from my chest.

He lowered his head and she pressed a noisy overexaggerated kiss to his forehead. She said something I couldn't make out, and he answered, "Yes, all better. Thank you."

Apparently, Sean was fluent in baby talk. Who knew?

"Down?" she asked.

Ah! That I understood. He set her on the floor, grabbed his mug and mine, and carried them to the living area. Setting them both on the coffee table, he sat in an oversized armchair and kept staring at Ava. Thoreau quickly hopped up next to him. I had no doubt who truly held the key to the little dog's heart. Our shared love for Sean was probably why we got along so well, Thoreau and me.

Fortunately for the cat, Ava gave up her pursuit of Grendel and clambered onto Aiden's lap as he gave Sean a quick run-down on how she'd ended up on his doorstep.

I crutched my way back to my chair and sat, grateful to sit down. My foot ached, but I'd rather eat Grendel's kitty kibble than complain about it. It seemed so trivial when compared to all Sean had gone through. Instead, I put my booted foot on the coffee table, sipped my coffee, and listened as Aiden told Sean of our plans.

"Did you search Kira's house yet?" Sean asked.

Aiden adjusted Ava on his lap. "Not yet. It's on the to-do list."

There was a lot on that list.

"This whole situation could be used as a case of what-not-to-do when a person goes missing," Aiden said. "And technically, I still don't know that Kira *is* missing. But I have a gut feeling that something is wrong. She packed only enough clothes for Ava to cover a day. That's long past. Kira should be back."

Gut instincts, so pure and simple, should always be trusted. And as I watched Ava—bright, happy, and healthy—relax against her father's chest, I had the feeling Aiden was right. Something was terribly wrong for her mother to have failed to return.

"Do you know of any other family?" Sean took a gulp of his coffee and winced as though it had burned his throat. "Maybe Kira's lying low for a few days."

Ava yawned and Aiden stood, holding her close to his chest. She buried her face in his neck, snuggling in. He swayed as he paced, lulling her to sleep. It was obvious that even though the pair had been together for only a couple of days, an attachment had been formed. A close one. They were strangers no more.

Waves crashed in the background as Aiden said, "Kira's dad died when she was young, and her mom died a year or two before I met her. She was an only child. I think she mentioned something about an elderly great-uncle in California, but who knows if he's even still alive."

Kira couldn't possibly have been raising this baby all on her own. Not with her job. "Someone had to be watching Ava while Kira was at work," I said. "That person is another lead, because most likely they have paperwork with emergency contacts, that sort of thing."

Aiden nodded, and I could practically see his thoughts whirling.

Sean said, "It would be nice to have a reference point. Is her disappearance related to a work story? Stalking? A bad relationship? A mental break?"

A stalker. It was something that hadn't yet crossed my mind. In Kira's line of work, it was an unfortunate reality. If that were the case, however, Kira's producer would likely be aware.

Sean set his mug on the coffee table and rubbed Thoreau's ears. "I can check Kira's house while you two go to the TV station."

My anxiety kicked up a notch as I set my foot on the floor. "You're supposed to be on bed rest. Taking it easy. Doctor's orders."

"Lucy," he warned.

"Don't use that tone on me. I almost lost you. You need to do exactly what the doctor said, so you can get better." I'd tried to keep my voice strong, stern even, but emotion cracked it wide open, revealing precisely how scared I'd been. How scared I still *was*.

He'd almost died in a fire at Valentine, Inc.

We'd almost died.

The building had suffered at the hands of the psycho, too, going up in flames. There had been heavy damage to the first floor vestibule and stairway, massive smoke damage to both the second-floor matchmaking offices and the PI agency on the third floor that was leased by Sean's brother, Sam. Fortunately for us all, the building was salvageable. It needed heavy renovations, but soon enough it would be good as new.

In time I hoped we would be, too.

Sean's gaze didn't waver as he studied me, and in that moment I knew he could see the tears that threatened to fall.

Finally, he said, "All right. I'll stay."

"You can help me from here, Sean," Aiden said. With two fingers stuck in her mouth, Ava had fallen asleep in his arms. His gaze slid to me. "That is, if you're allowed to use a laptop."

I rolled my eyes. "Yes, he can use a laptop. Smartass."

Sean smirked from behind the rim of his coffee cup. "You want me to run a full background check?"

"Yeah," Aiden answered. "That and also see what you can turn up on social media. She may have left a clue there, too."

All this speculation had me itching to get started. "When do you want to leave?" I asked Aiden.

"Now," he said. "As soon as you get dressed, and maybe brush your hair. No offense."

My hand went to my bedhead. "No offense," I echoed, "but I think you should be more worried about how *you* look. When was the last time you showered?"

He glanced toward the mirror near the door and winced. "You're probably right."

"Why don't you run home, shower, change, and shave?" I suggested. "After that, stop and file that missing persons report on your way back. And don't forget to talk to Em about taking care of Ava while we investigate. Until then, we can watch her for you while you're gone."

"I don't know about leaving her here," Aiden said. "Where will she sleep? What will she eat?"

"She can sleep on the bed." I stood up, grabbed my empty mug, and crutched into the kitchen for a refill. "We'll wall her in with pillows and cushions. And I have plenty of Twinkies."

He glared.

Laughing, I said, "Calm down. I have a whole box of Cheerios." I found no need to tell him I only had Cheerios on hand as treats for Odysseus. I didn't think he'd find it consoling that his daughter was sharing food with my hamster.

Silently, he kept pacing. His hand gently cupped the back of Ava's head as he made sharp pivots.

Steamy tendrils rose from my mug as I poured coffee. Softly I said, "At some point you're going to have to let Ava out of your sight if you want to find Kira."

After a long minute of silent deliberation, he abruptly stopped pacing. He said, "You'll call the security people?"

"I'll call."

Sean leaned forward and said, "I don't mind watching Ava while you two are out. I babysit my nieces all the time."

"Bed rest," I sing-songed to him. "I don't think chasing after a toddler is how the doctor imagined *taking it easy*."

"No, no," Aiden said, waving off my concerns. "This could work. Your place is small enough to not have to chase her much at all, and Sean's PI training is more likely to keep Ava safe. He probably has a gun here, too."

"Well out of reach of a toddler," Sean added.

I knew exactly what Aiden was doing, and I wasn't letting him get away with it.

I jabbed a finger toward him. "You are not getting out of telling Em. Good try, though. And you," I pointed at Sean, "are supposed to be resting."

What did he not understand about that?

"Lucy," he said softly.

Ugh. Not that tone again.

I tried to stand my ground. "Sean."

Then I made the mistake of looking into his eyes. I clearly saw his desperate need to feel useful. To help. Some of that probably stemmed from old wounds rather than new ones. Not long ago he'd been forced to retire as a firefighter because of the heart condition that nearly killed him while on duty. Being a PI was his second choice, and I couldn't help feeling that if he had the chance, he'd be back in that firehouse in a hot second.

I wanted to argue that recovering from his wounds was more important than feeling needed; but in his case, I wasn't one hundred percent sure he'd agree. And even though he didn't look it, he *was* recovering quickly. He was moving much faster today than yesterday and didn't look to be in near as much pain.

Letting out a defeated sigh, I said, "All right. You can watch her."

Sean said, "I knew you'd come around."

Aiden said, "Good, then we're all—"

He was cut off by the sound of two sharp knocks on the front door. Before any of us could move, it flung open.

Em was speaking even before entering. "Lucy, I saw Aiden's car and—" She abruptly broke off as she spotted Aiden standing there, a baby snuggled in his arms.

Her jaw dropped, then she spun around and went back out the door, slamming it behind her.

Ava's body jerked at the loud noise, but she didn't wake up. Thoreau started barking, and Sean shushed him.

Aiden shot me a look. "I told you she was going to freak—" Once again, he was interrupted by the door flying open.

Em rushed inside, her red hair flying out behind her, and stared at him. Then at me. Then at Sean. Thoreau leaped to the ground and ran over to her, his short tail wiggling happily.

Finally, she said to me, "I thought I might be hallucinating, but Aiden's really standing there holding a little girl that looks exactly like him, isn't he?"

"Yep," I confirmed solemnly. "But you can pinch him if you want. Hard."

He shot me an annoyed look.

In a flash, her distress switched to anger. Color a few shades darker than her hair rapidly infused her cheeks. Oh-so-slowly, her bright blue gaze—made even bluer by a sheen of tears—slid back to Aiden and narrowed dangerously. Her hands fisted tightly. Through clenched teeth she said, "I've been worried out of my mind. You've been missing for days on end. Not returning my texts or calls. Now this…?" She gestured wildly toward Ava. "Aiden Holliday, you have some explaining to do."

3

"You're not calling about the coffee date yesterday are you?" Jeremy Cross asked me a half an hour later. "Because I don't kiss and tell."

Jeremy was as mysterious as a person could be. In fact, Jeremy wasn't even his real name.

It was Jeremiah Norcross.

But he didn't know I knew that.

I sat on my porch swing, looking out over the ocean. It was a bright clear day, and the water looked like a wavy sheet of glass. Several barges floated on the horizon, dark blobs. A seagull swooped low and disappeared over the edge of the cliff. If Ava was going to be around much, we were going to have to make sure she didn't wander near the edge. It was a sheer fifty foot drop to the water, which might be fun for cliff diving, except for having to dodge rocky outcroppings below. There were only a few places safe to jump—and then only at high tide.

Inside the house, I heard Sean trying to get Ava to eat

some scrambled eggs. So far, she was refusing his airplane attempts. He switched to tug boat noises.

Aiden and Em had left for the time being. I wasn't sure exactly what had been said between them. For privacy, they'd gone for a walk. But, as soon as they returned, Em was smiling and announced that she had some shopping to do. Then she would split the time caring for little Ava with Sean (he'd watch her only while Em was studying or at school) until this whole matter was settled.

Before Aiden left to shower and stop by his office, he'd confessed he begged Em for forgiveness, which had been the smartest thing he could have done. He'd been instantly forgiven. If he had any lingering concerns about involving Em he was smart enough to keep them to himself.

"There was kissing?" I asked, hopeful.

"No," Jeremy stated.

"It didn't go well?"

"Did you hear a word I just said?"

Smiling, I could picture him, all tall, dark, and brooding. His grass-green eyes narrowed in annoyance. For some reason, irritating him amused me.

"No second date?" I pressed.

There was silence.

Fine. He could be that way. I'd just get the goods from Marisol later. "I wasn't calling about the date."

"I'm listening."

After playing a role in Sean's and my rescues from the arsonist, Jeremy had admitted ties to the FBI. He had to say something seeing as how he'd "borrowed" an FBI helicopter. But that was all he'd said. Not that he'd once been a profiler...or still might be. Not about having an alias. Not about what happened to his family. I'd learned that information on my own, and didn't feel the need to blab it. I hoped, as our friendship grew, that eventually he'd tell me everything.

"I need a favor," I said.

"You're high maintenance, you know that?"

"Yeah, well, you're grouchy."

He laughed. "What do you need?"

When it came down to it, we psychics stuck together.

Well, mostly. I shuddered at memories from the past week.

I gave myself a good mental shake. "The security team to come back."

There was another stretch of silence before he said, "What have you gotten yourself into this time?"

I wished I knew, but until I did, I had to prepare myself for the worst.

Later that afternoon, Aiden held open the door of the Channel 3 studios, an eight-story building located on always-busy Mass Ave.

Cars honked, T buses rumbled by, and pedestrians rushed past keeping their gazes fixed straight ahead.

The door behind us whooshed closed, blocking out the noise, insulating us against the roar of the street's hustle and bustle. Piped classical music serenely filled the cavernous lobby, bouncing off stately dark wood-paneled walls. As Aiden strode to the reception desk, I watched people zip in and out of the building. With each opening of the door, staccato bursts of city noise mingled with Mozart, creating an interesting harmony.

Frenetic energy swirled in the air. It had been a heavy news week due to the heat wave, the brownout, the fires, and the looters. The city had been through hell and back, but if there was one thing Boston had proven time and again, it was that it could—and would—recover. Stronger than ever.

Since the fires broke out, news coverage had been continuous and, for a Sunday afternoon, this place was hopping. As people hurried past me it felt as though it would be a long time before life around here returned to normal.

I glanced at Aiden and wondered when, or if, his life would ever be normal again. With a ramrod straight back, he waited in a long line for his turn with the receptionist. To a bystander, there was nothing on his face or in his stance that hinted at his impatience, but knowing him well, I could see it clearly. The thin stretched line of his normally relaxed lips, the intensity in his eyes, the way his shoulders looked starched rather than comfortable.

Except for the badge clipped to his belt, and the gun in a hip holster, he looked as though he could be just another executive in his gray suit, baby-blue shirt, and striped tie.

Before coming here, he'd filed the missing persons report on Kira. Subpoenas and search warrants were being sought; the search for her car was on. Our investigation had truly begun. This building was our first stop. We hoped Kira's producer, a woman named Nya Rodriguez, would have some answers for us as to what was going on in Kira's work and personal life when she disappeared.

During the ride here, I'd kept up a mostly one-sided conversation, telling him what he'd missed while holed up with Ava. He showed mild skepticism at Ebbie's arrival into my life; didn't question at all my newfound psychic ability to see scenes through scents (a bizarre mash-up of clairvoyance and clairalience); managed only a small smile during my anecdotes about Boobalicious Annie and ghoulish Dr. Paul of the Diviner Whiners; and appeared extremely troubled at the level of deception orchestrated by the arsonist. Yet Aiden said almost nothing in the hour-long trip into the city.

As he moved up in the reception line, I found myself worrying for him. He was a good man. Honest, decent, hardworking, and caring. I hated seeing him so...derailed. His life had gone off the tracks, and I had the uneasy feeling that he hadn't seen the worst of it yet.

After we were done here, we planned to search Kira's

house and interview her neighbors. It was her home I was most eager to visit. With my new ability to read scents, I should be able to find Kira fairly easily by sniffing an item of hers. A pillow. A blanket. *Something.* Through her scent, I'd be able to see through her eyes—if she were still alive.

At this point, it was a big if.

The towering walls of the Channel 3 lobby were filled with massive photos of its broadcasters, and it didn't take long to find Kira's image among them. Dressed in a sporty black skirt suit, she leaned against an old brick wall, her arms folded across her chest. A flash drive dangled in her hand. She was notorious for keeping all details of her investigations on the techy tool, taking it with her wherever she went, and never letting it out of her sight. The station played up the quirk. It had become something of a gimmick.

A heavy-handed edit had heightened the green coloring of her hazel eyes and added a bit of a mischievous sparkle to her irises. Her head was tilted in an I-dare-you kind of way. Her hair was styled in perfect waves around her shoulders, and her full lips were pressed into what seemed like a smile resulting from a private joke. Printed in big letters at the top of the poster was her name. And at the bottom was her tagline.

UNCOVERING THE TRUTH ON WHAT MATTERS.

"Lucy?" Aiden touched my elbow. "Ready?"

If he'd noticed Kira's photo, he didn't comment on it as he led me to a bank of elevators, slowing his gait to match mine as I crutched along. As the heavy doors slid closed, I couldn't help but feel that Kira's hazel gaze was watching our every move. It was a creepy feeling, and I shuddered.

"Cold?" Aiden jabbed the button for the fifth floor as others joined us, going up.

"A little," I lied. I didn't want to sound like a complete nutter telling him the truth.

As the elevator rose slowly, stopping and starting at each floor, my heart beat a little faster. Sweat dampened my hairline, turned my hands clammy. I was trying my best to breathe normally.

The city wasn't the only thing that had been to hell and back recently. I had been as well.

Yes, my foot would heal, but I was afraid my emotional recovery would take longer than I ever imagined. Because, with each stop of the elevator, the dings of arrival, and the sliding of the doors, more and more anxiety crowded out rational thought.

Inhale, exhale.

It was in an elevator at Valentine, Inc. that I had come face to face with the demented arsonist who'd almost killed Sean and me. There had been a life and death battle. Good versus evil.

Even though I'd ultimately won, it was not without acquiring a few scars, both physical and emotional. Scars so deep I was afraid to fully explore them. Afraid to discover exactly how painful they might be.

81/9 is 9.

Lately I'd been doing so well trying to break my habit of turning to simple math problems in times of stress. It was an idiosyncrasy I'd had since childhood and was proving to be a stubborn trait.

I shouldn't have been the least bit surprised. Valentines were nothing if not stubborn.

As the elevator stopped on the fourth floor, I silently told myself to get a grip. Squishing my eyes closed, I focused on breathing instead of math and bad memories. *In, out. In, out.*

"Lucy?"

I cracked open an eye. Aiden stood in the opening of the elevator, waiting for me by holding the door open with his body.

Feeling silly, I tried to laugh, but it came out as more of a squeak. I quickly crutched into the open, airy hallway and sucked in a lungful of chilly air-conditioned oxygen.

A shiver rippled through me as the elevator doors slid closed behind Aiden. He studied me carefully. "You okay?"

"Yeah, I just..." Biting the inside of my cheek, I struggled with what to say. How to explain. Letting out a windy sigh, I finally said, "Elevators."

Understanding dawned in his red-rimmed eyes. "Sorry. I didn't realize."

"Neither did I." I wiped my clammy hands on my skirt. "It's new."

I could have sworn I heard him mumble "son of a bitch is lucky to be dead" under his breath as he strode over to the reception desk for this floor.

Truthfully, I'd been expecting to see a fully-operational TV news studio when those elevator doors opened, but apparently this floor was solely made up of office space. From this central spot, three corridors branched off, all nondescript in their *beigeness*. There was no piped music and no one around except for the receptionist, who had promised she'd let Nya know we were here. I found the silence unsettling and suddenly missed the chaos of the busy lobby.

Aiden popped a Tic Tac in his mouth, then jammed his fists into his pants pockets and rocked on his heels as we waited. It wasn't long before I spotted a woman hurrying down the carpeted hallway, her dark hair trailing behind her, her high heel strikes silent on the beige carpeting.

Startling white teeth gleamed against beautiful light caramel-colored skin as she approached and said, "Lieutenant Holliday?"

"Yes. Ms. Rodriguez?"

"Nya, please." She shook his hand.

Nya Rodriguez was a beautiful woman. Late thirties to early forties, with high cheekbones, dark intelligent eyes, and ruby-red lips. Her hourglass figure was shown off in a tight-fitting violet wrap dress that hugged her generous curves. She turned her attention to me.

Before I could say a word, Aiden said, "This is my colleague, Lucy Valentine."

Fortunately, she didn't reach out to shake my hand—a perk of the crutches, no doubt. Though the extent of my abilities was still being explored through psychic lessons from my mentor, Orlinda Batista, and the other Diviner Whiners, my primary skill was being able to see lost objects via the energy in someone's palm. When shaking someone's hand I never knew what would be thrown my way.

Nya tipped her head. "Have we met? Your name and face are familiar."

"I don't think so," I said, not elaborating. I had no doubt she'd put it together soon enough. I'd been in the news frequently over the past year. Until then, however, I didn't want to volunteer the answer...and have to face the inevitable questions.

"Hmm," she said, still eyeing me suspiciously.

Aiden saved me from explaining by saying, "Thanks for agreeing to meet us on such short notice."

"I have to admit your call came as quite a surprise," she said. With a jerk of her chin, she motioned for us to follow her down the hallway. "You neglected to tell me what this meeting was about exactly, Lieutenant. Has Kira somehow offended the state police?" She glanced back, a wry smile on her lips. "It wouldn't be the first time."

"No," Aiden said, all business.

She kept a brisk pace, and I struggled to keep up. Aiden

stuck by my side as we passed closed office door after closed office door before finally coming to one that stood open. Nya ushered us inside, and Aiden held a chair out for me while I set my crutches aside.

The windowless office was small, barely big enough for her desk and a few chairs. Two diplomas hung on the wall, an undergrad degree from a college in Florida, the other a Master in Film and Television Studies from Boston University. There were a half-dozen family photos crowding her desk, mostly of a pair of grinning children and a sheepish-looking retriever. Other than those, her desktop was clear, her computer screen off, her trash bin emptied. I'd bet money she had OCD.

Nya closed the door before scooting around her desk and sitting in a leather chair. "Then why are you here?"

Aiden unbuttoned his suit coat and sat next to me, his back stiff and his jaw clenched. Although he'd showered and shaved, he still looked like he hadn't slept in days. His haggard appearance was working for him, though, making him look more formidable. As if the badge and gun weren't enough.

He didn't beat around the bush. "We're actually looking for Ms. Fitzpatrick."

Nya leaned back in her chair, steepled her long fingers, and said, "You and me both. She's not returning my calls. Are you looking to ask her about one of her previous stories? Because I might be able to help you with that. Otherwise…" She shrugged. "I'm afraid you're out of luck. She's not here."

There was a steely undertone to Aiden's voice as he said, "We're investigating her disappearance, Ms. Rodriguez. She's missing."

So much for calling her Nya.

Color drained from her face, leaving her ashen. She leaned forward. "Wait. You're *literally* looking for her? I thought you meant you wanted to *speak* with her. How long has she been gone?"

I saw the instant she went from humoring us to being an interested news veteran.

Aiden said, "A few days. When was the last time you saw her?"

"Thursday afternoon." Her gaze went to a notepad, and I had the feeling she was itching to take notes. "Where's Ava?"

"Safe in police custody." Aiden's jaw clenched, released.

She let out a relieved breath, a hint of humanity. "Thank goodness."

Fidgeting in my seat, I asked, "What time did you last see Kira?" We needed to start piecing together some semblance of a timeline.

"It was around two o'clock."

Her gaze zipped between the two of us, and I could practically see the internal debate being waged within her about how much to reveal.

Finally, she said, "It was right after she was fired. She left the building with nothing but Ava, her purse, and her laptop. I've been calling her practically every hour on the hour since she left. My boss is harping on me to get that computer back as it is company property."

Aiden's eyebrows rose. "Fired? Why?"

Wow. If Kira had been fired, she might have taken it badly and left Ava with Aiden as some sort of temporary situation until she got her head together. It would also explain why she'd been angry. But the more I thought of that scenario, the more I believed it unlikely. Being fired wouldn't have explained her fear for Ava's safety.

Nya let out a small sigh and said, "Official word is that the higher-ups came down hard on Kira for her interoffice romance with Trey Fisher. Using her to set an example, that sort of thing."

I recognized the name. Trey "Fish" Fisher, a former hockey player. He'd started at the station as a freelance sports reporter, but had recently been promoted to a full-time reporter. With thick wavy blond hair, sheepish smile, devilish blue eyes, and bad-boy persona it was no surprise that he ranked as high with the female demographic as he did the male. His egotistical playboy reputation only seemed to make him more popular. Not with me. I had a low tolerance for jerks.

"Was Trey fired as well?" I asked. News like that should have made headlines, as both were extremely popular, but I'd heard no gossip. I had to admit, though, that I—along with the rest of the city—had been a little preoccupied during the past week.

"No," Nya answered. "He received only a warning."

I stretched out my aching leg, wishing I'd taken some ibuprofen before I'd left the house. "A bit of a double standard." An understatement to be sure, but I wasn't ready to go hurling accusations of sexism quite yet.

"Not really." She adjusted the corner of her mouse pad so it was in perfect line with the edge of her desk. "Everyone around here knows it wasn't the real reason Kira was fired."

"No?" Aiden questioned.

Her gaze flicked to the closed door. After a second's hesitation, she said, "Kira was fired for her work on the McDaniel story." She quickly added, "You didn't hear that from me. I need my job."

Pale eyebrows dipped low on Aiden's forehead. "Dustin McDaniel?"

Nya said, "That's right. Kira claimed she was close to cracking his case."

Dustin McDaniel. Two years old. Blond hair. Blue eyes. Exactly how long he'd been missing from his Randolph home remained a mystery. He'd fallen through the cracks at the office of the Norfolk County Children and Families Coalition, commonly known as the CFC. It was a subsidiary of the Department of Children and Families (DCF), the state's go-to agency for protecting children.

His disappearance had finally been reported by his grandmother six weeks ago when she became suspicious about the evasive excuses her daughter gave as to his whereabouts. His father was in prison. His mother had tragically died from a drug overdose a month ago. He was still missing.

I knew all that because he was next on my docket of missing person cases. Aiden and I were to begin our investigation the following week. It seemed fate had stepped up our timing.

"What was Kira's theory?" Aiden asked.

"I wish I knew," Nya said, fussing with a slim watch on her wrist. "Kira never revealed anything to me until she was ready to film. She was a lone wolf, even though it earned her no favors around here. However, it was hard to argue with the ratings she brought in."

"Why would she be fired then?" It didn't make any sense. "I imagine cracking the McDaniel case would bring in blockbuster ratings."

"It would, for certain," Nya said. "But there are some here that didn't want to deal with the cost of those ratings. Since she received an anonymous tip about the case two weeks ago, Kira's been like a dog with a bone. Obsessed is too mild a description. Almost immediately, she began getting pressure from above to drop her investigation. As you probably know, the DCF has recently undergone an internal overhaul to clean up its image after a period of bad press."

The department had been plagued with troubles, mostly from being understaffed. It was one of the reasons why the county branches of the department were added—to help with the overflow of caseloads. The CFC handled low-risk families so the DCF could focus their time and energy on high-risk children. It was a partnership that was proving successful.

"Rumor has it that certain people within the state government were concerned that Kira's investigation would reopen old wounds and undo the recent accomplishments of DCF and CFC."

"Would it have?" Aiden asked.

"Like I said, I don't know for sure." Nya bit her lip, leaving a red lipstick stain on her front teeth. "But my guess is yes. Even though the boy's mother remains the number one suspect in his disappearance, no one is denying that his caseworker, and therefore the CFC, was negligent. But it's never been revealed to what extent. Everyone wants this case to go away. If Kira uncovered something that proves how badly the CFC screwed up, then all hell could break loose because both that agency and the DCF have been bragging about their accomplishments."

"How high up did the pressure go?" Aiden asked.

"High," she said gravely. "I don't know exactly how high, but it has to be way up there for management to behave this way."

Governor? Senators? It would take only one call from someone of that status to put pressure on station sponsors. Although this station was in the business of reporting news, they were also a business intended to make a profit. At the thought of losing money, they would bend to the pressure like a reed caught in a windstorm.

"The computer," I began, "are her notes about the case in it? Is that why your bosses want it back so badly?"

I wondered if I could get a reading on the laptop's location, but I doubted it. In order to do so, I'd need to find who the computer truly belonged to, and in a corporation like this that would be nearly impossible.

"They think so," Nya said, "because they obviously don't pay attention. Kira always kept her information on a flash drive. She didn't trust anyone enough to leave her notes where they could be compromised."

"Then why take the computer with her?" Aiden asked.

"All I can think of is that she hadn't had time to transfer her notes from that morning. Kira had been working on them when she was called into our supervisor's office. Earlier that day she'd met with someone about Dustin's case and was practically vibrating with excitement. She said she was close to cracking the case wide open and it was a shocker. When word reached management, she was called in and given an ultimatum. Either drop the case or she would be let go. She left. And before you ask, no, I don't know who she met with."

"Did she have an electronic calendar? Or paper planner?" Aiden asked.

Nya shook her head. "No. Her appointments were kept on her Blackberry."

Undoubtedly, that phone was still with her wherever she was. I shifted in my seat. "You said she took Ava…is there a daycare in the building?"

"Second floor," Nya said. "Ava's been attending since she was born. On the occasions that Kira had to work late, a neighbor friend picked up and cared for the baby. Morgan something. The baby wasn't left alone, was she?" Her anxious gaze darted between us. "Kira would never have done that willingly."

"Not alone," I said.

"When? Where?" Nya threw another glance at her notepad.

"We can't divulge that information at this time," Aiden said. "We'll need to speak with the daycare staff today," Aiden said. "Could you let them know we're coming?"

"Sure, I'll give them a call."

I refused to look in Aiden's direction as I said, "You mentioned Kira was in a relationship with Trey Fisher. Is he Ava's father?" I knew he wasn't, but I wanted to learn how much Nya knew.

"No," she said. "She was born long before Kira started dating Trey."

"How long have they been a couple?" Aiden asked.

"Not long. Maybe two months? At least publicly." Her eyebrows went up. "Two months ago is when his divorce papers were filed."

Had Kira broken up the marriage? If so, it would be wise of us to talk to Trey's soon-to-be ex-wife. Women scorned were notoriously vengeful.

Aiden couldn't quite hide his wince. "Where can we find Fisher?"

She glanced at the clock. "He's at the Sox game right now, prepping to report from the field for the afternoon game."

Aiden slid his card to her. "Have him get in touch with me."

"Absolutely," she said. "This is unbelievable. Has she been officially reported missing?"

"Yes." Aiden narrowed a stern gaze. "However, we'd appreciate keeping her disappearance off the news for the time being."

"But," she tipped her head, "if it helps locate her..."

Aiden leveled her with a hard glare. "We have to think of Ava's safety right now as well."

After a brief hesitation, she said, "I won't say anything, but I can't make that promise of anyone else."

Aiden didn't look too happy about her statement. Before he lost his temper, I asked, "Did Kira mention anything happening in her life lately that was unusual? Anyone bothering her? That kind of thing?"

"Nothing I can think of. Are you thinking she met with foul play?"

Apparently ready to leave, Aiden stood. "It's too early in the case to make any presumptions."

Suddenly, her head jerked up. "I just thought of something that had been bothering Kira. You might want to check with Danny Beckley in the station's garage.

There was some sort of incident down there with Kira's car a few days ago."

I reached for my crutches. "What kind of incident?"

"A flat tire on Wednesday. Kira was upset by it for some reason." She shrugged. "I didn't think it was that big of a deal. Everyone gets flats, but now, in light of her disappearance…"

"Danny Beckley, you said?" Aiden asked.

She rose to see us out the door, which was completely unnecessary considering the size of her office.

"Yes," she said. "The garage is around the corner on Boylston. You can't miss it."

Aiden gave a sharp nod. "Call me if you think of anything else that might be important."

"I will," she promised. "This is so upsetting."

We said our goodbyes and left her in her office as we headed down the hallway. I had to wonder how upset Nya truly was…versus how much she wanted the scoop on the story.

In my opinion, she'd spoken volumes about her relationship with Kira when she revealed she hadn't thought the incident with Kira's car had been a big deal. If she'd been a true friend, she would have cared simply because Kira had been upset.

Aiden said, "Kira's disappearance will be on the six o'clock news."

"You're being generous," I said. "I was thinking the noon broadcast."

He smiled a humorless smile and glanced at the elevator bay. "Stairs?"

"Yes, please." Navigating steps with crutches was never fun, but it was infinitely better than getting back into that elevator.

As we headed for the daycare on the second floor, all I could think about was Kira's tagline. *Uncovering the truth on what matters.*

The truth.

If there was one thing I knew about the truth it was the great lengths evil would go to keep it hidden...

4

The visit to the daycare had proven rather uneventful. It turned out that the providers hadn't thought anything of it when Kira had collected Ava early on Thursday afternoon and figured Kira had simply forgotten to tell them of upcoming vacation time when the little girl didn't return Friday morning. Not a single employee had noticed any unusual behavior from Kira in the previous weeks, and everyone seemed to genuinely care for the well-being of mother and daughter.

Ava's records revealed no additional leads. There was no father listed for a contact; the medical information was the same as in the folder Kira had left with Aiden; and her emergency contact was Morgan Creighton, the neighbor we already planned to visit.

The daycare employees had repeated that it wasn't unusual for Morgan to pick up Ava on occasion, and with that news, Aiden seemed to pull even farther into himself. I could only imagine the thoughts going through his head.

The emotions. Wondering why Kira had never told him of his daughter. He could have been the one picking her up.

As we exited the Channel 3 studios, heat haze rose from the sidewalk, and I squinted against the bright sunshine.

"You doing okay?" Aiden asked.

"Fine," I said, lying through my teeth. "You?"

He eyed me as though wise to my Pinocchio ways. "Fine."

We were both decent liars.

"Let's interview the garage guy," he said, "then find some lunch before we head to Needham."

Needham. To Kira's house. Where we'd hopefully find some answers—and not more questions.

Lunch sounded like a great idea. My stomach was starting to make gurgling noises so loud they could startle passersby. I should have had something more to eat instead of all that coffee this morning. Refueling would be necessary to finish what was going to undoubtedly be a long, long day.

My phone buzzed. I stepped aside, using the building for balance as I dug around my tote bag to find my cell.

"Preston," I said to Aiden as I answered.

"Bed rest might kill me," she said.

"How are you talking on the phone?" I asked.

"One syllable at a time."

I sighed. "I thought Dovie confiscated your phone."

"I found it," she said. "You're not the only one with locating skills."

I could picture her tucked into bed, her blond hair spiked, her cheeks flushed, and a scowl on her face. "Dovie wants to watch ballroom dancing."

"Fun!" I said, trying to sound like I meant it.

"I might have to fling myself into the ocean."

"It's not that bad."

"I want to come back," Preston said shrilly.

"Think of the baby. You need to rest. To relax. Heal."

She didn't say anything.

"You don't want another visit from Dr. Paul, do you?" I said, pulling out the big guns.

Preston had nicknamed Dr. Paul McDermott, one of the Whiners, Dr. Death. She thought he might be a serial killer. Her stance hadn't softened, even though he'd saved her and the baby's life.

"Fine," she said. "But I'm not happy about it."

She hung up.

I glanced at Aiden. "She's having a great time."

His lip twitched—almost a smile. "Sounds like it."

As we blended into the foot traffic on the sidewalk, the cloying scent of smoke stubbornly clung to the humid air, even though the city's fires had been extinguished. The warm breeze did nothing to dispel the scent, seeming only to spread it around.

What we needed was a good soaking rain to wash away the thin layer of ash that seemed to cover the city like an unwanted smelly topcoat and replace the acrid smoke with normal summery scents around these parts. Wisteria, salty sea air, watermelon...diesel fuel. I'd gladly take even the latter right now.

The television station's private parking garage was only a three-minute walk, but I managed to break a sweat during the trek there, and my skirt was starting to stick to my legs. A young black man sat in a booth lodged between matching swinging gates that allowed vehicles entrance and exit from the surprisingly airy structure. He watched us warily as we approached.

I imagined he didn't get too many walk-up customers.

A box fan on high speed whirred noisily behind him as he leaned out of a narrow window and said, "Can I help you? Need something?"

Aiden flashed his badge. "Are you Danny Beckley?"

"Nope. Over there." He jerked his hand toward a glass-walled office off to one side, tucked neatly into a concrete wall. Fluorescent lights flooded the space, glinting off the bald head of a man staring intently at his computer screen.

"Thanks," Aiden said, then looked back at me as he navigated the curbs and gates to make sure I was managing the obstacle course.

I was, but not without a couple of grunts and choice curse words beneath my breath.

Aiden's sharp knock on the closed steel door lifted Danny Beckley's gaze from the computer monitor. He motioned us inside, and Aiden stepped back to allow me to go in first. Air-conditioned gusts immediately cooled my heated cheeks. It took everything in me to fight the urge to stand in front of the unit with my arms over my head.

Beckley rose and held out his meaty hand to me. "Ms. Rodriguez called down to tell me you were coming. Danny Beckley."

I eyed his hand as warily as his attendant had eyed us only moments ago. Seeing no other option, I balanced my body weight to let go of my crutch. "Lucy Valentine."

As our palms touched, nothing flashed behind my eyes, and I thanked my lucky stars. As Aiden introduced himself, I quickly sat in a metal chair and almost yelped as my legs touched the cold steel. It had to be sixty degrees in here, and goose bumps quickly rose on my arms. My body didn't quite know how to take the quick change in temperature.

Aiden sat next to me, and Beckley slid back into his chair, which squeaked under his weight. About fifty, Beckley had narrow-set eyes, plump cheeks, and one of the friendliest smiles I'd ever seen.

Beckley said, "Strangest thing with Ms. Fitzpatrick—or Ms. Fitz as she likes us to call her. Ms. Rodriguez said she's missing? Is that right?"

I shouldn't have been surprised at how fast Nya had spilled the news, but I was. It was bound to be on the noon newscast for sure.

"For a couple of days," Aiden confirmed. "Could you tell us what happened? We heard there was an incident down here a few days ago."

Beckley's expression sobered and his lips turned downward in a deep frown. "Two incidents. Wednesday *and* Thursday."

Thursday, too? "What happened, exactly? Ms. Rodriguez was a little fuzzy on the details."

"Wednesday's deal wasn't that unusual except looking back on it. It was late—a little past nine p.m. or so—and Ms. Fitz was on her way out when one of my attendants noticed her back tire was real low, almost flat. He put her spare on for her and sent her on her way."

"Flat tires aren't that unusual," Aiden prompted, echoing Nya's earlier thoughts on the matter.

Beckley raised a dark unruly eyebrow. "Truth. But in tandem with what happened Thursday they are…and now she's missing. I can't help but wonder if someone messed with that tire. A slow leak would mean that Ms. Fitz would likely have pulled over somewhere on her way home with a flat."

If someone had been following behind her waiting for that moment…

That scenario made the goose bumps on my arms double. I glanced around the garage. The first floor was street level, with only waist-high concrete barriers and tall pillars separating the back of the garage from the street behind it. It would take only seconds for someone to jump that wall and pop a hole in the tire.

"Did she have her little girl with her?" Aiden asked.

"Not that night," Beckley said. "She must've been picked up earlier. That happens a lot."

"What happened Thursday?" Aiden asked through clenched teeth.

"It was a little before three, not quite quitting time for Ms. Fitz, but there she was, coming off the staff elevator and walking like the devil was on her heels, her little girl in one arm, her laptop in the other. Didn't wave to me like usual, just stormed over to her car, then kind of froze."

"And?" Aiden pressed.

"I immediately knew something was wrong, so I went to see. All the color was gone from her face." He took a breath. "I think the only reason she wasn't yelling was she didn't want to scare the baby."

Surreptitiously, I looked at Aiden. His lips were once again pressed in a thin line, and I could see his pulse jumping at his temple. His patience was wearing thin with Beckley's windy storytelling.

"What was wrong?" I asked.

"Never saw anything like it, and I've been working here for fourteen years now." He clasped his hands and kept shaking his head. Back and forth. Back and forth.

"Saw what?" Aiden ground out.

"There was this doll..." He kept shaking his head.

"What doll?" I asked, wondering if I had the strength to hold Aiden back if need be. I should have had more breakfast. Wheaties or something.

"The doll sitting in the little girl's car seat," Beckley explained as though we were both as dense as three-day-old donuts. "It was a cute doll, looked a lot like Ms. Fitz's little Ava, but then I saw the note stuck to the doll."

Aiden's fists clenched. "What did the note say?"

"Something about worrying about her own kid." He shook his head again. "I can't quite remember, but it rattled Ms. Fitz but good. That doll hadn't been there when she went into work that morning. Someone broke in during the day and put it there."

Immediately, Aiden's head snapped upward and looked around. "You have cameras in here?"

"Of course," Beckley said. "I figured you'd be wanting to look at the footage, same as Ms. Fitz did." He swiveled the monitor to face us. "I have it queued up for you. Got it pinned down to when the break-in occurred. A little after noon."

Aiden and I watched the screen. The picture wasn't the greatest but it was easy enough to make out Kira's SUV parked at the back of the garage. Sure enough, we watched as someone hopped the small concrete wall and stealthily approached the SUV, did something to the lock, and pulled the doll out from beneath a baggy sweatshirt. After closing the door, the person stuck something to the underside of the car.

My blood went cold. I'd bet it was a GPS tracker. I didn't even dare look at Aiden.

"Can you zoom in?" Aiden asked.

"Yeah, but it just gets grainier. The surveillance equipment in here ain't the greatest."

Truth, as he would say. The zoom added nothing to the image of the culprit except static. At first I couldn't even tell if the person was a man or a woman. On the tall side, medium build. Black baggy sweatpants. Dark sweatshirt with hood up to help obscure any facial features. Which wasn't all that successful. "Pause there," I asked.

The frame froze on the face. It was grainy, sure, but it was enough to see that it was man, maybe mid-twenties. I didn't recognize him.

"I wanted to call the cops, but Ms. Fitz didn't want to wait around. The baby was getting fussy—probably feeling the tension in the air." Beckley gave me a knowing look. "Little ones pick up on stuff like that. Anyways, she asked me to save the video, and that she'd get in touch with the police. I gave her car a once over to make sure her tires were good and she left. I'm kicking myself for not calling the cops then and there."

Aiden said, "There's nothing else you can remember from that note on the doll?"

He shook his head, then his eyes lit. "But I have it. You want it?"

"Wait," I said, excitement surging. "You have the doll or the note?"

"Both." He shrugged. "Ms. Fitz was in such a hurry to leave that she left without them. I put 'em aside for her, figuring she'd be back for them after she contacted the cops. You want 'em?"

I thought Aiden might spring out of his seat and kiss Beckley on the lips. For the first time all day, I saw him loosen up, if only for the briefest of moments.

Beckley stood even before receiving an answer and turned to a closet behind him and reached inside.

"Wait," Aiden said, standing. "You don't happen to have gloves, do you? Or a plastic bag?"

He lifted an eyebrow. "Trash bags."

"They'll do." Aiden waited while Beckley went to another closet—clearly one used to store maintenance odds and ends. He handed a bag to Aiden, who slipped it over his hand and reached into the closet.

There was nothing to prepare me for the gut reaction of seeing the doll in his hand. I sucked in a breath as my heart lurched then raced.

The small doll was a sweet thing—full cheeks, blond hair. Very lifelike but soft and cuddly as well. I could easily imagine Ava loving on the toy. As easily as I could imagine Ava as the doll. Except for the size, they were nearly identical, all big blue eyes and baby-fine hair.

Clearing my throat, I said, "What does the note say?" It was stuck to the doll's chest with a safety pin.

Beckley said, "I've seen some bad grammar in my days, hell, I'm probably one of the biggest offenders, but that note is something."

Aiden placed the doll on the desk, and I leaned in to read.

    U SHUD B MOR WURRIED 4 UR OWN KID

Aiden's eyes sparked dangerously, and I wondered what was going through his head. Even though he hadn't known Ava long, he'd formed an attachment. The note was a blatant threat against her.

"I need to take this with me," Aiden said, sounding hoarse.

"Take it, take it," Beckley said, backing away from the doll as though he wanted nothing more to do with it. "Anything to help find Ms. Fitz. She was a nice woman."

Was. Did he even realize he'd referred to her in the past tense? It was very telling. He'd subconsciously spoken what we were all undoubtedly thinking.

It wasn't looking good for finding Kira alive.

Beckley rubbed a hand down his face and let out a gusty breath. "It's an evil world out there. Us good people are just living in it."

5

As Aiden and I ambled down Beacon Street toward the Porcupine, our lunch destination, I kept thinking of what Danny Beckley had said about the world being an evil place.

The perception ate at me, gnawing painfully. I knew many good people, but on the whole, were we surrounded by evil? Some days it felt that way.

Days like today.

Especially as we neared the Porcupine, which was housed on the first floor of the Valentine, Inc. building.

"Jesus," Aiden whispered as we neared.

Grateful for my crutches to lean on, I gazed at the building. It was my first time back since the fire two days ago.

The Porcupine, fortunately, had been spared from the flames, thanks to the fire-proofed walls. A little cleaning, and it had been good to go. The same couldn't be said for the rest of the building.

As a hot breeze blew down the sidewalk, the scent of smoke was nearly overwhelming. Across the street, at the Common, people walked dogs, ate picnic lunches, played Frisbee. So *normal* when life for me right now seemed anything but.

Yellow caution tape was stretched across a piece of plywood that covered the scorched doorway leading to the upper floors of the building. Soot darkened the brick façade of all three levels, and the windows above us had been sealed with plywood as well—some broken to fight the fire, others broken in a fight for life.

In my mind's eye, I could easily imagine the first floor vestibule. The cherry-wood stairs with an elaborately carved bannister. The old-fashioned elevator.

And just as easily as I imagined what it used to look like, I could picture it how I'd last seen it. The flames. The heavy smoke. Charred wood. Embers glowing. The face of evil.

The second and third floors were slightly better off than the first—heavily smoke damaged, but the flames had been mostly contained by the time they reached the upper levels. Some structural work would be needed—and a complete fire restoration.

"It'll be okay," I said, more to myself than to Aiden.

The building was more than a hundred years old. History had been lost with the destruction of the old craftsmanship, but my parents would do all they could to preserve what remained. No matter what, renovations were sure to be extensive. I had no idea when we'd be getting back to work.

Right about now, I rather missed my job as a matchmaker. I, along with Sean, ran Lost Loves, which focused on reuniting (appropriately) lost loves. Between Sean's PI work and my psychic abilities we had a good track record going, and it was often rewarding. Seeing people fall in love all over again was something I never took for granted. That kind of joy was hard to come by in this world, which made me yearn for it that much more. Happiness was possibly the best weapon to battle the world's evils.

But, of course, reuniting lost loves wasn't the only way to find joy. It was everywhere if one looked for it. Even here. In the shadows of this charred, scarred building. It was in the sense of renewal. Of survival. Of knowing what was truly important in life.

It wasn't things. Not fancy old elevators or carved woodwork.

It was people.

Good people.

My gaze swung to the restaurant, and through the big plate-glass windows I could see Raphael, my surrogate father of sorts, busily wiping off a counter as his fiancée Maggie took an order.

I tugged on Aiden's sleeve to get his attention. "Let's go in."

He held the Porcupine's door open for me. Cool air swirled as I crutched inside. Even though it was a little early for lunchtime, the restaurant was packed. Raphael glanced up from wiping the counter and a smile spread across his face, his slightly-crooked teeth flashing bright against his olive skin. Soft wrinkles spread from the corners of his brown eyes as they filled with happiness.

This. This was joy. I couldn't help but smile back as he came toward me, tucking a hand towel into the waist of the white apron tied low around his hips. He pulled me into a crushing hug, crutches and all.

He pulled back to scan for any new injuries, searching for wounds that weren't so easily visible. Apparently, he didn't like what he saw. He cupped my cheeks with warm strong hands and said in a dulcet soothing tone, "*Mi Uvita.*"

Shit. Only when feeling especially emotional did he resort to the use of "*mi Uvita*," translated to "my little grape." I must really look like crap.

"I'm fine, *Pasa*," I returned using my nickname for him. Raisin. The names had been coined back in olden days when, at five years old, I pitched a hissy fit on a field trip. He claimed I turned the color of a purple Concord grape. I'm not sure exactly when I began calling him *Pasa*, but the names stuck, becoming more and more endearing as years passed.

Unofficially, my parents had shared custody of me from the time I was four years old. A fifty-fifty split. My time with my mother was...free. She raised me to be nothing if not independent. Though she loved me fiercely, she often did her own thing and expected me to do the same.

My father...well, he didn't know what to do with me at all. So, he left my care to Raphael, who until recently had been my father's full-time valet. He'd cut back his hours only after falling in love with Maggie (thanks to a little matchmaking), and here he was, working by her side at her restaurant and happier than I'd ever seen him.

Raphael had been in my life for as long as I could remember. He'd been my caretaker. My playmate. My teacher. My friend. My partner in crime. The one person in my life I knew without a doubt I could count on. He'd been the one to bandage scrapes, to shop with me for school supplies, to take me to museums and zoos. He'd been the one to teach me to drive. He'd dried my tears when my heart was broken. It was his wallet I'd found that revealed my ESP after I thought all my powers were lost.

He was wise, kind, and the best kind of good.

He was joy.

"I'm good," I insisted, trying to reassure him, even though I suddenly felt like sobbing. "Really."

"Such lies you tell," he said with a chastising look.

"I'd never," I lied, beating back the tears with an emotional baseball bat.

"Mmm-hmm."

"Are you going to hog her all day?" a female voice asked from behind him.

With a sigh, he stepped aside to shake Aiden's hand and said to him, "Glad to see you're not missing after all."

Maggie Constantine gave me a hug. Her hair was pulled back into a long braid, and her eyes shone with a vitality that came from an energy that radiated within her. "You're doing okay?" she asked, echoing Raphael's concern.

"I'm good," I repeated and nodded enthusiastically, swinging that mental bat around like I was aiming for a Twinkie-filled piñata.

She searched my gaze, too, and gave me a smile. She didn't know me as well as Raphael—it was easier to be deceptive. Turning her focus to Aiden, she teased, "I thought we were going to have to send out a search party for you. I was taking up a collection of Tic Tacs."

Aiden's gaze flicked to me. "Word gets around fast."

I smiled. "Welcome to my world."

Another couple came in, blinking as they adjusted to the lighting after being out in the sunshine. Raphael said, "Let me get these customers settled, then I'll be back to see you."

"No rush," I said, crutching out of the way. "We're staying for lunch."

"Wonderful!" Maggie ushered us to a booth near the front windows. "Sit, sit."

As I set my crutches into the booth and slid in next to them, the scent of garlic wafted in the air along with something else, something nuttier. Roasted pine nuts maybe. It was so nice to smell something other than smoke.

"Hungry?" she asked, putting menus in our hands.

There was nothing Maggie liked more than feeding people.

Well, maybe Raphael.

"Starving," I said.

Aiden only smiled. He was humoring me with this lunch, but I wasn't going to complain. More than food, I'd needed the visit with Raphael. Aiden and I both ordered lemonades and Maggie rushed off. She rarely moved at any speed other than fast.

Aiden shook out his napkin and placed it on his lap and looked out the window. Even though he sat directly across from me, I could tell he was somewhere far, far away.

"We'll find her," I said.

His gaze snapped to me. "What then, Lucy?"

What then? It was a good question—one I didn't have an answer to.

"If she's alive, is she going to fight me for shared custody? Because I'm not letting Ava go. Now that I know about her, I'm not stepping aside to let her slip seamlessly back into her old life."

I hadn't needed any kind of psychic ability to predict that Aiden wouldn't let Ava out of his life after all this was said and done. All it had taken was one look at him this morning cuddling the little girl to know he'd fallen head over heels for her.

"And sure as hell," he added scathingly, "I'm not letting that jackhole *Trey Fisher* raise my daughter…"

I lifted an eyebrow and fought a smile. Fought it hard. Aiden rarely cursed. "Jackhole?"

A smile teased the corners of his lips. "I might be being a bit harsh, but you know his reputation."

I did. Womanizer. Temperamental. Conceited.

Not exactly a father figure.

"They haven't been dating long," I said. "I doubt marriage is on the table at this point."

He glared.

I got the message. He needed to vent.

"Carry on," I said.

"On the flip side of that, if Kira's dead…," he began, then shook his head. After a second, he cleared his throat. "If she's dead, how can I explain to Ava that I waited days to look for her mother?"

"Aiden, you can't—"

"Here you go," Maggie said, sliding two frosty glasses of lemonade onto the tabletop. She quickly rattled off the daily specials, and the passion she had for her food was evident in the way she described each meal. I ordered a chicken spinach wrap, and Aiden ordered gazpacho. She rushed off, and I couldn't help but smile at her zest for life.

On the surface, it didn't seem like she would be a good fit for Raphael. He loved the Red Sox, she loved the Yankees. He loved eighties music, she loved classical. He was quiet, she was loud. Yet, the undeniable chemistry between them was palpable. And, of course, there were the auras. My father had known from the moment he met Maggie that she was the one to fill the void in Raphael's heart. Dad had leased this space to her at the fraction of the cost so she and Raphael could find their way to each other. Turned out, their internal navigational systems were a wee bit off course. It had taken *my* interference (I wanted full credit) to get them to finally look at each other. A whirlwind relationship later and they were engaged and living together.

It never ceased to amaze me how little it took to completely change the direction of someone's life. For good…or for bad.

I ran my fingers up and down my glass, drawing in the condensation. "You can't hold yourself responsible for what might or might not have happened to Kira."

His jaw jutted.

Because he knew I spoke the truth, I didn't press. Instead, I refocused the conversation. "It sure seems as though that doll was a warning to Kira about the McDaniel case."

"Yes." He ripped the paper from his straw and jabbed it into his drink. "I keep thinking about that note. It feels like someone went to an exaggerated length to make us believe they were uneducated. Why?"

It did, in fact, seem that way. I was fairly sure a third grader had better writing skills than whoever penned the note. "If I had to guess, someone well-educated wrote it."

"That's what I was thinking, too."

Ice cubes clinked against my glass as I slid it between my hands. "How much do you recall about Dustin McDaniel?"

"Not as much as I'd like right now. My files on him are at the office."

"Do you recall the parental situation?" I asked. "How did the state get involved in the first place?"

He said, "Mother had a problem with drugs, father is in prison. I don't know how the CFC became involved. There was supposed to be regular checks by his social worker, but somewhere along the line, he fell through the cracks in the system. After his disappearance was uncovered, his case worker was fired and her supervisor was suspended."

Sometimes the cracks in the system felt like chasms. "We're going to have to talk to Dustin's case worker and possibly her supervisor."

Aiden slowly shredded his straw wrapper. "It might be best if we split up tomorrow. Can you drive with that boot?"

"Yep. I mastered it last week."

Raphael set two plates on the table. He slid into the booth next to me. "You two look quite serious over here. Working?"

"New missing person case," I said.

"Adult? Child?" Raphael asked.

"Both," I said.

I was about to launch into the whole story when the front door swung open and a loud female voice said, "You're impossible!"

The man she was with said drolly, "So I've been told a thousand times."

"If the truth fits," she returned.

"A thousand and one." The man sighed.

Raphael smirked and elbowed me. "True love."

"Where's Raphael?" the woman said as she spun around. "He'll agree with—LucyD!" my mother squealed when she spotted me. She rushed over to the table, immediately abandoning her companion.

He didn't look fazed. My father was used to it.

Raphael scooted out of the booth, and my mother gave him a quick hug, and set a pile of binders on the table before taking his spot next to me.

"Let me look at you," she said, tucking a lock of hair behind my ear. She *tsk*ed. "You look tired."

"Thanks, Mum."

She beamed, her hazel eyes bright and shiny. "What are mothers for if not telling the truth?"

I was about to give her a whole list that didn't including telling their daughters they essentially looked like crap, but then I glanced at Aiden and remembered a little girl who didn't know where her mother was. I took another bite of my sandwich as Mum launched into hellos with him.

My parents were also a case of opposites attracting. Dad was polished whereas Mum was wild. Her platinum hair was cut short in a messy pixie style, and her eyelids glittered from sparkly eye shadow. A deep purple tunic with white embroidery flattered her shapely figure, and bangle bracelets clanked on her arm as she spoke with her hands. She was a flowerchild at heart and was a tireless defender of every cause around. She loved fiercely. Everything from the sound of the ocean to delectable desserts; her music students, her family, and her strange complicated relationship with my father.

My dad and Raphael had their heads bent—no doubt my father was ordering something not on the menu. My dad was classic Hollywood handsome. Tall, dark and debonair. Montgomery Clift with brown eyes (minus the addiction problems). Impeccably dressed, his silver-flecked hair was slicked back, and as his gaze turned to me, his eyes warmed. He leaned across the table to give my forehead a peck, then shook Aiden's hand and sat next to him.

"I hear you're being impossible," I said to Dad.

He straightened his tie. "I fear people across town heard as well."

My mother silently mimicked him, then said, "It's good to see you, Aiden. I heard you were missing for a while."

Aiden looked at me. "It doesn't get old." Sarcasm dripped from his words.

"Were you undercover?" Mum asked him. "Dressed as a motorcycle gang member or infiltrating a drug cartel? Did you get a tattoo?" Before he could answer, Mum turned to me. "I'm thinking about a tattoo."

"Dear God," my father said.

My mother wiggled her eyebrows. "Maybe Dovie and I can get matching tattoos of your father's face, so he can always be with us."

Now I knew she was only kidding. Despite their current reconciliation, the only long-lasting tribute to my father she wanted was me.

My father's strong jaw slid to the side and stayed there as his nostrils flared—a sure sign he was reaching his tolerance peak. "I'm not dying."

"Not yet," my mother replied, smiling sweetly, a murderous glint in her eye. "Give it time. Five, ten minutes or so."

Ah, love.

"Amusing," my father intoned.

Mum arched a thin blond eyebrow and returned her attention to Aiden. "Have you spoken with Em yet? She was quite worried."

"This morning." His mouth went back to being tight again.

"Good, good." She narrowed her gaze on him. "*Is everything good between you two?*"

Aiden gave me a "help me" look.

It was Dad who came to the rescue. "Good god, woman, let the man breathe."

"Impossible," my mother mumbled.

"Raphael says you're working, Lucy," Dad said, turning the focus on me. "I thought you were taking some time off?"

"There are some cases you can't say no to," I answered with a shrug.

"You can always say no," my father said quite seriously. "You should go home and rest."

"No," I said.

My mother tipped her head back and laughed.

"Not funny, Lucy," Dad murmured, rubbing his temples.

I was quite certain my mother and I were the sole source of his migraines.

"Oh, lighten up, Oscar," Mum countered. To Aiden and me, she added, "He's cranky."

He was cranky. She was murderous. It was just another day in their relationship.

"Why?" Aiden asked, pushing aside his empty soup bowl.

I was happy to see he'd eaten something. I had the feeling it was the first food in days.

Mum said, "Because I vetoed his renovation plans."

My father let out a loud sigh. "In an autocracy, there is no veto power, Judie."

"This King of Love stuff is going to your head, Oscar." My mother looked at me and said, "He wants to combine the second and third floors into one space with lots of glass and teak and no. No, no, no." She pulled a print of a floor plan from one of her binders.

I studied the page. "I kind of like it."

"The betrayal!" my mother said softly, clutching her heart.

"Not the glass or the teak, but the layout," I explained. The space combined the matchmaking and investigation offices.

"You're two-thirds forgiven," Mum said. "The character of the building cannot be sacrificed. The wood, the brick, the *charm*."

"Agreed, agreed, agreed." I liked the idea of us all being one big team, but I didn't know how Sam would take losing his space. "You'll want to run this by Sam before settling on any certain plan."

"It's my building," my father said. "I'll make the decisions."

I glanced at my mother. "The king thing *has* gone to his head."

"He's impossible these days, I'm telling you." She let out a deep breath. "I think it's the grandpa thing. He's not adjusting well to the news that he's old enough to have a grandchild."

My father looked at Aiden. "Kill me now."

I smiled. "Aw. Grandpa. So cute. But he looks more like a Grampy to me."

"Don't make me disown you," he snapped.

"How's Preston doing?" Mum asked. "Have you heard from her today?"

"Earlier. She's feeling fine, but Dovie's trying to make her watch ballroom dancing. She's thinking about flinging herself into the ocean."

"Smart girl," my father muttered.

I heard my phone chirp and fished in my tote bag for my cell.

"Is that Sean?" my mother asked. "How's he doing?"

It was Sean—a text message. "Better," I said, swiping the screen until Sean's message appeared. I read the words, looked up at Aiden, and said, "We need to go."

He looked more than ready. My parents in a tiff tended to have that effect on people.

My father stood out of the way as Aiden pulled his wallet from his inner coat pocket.

Dad put his hand on Aiden's. "I've got it."

"Thanks, Oscar," Aiden said.

"What's going on?" Mum questioned as she inched out of the booth to let me pass.

I dragged my crutches out. "Just something with our case."

"Oh, top secret. I get it," she said. "Tattoos?"

"No," I said. No way. No how. No needles. Never. Ever.

Then she whispered to me, "You'll tell me later?"

I kissed her cheek, then my father's. "Don't kill each other, okay?"

They glanced at each other, then at me. "No promises," they said at the same time.

I was shaking my head as I crutched away. I said my goodbyes to Raphael and Maggie, and as Aiden held the door open to me, a blast of heat nearly had me backtracking into the cool air.

"What's up?" Aiden asked once we were alone.

"That was Sean. He said Channel 3 is airing breaking news coverage of Kira's disappearance. We need to get to her house before every news van in the city does."

6

Needham was a good half hour drive in decent traffic. Southwest of the city, it was an upper-class town where people took pride in their homes, their yards, and their privacy.

Aiden hadn't needed directions to Kira's place—leaving me to assume he'd been there before. Once off the highway, it was like he was on autopilot. Right, left, left, straight. Finally, he turned right onto a residential tree-lined street, pulled across the street from a large picture-perfect Cape Cod-style home, complete with a white picket-fenced yard and tall trees shading the yard.

"No one's here yet," he said, stating the obvious as he tossed a Tic Tac into his mouth. He offered one to me, and I waved it away.

We crossed the street, the sound of my crutches clunking on the asphalt. I stopped to hitch my tote bag higher on my shoulder and wished I'd left it in the car, but I wanted access to my phone in case Sean called again, and my skirt had no pockets.

"I'm sure we don't have long." Ten, fifteen minutes. Tops. When the news vans arrived, chaos would ensue.

On the ride over, Aiden called his office to verify the search warrant had been secured and used his dashboard lights and siren on the way here. He'd cut the siren once we hit the suburbs, but he left the lights on. Blue flashes burst across his face—as surely as they did mine—at even intervals.

"I don't suppose you still have a key," I said.

"I never had a key, Lucy," he answered, his voice tight as he stepped onto the sidewalk.

"Sorry. I just..."

"I know," he said, "but it wasn't like that. It was...casual."

I didn't really understand "casual" dating. I was a monogamy type of girl. I didn't share well with others. Even the *thought* of Sean with someone else made my skin twitch.

A nearby sprinkler bathed the street, causing a stream of water to fill the gutters. I stepped over it, and crutched quickly to catch up with Aiden as he strode up Kira's empty driveway.

Her yard was neat and tidy. The lawn was well-kept, there were urns overflowing with colorful flowers flanking a brick walkway, and there were no signs at all that Kira hadn't been home in days. Papers weren't piled up. Mail wasn't spilling out of the box at the curb.

Anxiety and nerves coursed through me, and I closed my eyes, hoping calm would come over me. My scent-reading abilities were new, and I needed all my wits about me to concentrate. I wondered which house belonged to Morgan Creighton—Kira's friend and neighbor. If they were especially close, she'd know much more about Kira's daily activities and if she'd experienced other threatening events lately.

Somewhere nearby, a dog barked, alerting all the neighborhood canines that something was amiss in the neighborhood. A chorus of barks echoed back. It reminded me of a scene in *101 Dalmatians*, which made me smile, and just like that, my nerves calmed. *Good.* I hoped that within the hour Aiden and I would have a much better idea of what we were up against with Kira's disappearance.

"Hey!" someone shouted from nearby. "It's about time you showed up."

I turned and found an angry man scowling from the other side of a short picket fence that separated his yard from Kira's.

Aiden took off his sunglasses and said, "Pardon?"

"You're the cops, right?" the guy asked, jerking his chin toward Aiden's car where the lights still flashed. "I've been calling for days, and it's about time they sent someone out."

Aiden pushed open a gate and crossed the small patch of lawn, toward the fence. I followed along, hoping my crutches wouldn't sink into the ground.

"And you are?" Aiden asked, giving the man an intense stare down.

"Morgan Creighton," he said, straightening to try and match Aiden's height.

I pegged him to be five feet eight or so. Matching Aiden's height was impossible.

I'd assumed Morgan had been a woman. Color me embarrassed. Instead, he was a good-looking guy. Mid-to-late-thirties. Light skin with a sprinkle of freckles and light brown beard stubble. Brown hair, loosely styled. He wore khaki shorts, a wrinkled short-sleeve shirt, and Nike sandals. No wedding ring.

Aiden held out his hand. "Detective Lieutenant Aiden Holliday."

Morgan's face flushed red as a maraschino cherry and his hand stalled on the way to meet the handshake. His brown eyes widened. It was quite evident from his reaction that he knew exactly who Aiden was.

Morgan's house was a traditional colonial, its clapboard freshly stained a slate blue. White trim popped against the color, and fieldstone accents cemented its New England charm. A beautiful collie that looked exactly like Lassie stood behind a closed screen door, letting out random barks at our interaction.

"This is a colleague of mine, Lucy Valentine," Aiden said, introducing me.

"Hi," I said, gripping the handles of my crutches so I wouldn't have to shake hands.

"I don't understand." Morgan set his hands on his hips. "Are you here because I called? Or here because..." He seemed to struggle to finish the statement without coming right out and calling Aiden on his former relationship with Kira.

Aiden barely mollified the man by saying, "I know nothing of your calls to the local police."

"Then why...?" Morgan asked.

"I suspect," I said, "we're here for the same reason you called the police in the first place. Kira's missing."

The man seemed to slump in relief. "Yes. Kira and Ava. I got home late Thursday night to find Kira's dog in my backyard with a half a bag of food and some toys but no note, no explanation. Kira's not answering calls, and I've been collecting her papers and mail. This isn't like her," he said. "And I'm worried."

"You're close friends?" Aiden asked, a lift to his brow.

Morgan said, "We're close friends, yes, but not dating if that's what you're getting at." He added, pointedly, "Her type is apparently six-feet, blond hair, blue eyes."

I bit back a laugh. It appeared he was right. The description fit both Aiden and Trey Fisher.

"I waited a day," he continued, "for her to come back then called the police to report her missing, but you wouldn't believe the hoops you have to jump through to prove someone is actually missing and not missing because they want to be missing." He tipped his head. "Did that make sense? I filed a report yesterday, but can't help but feel like no one took me seriously."

I knew all about the hoops. It bordered on ridiculous.

"No one wants to believe something's wrong. But something is. Kira wouldn't leave Scout with me all this time otherwise—she knows I'm allergic."

"Scout?" I echoed.

"The dog."

I glanced over his shoulder at the dog in the doorway. The collie pranced back and forth. Ava's sweet voice echoed in my head. *Scow, scow, scow.* She'd been calling Thoreau by her dog's name—Scout.

Morgan searched our faces. "Something is wrong, isn't it?"

"We think so," I said, glancing at Aiden. I didn't know how much to tell this man.

"Kira came by my house Thursday night," Aiden said. "She handed me Ava and left. She hasn't been seen since."

Color drained from Morgan's face. He grabbed on to the fence. "I don't understand. Why?"

"We're trying to figure that out," I said. "Did you know of any problems going on in her life? Had she gotten any threats? Anything of that sort?"

"I know she was going through something with Trey—Trey Fisher," he added. "They've been dating for a couple of months now. They had a fight recently."

"About what?" I asked.

He shrugged. "Kira didn't elaborate, but I had the feeling the relationship wasn't going to last much longer. Kira doesn't suffer fools easily, so I'm extremely surprised she stayed with him as long as she has."

Trey had quite the reputation.

"What about Trey's wife?" I asked. "Any problems with her?"

I didn't want to let go of my scorned woman theory just yet.

"Not that I know of, but I wouldn't be surprised."

"Did Kira break them up?" Aiden asked.

"I think Trey Fisher's wandering eye is more to blame," he answered.

"You don't like Trey Fisher?" Aiden asked.

Morgan clenched his fists. "I barely know the man, but I don't think he's right for Kira. That's all. She needs maturity, not an attention seeker. At least she had the foresight not to let Ava near him."

A cloud passed in front of the sun, and I was grateful for the sudden shade. "She didn't?" I asked.

"She has a rule about not bringing guys around unless she thinks it's serious. Doesn't want Ava to get attached if a relationship is short-lived. That kind of thing. As far as I know, Trey's never spent time with Ava except maybe a minute or two in passing."

"Did Kira bring many guys home?" I asked, because I was afraid Aiden wouldn't go there.

"No," Morgan said. "She's highly selective about the men in her life. In all the time I've known her, no one's lasted more than a few months."

Well, except for him.

If I read him right, he cared for Kira as more than a friend.

I cleared my throat. "Did Kira mention anything to you about her current case?"

"Dustin McDaniel? Not much. She doesn't like to talk about her stories before they air. She was excited by it, though. Had that look in her eye that she gets when she's close to solving something big."

Aiden jerked a thumb toward the house. "I'm going to look around a bit before everyone gets here." He stalked off, walking around the house, examining the ground around the foundation.

"Gets here?" Morgan said. "Who?"

"Channel 3 ran a breaking news report on Kira's disappearance at noon."

Morgan closed his eyes. "Sweet Jesus. She'd hate that."

"Why?" I asked, losing sight of Aiden as he went around the back of the house.

"Kira strived to keep her personal life separate from work. Which became harder when she started seeing Trey. She loved her job, investigating and reporting the news. She never wanted to *be* the news."

"How long have you known her?" I spotted Aiden reappear on the opposite side of the house.

"As long as we've been neighbors. Five years now."

"And what do you do for work?"

"I'm a food writer for an online magazine. I work from home."

Well, that explained why he was home during the day. "Have you noticed anyone coming and going from Kira's in the past few days?"

"Only the usual mail and paper deliveries. Though I did wake up last night to Scout barking his head off at the window. I looked outside but didn't see anything unusual. I can't keep him much longer. Scout, I mean, but I don't know what to do with him. I don't want to bring him to the pound."

"Kennel him?" I suggested as Aiden overturned rocks and ran his hand along the top of the doorframe. He was looking for a hidden key. It never failed to amaze me how many people hid keys in obvious places.

"He can't," Morgan said. "He has a delicate immune system. Gets sick too easy."

I was such a sucker for a sob story. I reached in my tote bag for a pad of paper. "I might know someone who can help." I jotted down the name of the vet clinic where Marisol worked. "Bring Scout here, and ask for Marisol Valerius. Tell her I sent you."

Aiden tipped one of the flower urns, bent down, and pulled something off the bottom of the pot. He came up holding a key. I guessed taping the key to the bottom of the pot was better than simply leaving it under the pot, but still…

"This isn't some kind of shelter, is it?" Morgan questioned.

"It's a vet's office."

He frowned as though he didn't believe me. "Okay."

At the sound of a loud rumble, I looked down the street. A news van was headed this way. I turned back to warn Aiden just as he put the key in the lock and turned to call me over as he pushed open the door. With a fiery flash, a soul-ripping *KABOOM* blew me backward over the fence.

7

For a dizzying, disorienting moment, it felt as though I was mired in a strange sort of suspended animation, almost like swimming underwater. Sounds were muffled. My vision was blurry. It was hard to breathe.

In a haze of confusion, smoke, and pain, I wondered what in the hell had just happened.

As I looked around it became shockingly obvious.

Kira's house had exploded.

Her front door, at least. What was left of the home was now engulfed in flames. Jet black smoke plumed into the sky, turning midday into midnight.

Squinting, I noticed everyone else seemed stuck in that same strange suspension as well. Then all at once, as through the movie before me un-paused, neighbors started running, shouting frantically. Pops and crackles emitted from within the house.

Choking and sputtering, I covered my nose with my arm and gasped for air. I felt a trickle of moisture sliding down the side of my face and wiped it away. My fingers came back red.

I glanced again at the house, at the shattered window—*Aiden*! Where was he?

Adrenaline flooded my veins as I struggled to stand. My gaze swept the area. Behind me, Morgan lay moaning and holding his head. Debris littered his perfect yard.

"Aiden!" I shouted, a guttural sound pulled from the very heart of me. I tested my balance by taking a step, two. I carefully climbed over the fence, back into Kira's yard. Leaving my crutches on the ground, I started for the front of the house, my arm up to protect my face from the heat and flames.

"Aiden!" I cried. I stumbled forward, trying to ignore the gaping hole where Kira's front door had once stood. Where Aiden had last stood. He wasn't there. I whipped around, trying to figure out where the blast would have thrown him.

My eyes watered from the thick smoke. Hobbling along, I crouched low, scanning the ground. I finally saw movement near one of the trees. I quickly limped over and dropped down next to Aiden's writhing body.

"Aiden," I said, reaching out to touch him but ultimately pulled my hands back. I didn't want to hurt him any more than he might already be. To look at him, he didn't appear severely wounded. His skin was red from minor flash burns. There were a couple of scrapes on his face, his hands. All his limbs were present and accounted for. He seemed like he could get up, dust himself off, and be on his way...

But I knew blast injuries, and almost always they were internal. Internal and deadly.

Groaning, he pried open his eyes. He rasped, "What's with you and fires these days?"

I sniffled, then laughed. "I can't believe you're joking at a time like this."

He tried for a wry smile but ended up grimacing. "Who's joking?"

Movement in my peripheral vision switched my attention from him to what was going on around us. It seemed like absolute mayhem as people rushed toward the burning house. The news crew was scurrying to set up feed. Sirens screamed in the distance, and I fought the scream rising in me.

Aiden reached out his hand, touching my arm. "I'm fine."

I clasped his hand. "Yeah," I agreed. "You're the picture of health."

A smile twitched the corners of his mouth. He struggled to get up, but couldn't quite.

"An ambulance will be here soon."

"Lucy, I don't need—" he began.

I glared, silencing him. "No arguing."

Leaning against the tree trunk, he said, "You're bleeding."

"Only a nick." I didn't know if that was true, but I

didn't have time to worry about myself.

The next twenty minutes passed in a blur of emergency services. I'd managed to collect my tote and crutches before being loaded into the same ambulance as Aiden; neighbor Morgan was in another right behind us.

As the rigs pulled away, through the back window I watched as firefighters tried in vain to save the house.

It was a lost cause.

It wasn't the only thing. Any hopes I had of reading Kira's scent had also gone up in smoke.

It was nearing sunset by the time I made it home from the hospital. I paid my cabbie a small ransom, refused his help to my front door, and as he drove off, I shouted, "Fuzzy navel!" (the previously agreed-upon safety code phrase) to let the security team know I was friend not foe. The last thing I needed today was to be tackled by heavily-armed security forces.

Earlier I'd called Sean from the emergency room to assure him I was mostly fine. I had some bruising and minor cuts and scrapes. I'd convinced him to stay home and watch Ava so Em could go to the hospital to be with Aiden. Sean had reluctantly agreed. A frazzled Em planned to stay by Aiden's side. He was going to have to stay the night, much to his dismay. He wanted out. His body, however, wasn't cooperating. At last check, he'd been diagnosed with minor burns, two broken ribs, and was about to get scanned for more internal injuries.

Em promised to call with an update later.

Sean wasn't going to be pleased that I'd taken a taxi home, but the thought of calling my mum or dad or Raphael to come back to the hospital after they'd just left... And then having to chit-chat about the explosion for the forty-five minute drive back here had been enough for me to break out in a cold sweat.

The cab fare had been worth every penny.

A cool sea breeze whipped loose strands of hair against my face as I adjusted my tote bag and turned to crutch into the house. The front door opened and Thoreau bounded out, quickly followed by Rufus, an energetic golden retriever that belonged to Dovie's boyfriend, Mac Gladstone. He filled the doorway, a broad smile on his weathered face.

I worried about his appearance here, wondering if Dovie had learned of the case.

"You're a sight," he said.

I stopped to let the dogs race around my legs and sniff the heck out of them. "For sore eyes?"

"Just a sight." His smile broadened even more, and the wrinkles around his eyes multiplied. When I first met him, he had thick dark hair and a beard that reminded me of the Gorton's fisherman. But one of the side effects of his chemo treatments for liver cancer hadn't been losing his hair—it had been turning it a shocking white.

"Such a charmer," I teased. The dogs darted away, off

to explore the garden.

"Your grandmother is rubbing off on me."

"Undoubtedly." I added, "She doesn't know about..."

"No, no," he said. "My lips are sealed, and you know I can keep a secret."

I did. He'd kept a big one not long ago.

I crutched up the steps and he kissed my cheek. Under the soft glow of waning daylight it was hard to see the jaundiced tint to his skin, but I knew it was there. His cancer treatments were going well, but he was on borrowed time.

He wrinkled his nose. "You don't smell so great, either."

Eyeing him, I said, "I'm not sure Dovie is a *good* influence on you."

He laughed. A deep belly chuckle that was usually infectious.

Only I hadn't been kidding.

"I'm surprised to see you here," I said as I kept an eye on the dogs as the sky slowly darkened.

"Raphael called earlier. Asked me to stop by to help babysit."

"I thought Sean had that covered?"

Gently, he pushed open the front door. "I think I was sent over to watch both of them."

Light spilled across Sean's face as he snoozed on the sofa with Ebbie stretched out alongside of him. I noticed a small portable crib set up in the corner of the dining room and assumed Ava was in it—I couldn't see beyond the bumper pad and the herd of stuffed animals standing sentry.

"Good thing you're here," I said.

"Nah," Mac said. "Sean had it handled. But since I was here, he went ahead and took his pain medicine. That stuff kicks in fast. Knocked him out but good."

I hated thinking of the pain Sean must have been in. He didn't like taking medicine and used it only when absolutely necessary. "How long has he been out?"

"Both of them have been asleep for about half an hour."

"Did Ava eat supper?"

"She did at that. Spaghetti. She had a little help from the dogs. And Grendel."

I smiled. Grendel was the worst table beggar of the lot.

"You want me to stick around?" Mac asked.

Sean's face was slack from deep sleep. He looked at peace. A rarity. His demons didn't usually let him fully rest. "That's okay. I've got it. Thanks for staying with them."

"No problem. You'll call if you need anything?"

"Yep."

He gave me another kiss and whistled for Rufus, who galloped over. Together, they headed up the lane to Dovie's house. I called for Thoreau, who ran inside ahead of me.

I set my tote bag by the door and kicked off my ballet flat. I set the crutches against the wall, sick to death of using them. Grendel came running over, meowing pathetically. He looked up at me accusingly—he hated when I was gone all day.

I scooped him up—not an easy task with him being such a big boy. A good twenty-five pounds of pouting kitty. "Sorry, G." I rubbed his ears and nuzzled with him as I gimped over to the sofa. One-handed, I pulled a throw blanket up to Sean's chest and scratched Ebbie's chin as she gazed sleepily at me.

I bent and kissed Sean's forehead, then flicked a gaze toward the kitchen. My stomach was rumbling, but Mac hadn't been kidding when he said I smelled. A shower definitely took precedence over food.

Setting Grendel down, I hobbled as quietly as I could toward the crib in the corner. Em had gone overboard with shopping. Besides the crib and stuffed animals, there were toys scattered about, piles of clothes, a box of diapers, a baby gate, and some sort of plastic booster seat that attached to one of my dining chairs.

The crib had been done up in a playful monkey theme. Monkey bumper pad, monkey sheets, monkey blanket. Monkey everything. It smelled as though it had been freshly laundered and it all looked soft and cozy. I wanted to climb in there myself, but Ava was a bit of a bed hog.

Dressed in a tank-and-shorts pajama set adorned with smiling suns wearing sunglasses, she slept with wild abandon, her arms flung out, her legs askew. Her blond hair shone like spun gold, but contrarily stuck up from the top of her head like the crown of a pineapple. Her sweet face was turned to the side, her cheeks flushed pink.

As I stood there, I tried not to think too hard about what could have happened to Aiden today. I wasn't much the praying type, but as I watched Ava, I couldn't help but say a small plea for this little one—that she always be as worry free as she was at this very moment.

It was an impossible request. More of a wish.

Ava's eyelid twitched and she let out a quiet sigh from slightly parted lips.

Such innocence. Such…perfection.

Her jammie theme was appropriate. She was the sunshine on this stormy day.

I tugged her monkey blanket a little higher toward her chin, whispered "Goodnight," and went into the bedroom, shedding clothes as I limped along.

I didn't think my skirt suit would be salvageable. Between the rips, tears, and smell…it would probably appreciate being put out of its misery.

I winced at the loud noise of the Velcro on the boot as I took it off. I inspected the bruising on the top of my foot—it was definitely starting to fade despite my less-than-stellar crutch usage. Those crutches were getting on my last nerve, and I wondered if I could get away with using only one of them. Or a cane, even. I decided I'd check with my orthopedic doctor as soon as possible.

On my way to the bathroom, I stopped at the cage sitting atop my bureau and made kissing noises at Odysseus, who was busy taking his own bath. He licked his tiny hands and rubbed them over his head, causing his fluffy black-and-white fur to stick up much like Ava's had. He paused in his ablutions to give me the stink eye, which wasn't entirely his fault considering he had only one eye to begin with. His expression seemed especially cranky, however, and in an attempt to cheer him up, I promised him a piece of cantaloupe as soon as I was done with my shower. He didn't seem placated.

In the bathroom, I turned on the shower for the water to warm up, took a deep breath, and faced the full-length mirror hanging on the back of the door. I'd been avoiding my reflection all day.

With one eye closed, I peeked at the mirror with the other. The slice near my temple was the worst of the cuts. My skin was red—like a light sunburn. I reluctantly opened the other eye. A couple of strands of hair had been singed, leaving behind brittle frizz. I glanced over my shoulder and saw enormous bruises starting to form on my shoulder blades and hips—from when I hit the ground after being blown over the fence.

Steam began to fill the bathroom as I took one last look.

All in all, I was extremely grateful. It could have been so much worse.

I carefully stepped into the shower and breathed deeply as the hot water coursed over my skin. A layer of grime washed down the drain as I kept thinking about that explosion. No cause had been determined yet, but I doubted it had been an accident. The timing was too coincidental to Kira's disappearance, and happening when Aiden opened the door... No, the explosion had been planned to keep people out. But by whom? And why?

I racked my brain but couldn't come up with anything that made sense. Suddenly, I was so tired that I fully understood the meaning of "bone-weary." I leaned against the aging tiles and let the hot water run down my body, washing away the stress of the day. I didn't want to think about explosions or fires or babies who didn't know where their mothers were.

There was a soft tap on the door, and a second later Sean poked his head in the shower. Even sleep rumpled, bleary-eyed, and busted up, he still made my heart lurch.

He said, "You should have woken me, Ms. Valentine."

"You looked too peaceful."

He ducked back out and said, "When did you get back?"

"Not long ago. Fifteen minutes or so."

A moment later, the shower curtain pulled back and Sean stepped in with me. I couldn't help but smile. "Nice hat."

He smirked. "It's the latest fashion."

He wore a clear plastic shower cap to protect his head wound from the water.

"Now," he said, "let me look at you."

He cupped my face and tipped my head back and forth. His right thumb swiped under the cut on my temple.

"Flying glass," I said, shifting to the side so the water could reach him.

The shower hadn't been made for two. In fact, it hadn't been updated since the little cottage had been renovated in the seventies. A few of the tiles were loose, the enamel on the cast iron tub was chipped, the grout was...dismal. But right now it felt like paradise.

His eyes crinkled. "You've had a stressful day. I thought you might like some help in here."

"That's very...thoughtful of you."

"I'm nothing if not thoughtful."

"Oh, I'm aware." I wrapped my arms around his waist, clasping my hands behind his back, loving the feel of his skin against mine.

Smiling, he reached for the shampoo, squirted some into his palm, and then worked it into my hair as I told him about the explosion. As the shampoo lathered, he massaged my head, using exactly the right amount of pressure. Pleasure instead of pain.

"I saw the footage on TV. I'd bet money that house had been doused in accelerant. It went up too fast." He angled my head into the spray to rinse the shampoo.

"Makes sense. It was fully engulfed in minutes."

"Any leads on Kira yet?"

I told him all we'd learned, starting with Trey and his

soon-to-be ex, the doll, and Dustin McDaniel.

I braced myself for a possible reaction to that last bit. Sean had once been in the same system as Dustin, in and out of foster care before running away with a friend. It was fate that put him—and Sam—in the path of the Donahues, whose big hearts welcomed the pair into the family without a second thought.

He reached for the conditioner. "So, you're essentially working on two missing person cases now."

"Yes."

"If the two are connected, this case is..."

Explosive. We both left the words unsaid.

Finally, he said, "Productive day." He rinsed the conditioner from my hair and frowned at the singed ends.

"Well, except for the part where it blew up."

Grabbing a bar of soap, he built a lather, then ran his hands down one of my arms, then the other, stopping just shy of my hands, but even so, I felt little zaps.

"When I saw what happened on TV...." He shook his head.

I caught his chin. Stilled it. "I'm fine. A little achy but fine."

His arms went around me. "Achy? Where? Here?" He pressed a kiss to the side of my face.

I let my head fall to the side. "Mmm-hmm. A little lower, too."

His lips slid down my jawline. "Here?"

"Yep." I ran my hands across his wet chest, loving how

easily my fingers slid over his hard muscles. I loved him. It was that plain and simple. "There and lots of other places."

His head dipped to my breast. "Here?"

I sucked in a breath. "Really, Sean, this could take all night."

Looking up at me, his dimples popped as he smiled—a smile so full of promise that my knees went weak. "That's okay," he said. "I had a nap."

8

Later that night, Sean was sitting up in bed reading, and I was trying to watch news footage on my iPad. Try, because there was a cat stretched across my chest making the task difficult.

Ebbie playfully tapped my chin, and I scratched her head as I listened to Kira's voiceover on one of her exposés last year. As a result of her investigation, an election official had been arrested and charged with voter fraud.

Her voice was calm, smooth, confident. She came off as completely earnest, and it was easy to see why she was so popular—she elicited trust from those who watched her.

I noticed, too, that Ava had her smile.

With a few swipes of my fingertip, I called up another search. This one of Dustin McDaniel. I read article after article. Watched video after video.

The media had certainly made it seem as though Alisha McDaniel had been guilty of whatever happened to her son. The court of public opinion had tried and convicted her. But Alisha McDaniel was dead... So what had prompted the anonymous tip that Kira had received? And where had it led her?

Ebbie's purrs vibrated against my chest, and I smiled down at her. She was settling in just fine. Grendel had no time for affection as he needed his beauty sleep. He was curled with Thoreau at the foot of the bed; their two bodies so close that it was hard to see where one ended and the other began. Odysseus was running a marathon on his wheel, his piece of cantaloupe stored away in his plastic igloo for a midnight snack.

I queued up news footage, taken shortly after the original story broke (thank goodness for YouTube). Cameras had followed police as they took Alisha in for questioning. She, of course, had denied any culpability, laying the blame squarely on the CFC. She claimed they'd taken custody of Dustin months before, in January, yet she'd told no one about it. For *months*. I had to admit, she seemed guilty as hell.

I clicked on another video, this one of Dustin's caseworker as she left the district attorney's office after being questioned. Catherine "Cat" Bennett was twenty-five years old and looked fifteen. Young and pretty with light brown hair and big brown eyes. She'd been crying as she raced to her car, her husband at her side attempting to shield her from cameras with his suit coat. When he dropped his car keys and bent to pick them up, photographers swarmed as they tried to capture Cat's tear-stained face. The encounter had her hysterically sobbing by the time the pair had driven off.

Cat Bennett claimed the last time she had seen Dustin was December, and he'd been alive and well. She fully accepted her role in the case—that she had let Dustin fall through the cracks by missing months and months of check-ins.

The next video was of similar footage, except this time of Elliman Bay, Cat Bennett's supervisor, as he exited the police station with his lawyer. He wore a baby-blue button-down shirt that complemented his dark skin. His lawyer kept repeating "No comment" to the reporters as he headed for a dark SUV.

My phone rang, and I leaned so far off the bed to grab it from the nightstand that I nearly fell off. Laughing, Sean grabbed my arm, pulling me back up.

"Dovie," I said to him.

"Good luck." He went back to his book, a nonfiction account of hikers lost in the wilderness. Not my idea of light bedtime reading.

"You need to come down here," Dovie said, her voice going up an octave. "I need reinforcements."

I let out a breath of relief that she hadn't learned about Kira's investigation. "What'd Preston do?"

"It's what she won't do. She doesn't want to watch TV, doesn't want to play Scrabble, doesn't want to do a puzzle. She keeps sneaking out of bed to try and find her phone. I finally had to bury it in the sand."

"X marks the spot?"

"Not funny, LucyD."

"It's only a couple of weeks," I said.

"I need help."

"Cutter's there." I still needed to call him.

"He's the only reason she's eating."

Preston was as stubborn as they came.

"You'll come?" Dovie pressed.

"I can't."

"Why?"

"I can't leave Sean. He needs me."

He raised an eyebrow. I shrugged. Any port in a storm.

"Bring him. There's plenty of room."

Ebbie swatted the phone. "The pets…"

"Bring them," Dovie repeated.

"I have some readings scheduled…"

"Reschedule them."

"Dovie, you'll be fine without me. You might want to rent a bunch of musicals—Preston loves those. Then go to the bookstore. She loves to read. Anything and everything. Buy her lots of trashy magazines. And ice cream. Gallons of ice cream."

Dovie sniffed. "Fine, but if none of those work, then you're getting your ass down here even if I have to drag you myself."

"I love you, too." At the click in my ear, I hung up, and glanced at Sean. "She might disown me when all this is said and done, and she learns the truth."

"That's a lot of disowning in one day."

I'd already told him about my father. "I'm lucky that way, I guess."

"You still have your mother."

"Until she wants to get matching tattoos."

He laughed and switched off his bedside lamp. Ebbie slid off my chest and went over to curl up against his.

I looked at the iPad screen one more time before shutting it off. On the screen, the video had been frozen on Dustin's adorable face, all big blue eyes and long blond hair.

I thought about the doll in Kira's SUV, her fear for Ava, and the way her house had exploded. I wasn't yet sure what had prompted the anonymous tip that Kira had received, but I could only hope it hadn't led to her death.

At a little past seven the next morning, I woke to an unfamiliar sound. It took me a moment to place the noise. Thoreau, lodged between Sean and me on the bed, heard it, too. He launched to his feet, his ears perked.

Sean slept face-down, one arm flung over the side of the bed, the other stuffed under his pillow. Morning light crept under the window shade, highlighting the hollow of his back.

I resisted the temptation to kiss that area. Undoubtedly, it would wake him up—and he needed the sleep.

I yawned and listened for the noise again.

There. A *hummm-hummm-hummm*. I smiled.

Ava was awake.

Tossing the covers aside, I held in a groan.

Holy hell. My body ached something fierce. I winced at the pain as I slipped into my robe and fastened my boot. I hoped a couple—or five—ibuprofen would take the edge off the hurt.

Ebbie stayed glued to Sean's side like a barnacle to a skiff. I was beginning to think her decision to live with me had more to do with Sean than anything else. I couldn't blame her much—she obviously had excellent taste.

Then I shook my head at my thoughts. Jeremy Cross's animal communication skills still amazed me. To talk with animals... It would be amazing. I glanced at Grendel, who glared at me for disrupting his sleep, and decided that maybe it was a blessing that I didn't have that kind of psychic gift.

I left my crutches by the bed and walked at a snail's pace toward the bedroom door, which was ajar. I nudged it far enough open to peek out into the dining room. Ava sat in the middle of her crib, a doll in her hands that she was bouncing up and down. The *hummm-hummm* noise seemed to be Ava's way of speaking to her new friend. She used it in a conversational pattern that was adorable to listen to.

Thoreau zoomed to the crib and stood on his hind legs to try and see in. Ava's head snapped up at the sound of his claws on the wooden floor, and she abandoned her doll and rose to her feet to look over the railing. She held onto the side of the crib and bounced. "*Scow!*"

My heart clenched at the thought of the real Scout. I hoped someone was taking care of him. After all, the last I'd seen of neighbor Morgan, he'd been getting stitched up in the emergency room.

"*Psst*," I said to get Ava's attention, barely catching her eye before I ducked back into the bedroom.

Slowly, I leaned forward—just far enough to see her. "Peekaboo!"

A smile crept across her face.

During the middle of the night Em had called with an update on Aiden. The scan had revealed he had a laceration of his spleen that would either heal on its own or require surgery. Time would tell, but until then the doctors needed to keep a close eye on his condition. He'd be in the ICU for the next couple of days, then if progressing to his physician's liking, he'd be moved to a recovery floor for a few more days of bed rest. Em didn't want to leave his side, which meant that Ava would stay with us for a while.

It also meant missing some of her exams. I knew choosing Aiden over the tests was a no-brainer, but I also knew Em. She was going to be stressed.

Until Aiden was released, I was in a bit of an investigative limbo. I usually worked with Aiden or Sean—both of whom were currently out of commission. Time was of the essence with Kira's disappearance, so I'd go solo if I had to. And it was looking like I had to.

I hid again, then popped out. "Peekaboo!"

Ava squealed.

I hid, smiling like a damn fool.

It was then that I noticed Sean sitting up in bed, staring at me, a soft glint in his eyes.

"What?" I asked him.

"Nothing." But his grin told me otherwise.

I waved him off and popped back into the other room. "Peekaboo!"

Ava threw her head back and laughed.

It might have been the sweetest sound I'd ever heard.

"Good morning," I said, limping over to her.

Reaching into the crib, I lifted her out. I racked my brain for any kind of morning lullaby but couldn't think of one.

Another reason my job at the daycare had been appropriately short-lived.

Softly, I began singing about my man taking a morning train. I clumsily danced around the living room as Thoreau ran circles around my feet, barking sharply.

He hated my singing.

Sean appeared in the bedroom doorway still wearing that bemused smile. "Sheena Easton?"

"Raphael's influence." His love of eighties music had rubbed off on me. I started singing again.

Ava's face crumpled and she let out a wail.

"What? What?" I asked her. "What's wrong?"

"It's probably your singing," Sean said.

I made a face at him.

He came over and held out his arms. Ava went willingly into them and immediately stopped crying.

My jaw dropped. "How—"

Smiling, he said, "I have a way with women."

I rolled my eyes and went to brush my teeth, wash up, and pull my hair back.

His laughter echoed through the cottage and soon Ava was giggling with him. It did my heart good.

By the time I emerged from the bathroom, Sean had a mug of coffee ready for me. A freshly-diapered Ava was sitting with a pile of blocks, carefully stacking them. I saw Ebbie eyeing the tower and had the feeling she was plotting to knock it down. Ebbie as King Kong versus toy skyscrapers. I took a picture of Ava with my cell phone and messaged it to Aiden—it was my way of showing him that Ava was perfectly fine.

A moment later, my cell phone rang, and I saw it was Em calling. I quickly answered.

After a minute of catching up on Aiden's condition (nothing's changed), and how she was doing (tired but fine and she didn't want to talk about school), she said, "Aiden wants to talk to you."

"Why does that sound like a warning?"

With a question in his eyes Sean glanced at me, and I shrugged.

"He's grumpy," Em said. "Brace yourself."

I mouthed, "Aiden's grumpy" to Sean, who was going about making breakfast. He nodded. I supposed Aiden had reason to be. Someone had almost blown him to bits. "I'm braced."

"I'll talk to you later," she said.

I heard a lot of static—probably the shuffling of the phone—and then Aiden's voice came on the line.

"How's Ava?"

I wanted to tease him about his manners and not saying hello, but I gave him a pass this time. "She's fine. Didn't you get the picture I sent?"

"Are those non-toxic blocks?"

"Nope. Full of arsenic."

There was silence on the line.

Finally, I thought I heard him mumble, "I need to get out of this place."

Then I thought I heard Em say, "Not until the doctor says so."

Then I definitely heard Aiden let loose a few choice swear words.

"Hello?" I said. "I'm still here."

Aiden's voice was tight, maybe from pain, maybe from anger. Maybe both. "Early report is in about the blast at Kira's house. Amateurish homemade bomb rigged to the front door. House doused with gasoline."

"Thank goodness it was amateurish," I heard Em say, "or we'd still be picking pieces of you off that lawn. Don't look at me like that, Aiden Holliday. You know it's true."

I could easily imagine the stern look she was giving him, and also the clenching of Aiden's jaw.

But Em was probably right. If that blast had been stronger or if he hadn't turned to face me at the last moment... I shook my head. I didn't want to think about it.

He said, "There's a team putting the pieces of the bomb back together to try and get prints."

"How long will that take?" I asked.

"Days, weeks, months."

"That narrows it down."

He didn't comment on my sassiness, but went on to say, "We hit a snag with Kira's SUV."

"What kind of snag?"

"She doesn't own one. Or lease one. There are absolutely no records of her owning a car since March."

"She got it somewhere. It's not Cinderella's coach."

"It's being looked into, but until we find out, there's no way to track it. No license plate number. Nothing."

Not good.

"Oh," he added. "I got a call earlier from Trey Fisher."

I was very curious as to what Kira's boyfriend had to say. "Oh?"

"You're meeting him at ten a.m. for an interview."

I straightened and almost let out a groan as my muscles protested the sudden movement. I didn't even mind so much that Aiden hadn't asked first. This was too important. "Where?"

"Coffee shop in Hingham." He gave me the address.

I jotted it down.

"After that, you have a meeting with Barb Manciello, the assistant director of the CFC." He rattled off that address, too.

"After that?" I asked, teasing.

There was no joking in his voice when he said, "I'll let you know."

"Any news on the doll?" I asked. Last night Aiden's unmarked car—and the doll we'd picked up at the garage—had been collected by the state police from in front of Kira's house.

"Not yet. Make sure you review Dustin McDaniel's file before going to CFC."

"I will."

"Send more pictures of Ava."

"I will."

"Lucy?"

"Yes?"

"Thanks," he grumbled.

"You're welcome." I promised to call him later.

I hung up as Sean went to the fridge for eggs and milk. He poured the milk into a sippy cup that must have been part of Em's haul that she left here because I'd never seen it before.

"How's Aiden?" Sean asked.

"I think the doctors will be transferring him from ICU to the psych ward soon."

Laughing, he put the milk back in the fridge.

"He just wants to be working," I said, glancing at Ava. "There's still so much to do."

"Was he calling about Kira?"

Between restorative sips of coffee, I filled Sean in about the latest on the explosion.

He motioned to the note I'd written. "You're going somewhere?"

I explained about meeting with Trey Fisher and going to the CFC office later today.

His dark eyebrows furrowed.

"I'll be fine," I said, knowing instantly that he was concerned about my going alone.

Meeting my gaze, he held it for a long second, and then nodded. He walked over and handed the cup to Ava. She happily sipped away. Thoreau sat next to her, watching her every move, and Ebbie was still eyeing the block tower. Grendel sat near his food bowl, his tail swishing back and forth.

As I went about getting food bowls filled, Sean said, "Take a look at this when you get a chance."

He pointed at his laptop on the breakfast bar.

Ebbie abandoned her desire to knock over the tower in favor of food. She rushed to her bowl. She was no fool—if she waited, she knew full well that Grendel would snarf her breakfast in a hot second. Thoreau's bowl was on the other side of the room which gave him a fighting chance against Grendel's thieving ways as well.

I washed my hands and pulled up a counter stool.

Sean had already told me that during his social media search of Kira Fitzpatrick yesterday he'd found someone hell-bent on smearing her name on every platform possible. Even when the comment was deleted by site administrators, other comments remained that referenced the original and the vitriol it contained.

I looked at Sean's computer screen. The Channel 3 Facebook page was loaded, and a post about the explosion was at the top. I skimmed to the comment Sean had highlighted. It was from a user named Barracuda Smith and read "Hahaha. Whore got what was coming to her."

Harsh. "Is that the same user you've seen on the other sites?"

"The name changes. Shark Smith. Piranha Smith. I've found posts on Facebook, Twitter, Instagram. All the same kind of thing. Slut. Whore. Etcetera."

"Etcetera?" I smiled.

"Trying to keep things PG in front of Ava. She's like a sponge right now, you know."

At her name, she looked over at Sean and started babbling up a storm.

"I've heard." Danny, the Channel 3 garage manager, had told me so yesterday. The memory made me think about that doll again. The sooner it was processed the sooner we might have a more substantial lead.

"Think it's a coincidence that the user name on those accounts is some sort of vicious fish?" I asked Sean.

"Nope."

"Trey Fisher's wife?" I speculated.

"I need a little more time to track the IP address but I'd say it's a good possibility." He cracked four eggs into a bowl and began whisking them to make scrambled eggs.

I knew my woman-scorned theory was a good one.

I took out bread for toast, supplemented my coffee with ibuprofen (only two), and let Thoreau out, clipping his lead to his collar.

I was surprised to see a dark pickup truck turn off Dovie's drive and head this way.

I felt Sean come up behind me. "Who is it?" he asked.

"Not sure. I don't recognize the truck."

Sunlight glinted off the windshield, making it impossible to see the driver. I glanced toward the woods. The rent-a-ninjas remained hidden.

The truck stopped and parked at the edge of my crushed shell lane—far enough off as to not interfere with Thoreau's exploration of the front yard.

Dressed in dark jeans and a snug polo shirt, the man stepped out of the truck and hitched a messenger bag onto his shoulder. Ah. That was why the ninjas hadn't come out.

Jeremy Cross was the one who hired them.

He bent to have a silent conversation with Thoreau, who happily wagged his stubby tail. Gulls squawked overhead and Sean hurried to the kitchen, muttering something about his eggs burning.

Jeremy slid sunglasses off as he approached. "Thoreau requests that you stop singing."

Sean let out a loud laugh, and I folded my arms and stared at the dog. "Is that so?"

Thoreau looked away and wandered over to sniff a rock. *Huh.* See if he got any treats today.

"Where are your crutches?" Jeremy asked.

"Inside."

"That'll speed healing."

I frowned at his sarcasm and folded my arms. "I'm a little surprised to see you here."

"I have a few things I need to discuss with you."

I didn't like his tone. "Is something wrong?"

"Yes and no."

"What's the yes?" I asked, instantly alarmed.

"There was an incident last night…"

"An incident? Where?"

Jeremy didn't so much as blink. "Here."

I looked at the woods, at the security team I couldn't see. "You'd better come in and explain."

9

"Coffee?" I asked as I led Jeremy into the house and motioned to a chair.

"No thanks."

He sat, but his gaze hadn't left Ava since the minute he walked through the door. Sitting at the dining table in her little booster seat, she played with more than ate the scrambled eggs in front of her. Sean set a halved piece of toast on her plate, and then came over to shake Jeremy's hand before going into the kitchen to refill Ava's sippy cup.

If he was vying for the title of Mr. Mom of the Year, he'd win, hands down.

Jeremy couldn't take his eyes off Ava, and I couldn't even imagine what was going through his head. Or the pain he'd lived through when his little girl had been murdered by a madman.

I grabbed my coffee mug from the breakfast bar and sat on the sofa. "That's Ava, Kira's daughter." I'd already told him all about the case when I called yesterday.

It wasn't until Ebbie streaked across the room and leapt onto his lap that Jeremy tore his gaze from the little girl.

He whispered to Ebbie, and she began purring.

"Does she hate my singing, too?" I asked.

"Not as much as Thoreau does."

"Yeah, yeah," I mumbled.

"What's this about an incident?" Sean asked, sitting next to Ava at the table, keeping a close watch on her.

Grendel was watching, too, hoping some scraps of food would fall. He was probably in luck today with the way Ava was flinging her food around. She reminded me a little bit of the Cookie Monster—and how most of his cookies ended up on the floor.

Setting his bag on the table, Jeremy reached in and pulled out a manila folder. "Someone tried to breach the perimeter here last night."

"Tried?" I asked.

Jeremy's tone was hard, unyielding. "It was not a successful attempt."

"Who?" Sean asked.

"Unknown. Intruder escaped by jumping off the neighbor's cliff."

My gaze went to the window. The cliffs along this stretch of the coast were quite high, and it was extremely rocky below the surf. "Did he live?"

"Unknown," Jeremy said. "No body has washed up."

Sean's eyebrows dipped. "Did your team find a car parked nearby?"

"Negative."

"Any description?" I asked.

Jeremy scratched Ebbie's chin. "White male. Tall, average build. Blond hair."

It sounded a lot like the description of the man who put the doll in Kira's SUV. Who was he? "Aiden was afraid this would happen. That someone might come after Ava."

"But why?" Sean asked. "What's she have to do with any of this?"

We all looked at her as she lifted a piece of toast toward her mouth. Bits of scrambled egg stuck to her chin, her hair.

It was an unanswerable question at this point. All we could do was continue to keep her safe. "Thank your team for us, Jeremy."

Jeremy said, "I heard about the explosion and Aiden's hospitalization. Thought I could be of help." He dropped the file on the coffee table.

I reached for it.

"This is Kira Fitzpatrick's banking history. I'm still working on getting her home and cell phone records," Jeremy explained.

My eyebrows shot up. "I'm not even going to ask how you got this."

"Good," he said without a hint of a smile, "because I wasn't going to tell you."

I frowned at him, and he stared back, his gaze unwavering.

Damn, I bet he'd been (and most likely still was) an excellent FBI agent.

Sean unbuckled Ava from her seat, gave her hands and face a quick wipe, and set her free to run around. She grabbed her doll and plopped down next to her pile of blocks which had been, suspiciously, knocked over. Grendel quickly snarfed all fallen crumbs.

Sean sat next to me and leaned over my shoulder as I opened the file.

"As you can see," Jeremy said, "there have been several withdrawals over the past couple of days from various ATMs."

I skimmed the details. Starting late Thursday night the daily max limit of five hundred dollars had been withdrawn. Fifteen hundred so far. The banks had been in Quincy, Milton, Braintree.

"She's alive?" Sean asked, glancing at Ava.

Jeremy said, "Appears that way. But appearances can be deceiving."

I thought about the bomb at her house. If she were hiding, she had good reason. "Any chance you have video surveillance?"

"Working on it."

My cell phone rang and Sean got up to grab it for me. He handed it over and I read the caller ID. Marisol. I silenced the phone—I'd call her back as soon as Jeremy left. She was probably calling to tell me how their coffee date had gone. It would be all kinds of awkward to talk about it in front of him.

Jeremy rubbed Ebbie's ears, then put her on the ground. He stood up. "I need to get back. I'll let you know when I hear something else."

He didn't know it, but I knew he owned a wildlife refuge in Marshfield. I suspected it was more of a refuge for him than the animals. I walked him to the door. I spotted my mother's car turning in at the top of the lane. I could only imagine why she was dropping by so early.

Jeremy hopped in his truck and slammed the door. He apparently didn't want to give me any time to question him about Marisol. I wanted to run to my phone to return Marisol's call and get the details of their date, but there was the small matter of my mother's arrival.

"Good morning, LucyD!" Mum said as she stepped out of her car. There was a covered dish in one hand and with the other she waved to Jeremy as he drove off. She yelled, "Fuzzy navel" toward the trees as she tottered up the walkway in strappy high heel sandals.

I eyed the plate as she climbed the front steps. "Are those cookies?"

"These aren't for you," she said as she set the plate on the porch railing. Again, she yelled toward the woods. "I baked you some chocolate chip cookies if you're interested! I'll leave them right here for you."

"Chocolate chip?" I said, trying not to drool. "I'm sure they wouldn't mind if I just had one... You know they're my favorite."

"I know." She kissed my cheek and reached inside her leather tote bag. "I have yours right here." She pulled out a plastic container which held at least two dozen cookies.

Suddenly suspicious, I eyed her. If she'd brought a half dozen—or even a dozen, I'd say it came from motherly love. Two dozen, however? It reeked of bribery.

"What are you up to?" I asked her.

"Me?" she asked, laughing as she linked arms with me as we went into the house. "Nothing. Nothing at all. There are a few things I want to show you..."

"What kind of things?"

She left me in the doorway and went to kiss Sean's cheek, and then coo over Ava. "She's the spitting image of Aiden, isn't she? Hello there, beautiful girl."

"Mum? What things?"

Mum knelt down on the floor next to Ava and picked up one of the stuffed animals—a lamb—and started making overdramatic *baa*ing noises. *Baa! Baaaaa! BAAA!*

My mother was highly skilled in the art of diversion.

At first Ava looked to Sean like she questioned my mother's sanity (I've questioned it a time or two myself), but then she laughed.

Not swayed by her lamb-tastic performance, I said loudly, "What kind of things?"

"*Baa!*" Mum answered, bouncing the sheep over Ava's legs.

"*Baabaabaa!*" Ava echoed, reaching for the lamb.

Miraculously, my mother handed it over. *Finally.*

Before I could ask her again about the things she wanted to show me, someone knocked on the door.

"Who could that be?" my mother said brightly.

Her tone told me she knew exactly who it would be.

Sean looked amused. I had the feeling my face did not show any amusement whatsoever.

I pulled open the door to find a skinny little man, upper middle aged and dressed in a three-piece suit, surrounded by three scary-looking men who wore dark clothing and carried big guns.

The skinny man's eyes were wide with fear, his forehead dotted with sweat, and his knees knocked as he clutched a satchel to his chest.

"Shit," my mother said, scrambling to her feet. "I forgot to tell him the safe words."

"Shit! Shit! Shit!" Ava echoed.

Oh, *that* she said perfectly.

Sean dropped down and began *baa*aing madly to try to distract Ava from repeating the curse word—Aiden would be seriously displeased to learn of the latest addition to his daughter's vocabulary.

I glanced from Sean to my mother to Mr. Shaky Knees and laughed.

"Lucy!" my mother chastised as she pushed past me saying "fuzzy navel" over and over in higher and higher octaves to the men in black.

I swiped tears from my face. "I can't help it!"

My mother grabbed Mr. Shaky's arm and pulled him inside. "Lucy, this is Reginald Bruce. He's an architect. Your father and I hired him to draw up the plans for Valentine, Inc."

"Hi," I said to him, doing my best to hold in more laughter. Another giggle bubbled out.

"Wh—Who are they?" Reginald asked, surreptitiously looking over his shoulder.

The three men in black still stood on the porch.

I wanted to say something like "Your worst nightmare" but poor Reg looked like he'd already had a time of it. I couldn't bring myself to tease him. "Security."

Reg's eyes grew even bigger. "Impressive."

"Come sit down, Reginald," my mother said, patting his hand.

One of the men in black said, "Everything good here?"

I said, "Depends on why my mother brought an architect by."

He stared.

"Yep," I said. "All's good."

I received three nods, then the trio turned and marched off the porch. One veered off and grabbed the plate of cookies before heading back into the woods.

By the time I let in Thoreau and closed the door, Sean had a whole farmyard of stuffed animals gathered around Ava. A duck, cow, and a horse had joined the lamb. He was doing his best Old MacDonald impersonation as he mimicked quacks, moos, and neighs.

Still in his jammies with his bandaged head and scruffy beard, he looked absolutely ridiculous lying on the floor playing with stuffed animals.

Yet…I fell a little harder for him.

"Lucy, come look," Mum said as she unrolled a large piece of paper on the table. Building plans.

"What is that?" I asked, trying to make sense of it. "It doesn't look like Valentine, Inc."

Reginald's head snapped up and he said to my mother, "You didn't tell her?"

My mother waved away his concern.

"Tell me what?" I asked, squinting at the plans.

"About the renovations," Reginald said, swiping his forehead with a monogrammed handkerchief.

"Right, the renovations. At Valentine, Inc." Why did I feel as though we were talking in circles? "Mum?"

"No," Reginald said, looking between us. "The renovations…here."

"Here *here*?" I pointed at the floor.

Sean stopped *moo*ing and watched us carefully.

Reginald tipped his head and said, "It's more like here *there*." He motioned upward toward the roof. "The plans are to renovate the first floor and add a second story." He looked at my mother. "Did I misunderstand, Judie? I've already hired a contractor..."

My gaze whipped to my mother.

She smiled ear to ear. "I brought cookies."

"There aren't enough cookies in the world," I said, folding my arms.

"LucyD, just listen to reason," Mum said.

"No. I don't have time for reason. I have somewhere I need to be soon."

"Five minutes," Mum persisted. "Five itty bitty minutes."

"No."

"Four, then. Reginald came all the way out here and the poor man is still shaking from being accosted outside."

"It's your fault he was accosted," I pointed out.

"A pesky detail," she said. "And they were chocolate chip cookies I brought, remember? Your favorite."

I looked at Reginald. He blinked beguilingly at me.

"Dovie's never going to agree to this," I said, pulling out my trump card. Dovie loved this place the way it was. Same as I did.

"LucyD," my mother reached over and patted my hand. "It was her idea."

"Shit!" Ava squealed.

I agreed wholeheartedly.

10

The Brew the Day coffee shop occupied a corner of an upscale strip mall not far from Hingham center. Large planters filled with colorful summer flowers hung from lampposts along the sidewalk, and the shop's pale-green awning flapped in the sea breeze. A decorative menu board boasted the lunch special of a tomato, basil, and mozzarella panini, which normally would make my mouth water, but I'd eaten half a dozen cookies on the way over. My stomach wasn't too happy about my lack of discipline when it came to chocolate chips.

I bought an iced coffee and crutched back outside to sit at a bistro table under an ivy-covered pergola. Trey Fisher was late.

Aching, I stretched my muscles and breathed in the sea air to try to let go of some stress. It was nearly impossible. Between this case and my mother...

My mother.

I sucked in a deep breath and let it out slowly, hoping

that would ease the tension gripping my muscles, my nerves, my…world. I waited a second. Nope. The breathing thing wasn't working. I eyed my iced coffee and suddenly wished it was a bottle of vodka. That *might* help.

Renovations. On my cottage. My sweet little cottage. I loved every inch of its 800 square feet. Yes, it was tiny. Yes, it needed updating. But it didn't need four bedrooms, three baths, and a balcony.

I blew out another breath, which might have sounded more like a monstrous huff to the couple sitting next to me. I apologized and stuffed the straw in my mouth.

The worst part of the renovation plans was that I didn't really have a say in what happened to my home. I rented the cottage from Dovie…so if she had planned this whole thing with my mother then I could expect contractors to show up in a few days.

I'd better start packing.

I was so lost in miserable thoughts I didn't hear the man approach until he started speaking.

"I was told to look for a blonde with curly hair who had a boot on her foot. The detective neglected to tell me how beautiful you are. Might I say that the cuts and bruises only add to your appeal?"

I glanced up into the sky-blue eyes of Trey Fisher.

He wore a fitted light-gray dress shirt tucked into tailored charcoal-gray dress pants. A black leather belt matched square-toed loafers. He looked every inch a professional, but his last comment zipped past acceptable and went straight to smarmy.

I frowned, wondering if he spoke to all women like this.

He held out a hand for a shake. "I'm Trey Fisher."

As though I needed an introduction. I'd seen his face on my TV for years. First as a Bruins forward, then as a sportscaster. I set my cup on the table and stared at his hand. He thrust it a little closer.

Bracing myself, I reached out and shook. "I'm Lucy Valentine."

His hand wasn't as big and beefy as one would think for a former professional hockey player, but it was strong, his skin rough and callused.

I didn't have any visions, for which I thanked my lucky stars. "Please sit," I said, trying to pull my hand back.

He was having none of it. I met his gaze. It was challenging—and dare I say it—a bit predatory.

I yanked my hand away, and he sat down, smiling.

"Did you see anything?" he asked, using air quotes around the word "see."

What on earth had Kira seen in him? Because I'd spent all of ten seconds with him and pegged him as a complete asshole.

Jackhole, Aiden had called him.

That fit, too.

Well, *okay*. Trey was a handsome jackhole. I'd give him that. Somehow, his slightly-crooked nose only added to his good looks. With his thick wavy blond hair, wolfish gaze, and sexy beard scruff...he was easy on the eyes.

"Well?" he said, leaning in. "You're a psychic, right?"

As Aiden didn't usually come out and tell people I was psychic, I wondered how Trey had known. Had he recognized my name from news reports? I supposed it didn't matter. He knew—and he'd been trying to test me. He hadn't done his homework, however, because he hadn't been thinking about an *item* he lost...or I would have seen it. I straightened and looked him dead on. "A psychic, yes. Your puppet, no."

His smiled broadened. "Feisty. I like that."

Dirtbag.

Reaching in my tote, I pulled out a small journal and a pen. The sooner this interview was over and done with, the better. "How long have you been dating Kira?" I narrowed my gaze. "And does she know how you shamelessly flirt with women you just met?"

Leaning back, he drew his left foot atop his right knee. Paisley-printed socks peeked out from beneath the hem of his pants. He'd come a long way from center ice.

His gaze hardened. "Don't flatter yourself. That wasn't flirting. If it had been, we'd be in my car by now and you'd have that pretty little dress up around your waist."

"You're charming," I said, oozing sarcasm.

Nonplussed, he shrugged. "I'm honest."

I had the feeling not too many women said no to him. Lifting my eyebrows, I said, "Then you can honestly answer my questions."

He didn't fidget, but he looked pained, like he'd rather be anywhere but here. "Kira and me? We've been dating for two months, give or take."

Tapping my pen, I said, "Exclusively?"

He hesitated only a second before saying, "Yes."

I studied him carefully. *Honest*, my ass. If I wanted, I could be in his car with him right now, having my way with him. The thought made me want to toss all those cookies I'd eaten. Why the pretense of being monogamous, then? What was he trying so hard to hide? "When did you file for a divorce?"

His eyelid twitched. "I didn't file. Tova did. A few months ago."

Tova Dovell Fisher, his stunning Swedish wife. "How long were you two separated before the filing?"

"Technically, we've never been separated."

Beads of condensation slid down my plastic cup and pooled on the table. "What's that mean?"

"It means that we still live together," he said. "Neither of us are willing to vacate our brownstone. Our lawyers are sorting it out while we sleep in separate bedrooms."

I couldn't imagine the stress of that living situation. "I take it Kira didn't spend much time at your place."

"Mostly when Tova was out of town for work." He grinned and winked.

I couldn't tell whether he was being honest or trying to get a rise out of me. "Did you and Tova have an open marriage?"

"It was open on my part."

I had the feeling that's all that mattered to him—what he wanted. "Why get married in the first place if you're not fond of monogamy?"

"Tequila and an Elvis chaplain."

Ah. "Vegas?"

"What happens there doesn't always stay there. Sometimes it moves in and then refuses to get the hell out without taking half of your life savings."

I knew Tova had her own money—lots of it. But Trey had more. He had all kinds of endorsement deals, a line of sports clothing, and was an investor in many businesses.

Personally, I kind of hoped Tova got more than half of his property. A jet rumbled overhead as I asked, "How's she feel about Kira?"

"We don't talk about it."

"That sounds like a copout."

"What do you want me to say? That Tova hates Kira? That she kidnapped and killed her?"

Interesting that he went there. "Does she? Did she?"

"Don't be ridiculous. Tova has a temper, but she's a woman who rescues a cricket if it gets into the house."

"Is she the type who'd leave vicious messages on social media?"

He chuckled. "She's not very subtle, is she? Barracuda? Piranha? It's laughable."

"You know for certain that she's the one who left those posts?"

"One hundred percent. Once in a while, she leaves her laptop open. I snoop. Sue me."

It wouldn't surprise me if Tova left it open on purpose so he'd know she was trying to hurt Kira. "Has she ever had a face-to-face confrontation with Kira?"

"Not that I know of."

"When was the last time you saw Kira?"

Without even taking a second to think about it, he said, "Thursday afternoon at work. It was the last I saw her."

I set the pen to rest in the channel between the pages of the journal. "I heard you two had a big fight recently. What was it about?"

"You're mistaken."

I tipped my head. "Am I?"

"Yes."

Interesting. Morgan Creighton seemed sure, which made me wonder why Trey would try to hide it. "Did she talk to you about her latest story?"

"Her whole world has been wrapped up in that case about the missing kid the last couple of weeks." He sounded jealous.

I asked, "Do you know who she was meeting with Thursday morning?"

He shook his head. "She doesn't like sharing that kind of information, but she keeps all her notes on a flash drive. Find that flash drive, and you'll find a lot of answers." He snapped his fingers. "I did hear her on the phone Tuesday night with someone, making plans to meet on Wednesday morning."

The day before all hell broke loose.

"She said a name," he said. "It was unusual, so it stuck in my head. Jarvis. And she promised to bring money."

"Money?" I asked.

"Reward money."

I lifted a brow. "For the McDaniel case?"

"No idea, but it wouldn't surprise me. Kira often made it known she was willing to pay tipsters for valid leads, and she was eating, drinking, sleeping that case."

Valid leads. What had this particular tipster told her about the McDaniel case? "Jarvis? Is that a first name or last name?" I jotted it down. If I could find Jarvis, it might be the break I needed.

Trey shrugged. "It's probably on her flash drive. Like I said, find that..." He trailed off as his attention was diverted by a pretty young thing walking into the coffee shop.

Find the flash drive. That was easier said than done. It could be anywhere—including in the ruins of Kira's home. If it had been incinerated, it wouldn't be much good to us now.

I switched to a different approach, my tried and true way of finding things. "Did you ever give Kira any gifts?"

He said, "Yeah. Of course."

"Anything she might have been wearing when she disappeared?" I could read his energy and find the object. Gifts were the only time an item had two owners. "Earrings, a ring, a handbag? That kind of thing?"

He tore his gaze from the young woman and focused on me. "I don't think so. The jewelry I bought her was high quality. Not the type of pieces to wear casually at work or around town."

I was both disappointed and relieved. As much as I wanted to find Kira, I really didn't want to touch him again. "Any chance she left some clothing at your place?" If she had, I could still do a scent reading.

"Nothing that I know of," he said. "She didn't have a drawer in my bureau if that's what you're getting at."

This meeting was going nowhere fast.

"Where do you think Kira is?" I finally asked him. He didn't seem all that concerned she was missing.

"I don't know, but I'm sure she's fine."

"You still think that way, even after her house blew up?"

"Kira...Kira is indestructible. If she got herself in a mess, she'll find a way out of it. I'm sure she's holed up in a fancy hotel under an assumed name and laughing her ass off at the media coverage. That *she's* the story. The talk of the town."

There was something in his tone that made me wonder if he knew more than he was letting on. Did he believe Kira orchestrated all of this somehow? It was the opposite of what Morgan had said. "You don't think—"

"Sorry," he said, holding up one hand as he looked at his buzzing smartphone. "I have to get this." He stood up and stepped out of earshot.

Was Kira's disappearance one big PR stunt? I thought about those bank records and recent withdrawals. Kira could be tucked into a very nice hotel for a few hundred dollars a night. I didn't want to believe it. For Ava's sake, I hoped Trey's indifference was more about his own self-involvement. He was so wrapped up in himself, maybe he thought everyone else was, too.

But then I thought about the alternative. That something terrible had happened to Kira, leaving a little girl without her mother. Suddenly, a PR stunt looked positively wonderful.

Trey came back to the table and said, "I have to go. One of the Patriots got himself arrested for trying to take a loaded weapon through airport security."

Even though I still had questions for him, I wasn't all that sad to see him go. "That's fine. I have more questions for you, and I'll also need to speak with Tova at some point, so I need a contact number."

"Is speaking to Tova necessary?"

I stood. "Yes."

After giving me a long once-over that made me want to shower, he tossed a business card on the table and used my pen to write Tova's number on the back. "Call me anytime, especially if you change your mind about getting a ride in my car." He puckered his lips in a faux kiss, winked, and strode off.

Yuck. I was starting to believe that he was called "Fish" not because of his last name but because he was slimy.

As I watched him saunter away, I could kick myself for not asking him anything about Ava and if he knew why Kira suspected she might be in danger. But I thought in light of her missing mother that it was more interesting he hadn't asked *me* about her.

11

Traffic-heavy side roads slowed me down as I navigated my way to Randolph. The twenty-five minute trip took nearly forty as Scarlett, my GPS, bossily guided me to the CFC's area office located near Central Cemetery. Clouds shaded the simple square brick building as I turned into the lot. My meeting with Barb Manciello, this office's assistant head honcho, wasn't for another fifteen minutes, so I was in no rush as I parked the car. I was here solely on a fact-finding mission. I wanted to know what Barb knew of Kira's involvement in Dustin McDaniel's case.

I needed a clear head for this meeting, so I forced myself not to think about Trey Fisher or my mother's renovation plans. Reaching across the console, I rifled through my tote looking for my copy of Dustin McDaniel's file.

Paper-clipped to the inside cover was a photo of the little boy. Longish blond hair, big blue eyes, pale cheeks. Thin bordering on too thin, and his far-off gaze looked to hold secrets instead of little-boy mischief.

Dustin David McDaniel had been born to Alisha (nee Keefe) and Corey McDaniel, both twenty-four years old. Dustin had been in the CFC system since he was born—when he'd tested positive for marijuana. The agency took custody of the baby, but later returned him after Alisha completed a court-ordered drug program. When Dustin was a year old, a neighbor had called in a report of negligence when she witnessed Alisha leave the baby in a playpen in the front yard unsupervised for a long period of time. It turned out Alisha been getting high in the house and had forgotten about him. Again, CFC had taken temporary custody of the child but Alisha completed another court-ordered drug program and was able to get the boy back a few months later.

Dustin's father, Corey, had been in prison on drug-related and assault charges for all of Dustin's short life—he'd been arrested while Alisha was pregnant. Corey still had four years left on his six-year sentence.

Dustin's disappearance might have not ever come to light if not for Alisha's mother, Patty Keefe. Patty, who was battling a terminal cancer diagnosis, hadn't seen Dustin since Christmastime and repeated requests to visit him had been shot down by her daughter. Dustin was napping; he wasn't feeling well; he was at a friend's house having a playdate. For months, there had been an excuse as to why Patty couldn't see him and the more her health failed, the more desperate she grew. She wanted to see her grandson—spend more time with him before she died.

My phone rang, startling me. I glanced at the readout. Sean. I answered, but all I heard in the background was utter chaos. Men shouting, the baby crying, barking, my mother asking about cookies.

"Sean? Hello?"

"Hold on," he said.

Smiling, I shook my head. Only he'd call me and tell me to hold on.

Finally, he came back on the line. "Okay, I had to move somewhere a little quieter."

It didn't sound that much quieter—I could still hear all the commotion. "What's going on?"

"Were you expecting a delivery of a dog today?" he asked.

"Of a what?"

"A dog. *Woof, woof,*" he said and I heard Ava quickly mimic him.

"A dog? Noooo," I said, dragging the word out. "Why?"

"A vet tech showed up from Marisol's clinic with a dog in tow. He said he was told to deliver it to you. Looks like Lassie. Collar has a tag that says his name is Scout, but no one is answering the phone number on the tag. The security team has the guy pinned to the ground. He's close to tears."

"Ohhhh," I said, dragging that word out, too. Maybe the dog—and not Jeremy Cross—had been why Marisol called earlier. "*That* dog. Shit."

I heard the smile in his voice. "Something you need to tell me, Ms. Valentine?"

"Was the dog overjoyed to see Ava?"

"How'd you know? We had to put the dog outside so he wouldn't jump all over her."

"You know how she keeps saying '*scow?*' She's actually saying Scout. The dog is Ava's. Well, Kira's, I guess. Kira's neighbor, Morgan, was supposed to bring the dog to Marisol at the clinic." I explained about how I'd met Morgan the day before—and why he couldn't keep the dog because of his allergies. "I don't quite know why the dog is at our house, but I missed a call from Marisol earlier…"

I heard Sean yell to let the guy up, that his story checked out. "I smell a lawsuit," he said to me.

"I'll have Marisol explain it all to him." I winced, having the feeling I might have to dip into my off-limits trust fund for a payoff.

"Can you call Marisol?" Sean asked. "This house isn't big enough for more pets."

"I told you so," I heard my mother yell.

I rolled my eyes.

"How'd your meeting with Trey Fisher go?" he asked.

"It went. He's skeezy."

"Do I need to kill him?"

"Not yet."

"That's probably good. I'm not exactly in top fighting condition."

"You could still take him."

"Thanks for that, Ms. Valentine."

"No problem. Hey, if you have a free minute in between changing diapers, walking dogs, entertaining my mother, and saving vet techs, can you search everything of Ava's that Aiden brought over? A thorough search, too. Cut open stuffed animals, check the lining of the diaper bag, inspect every bit of her car seat."

"What am I looking for?"

"A flash drive," I said, explaining how Kira was never without it. "If all her notes are on that flash drive, and she thought someone was after her…"

"She'd stash it somewhere safe."

"Right."

"It makes sense. It also might explain the explosion at her house."

"Go on," I said, not quite following.

"Okay, worst-case scenario? Someone confronts her, kills her, and can't find the flash drive. The killer goes to her house, searches it, and still can't find it. Could be it's in there, could be it's not, but the killer's not taking a chance that it is and someone else will eventually find it."

A chill went down my spine. "Do you think that's why someone tried to break in here last night? Because he or she had the same idea I did? To search Ava's belongings?"

"Possibly. But then we have to think about how the killer knew she was here. The killer would have to know that Ava was with Aiden and that he brought her here. It's a stretch."

Killer. Sean had prefaced what he said with "worst-case scenario" and he was right. It would be the worst. All this supposition was giving me a headache. "One step at a time, I guess."

The dogs set off barking again. Sean asked, "When are you coming back?"

"I have ten minutes until my meeting here at the CFC. I'll be home after that."

"I'll be waiting with a baby, two cats, two dogs, a hamster, three special ops, a litigious vet tech, and your mother," he said, letting out a laugh. "I know I volunteered to babysit, but I think this deserves hazard pay."

"I'll make it up to you," I promised.

His voice dropped low. "I'm going to hold you to that." He clicked off.

I bet he would.

I dialed Marisol, but it went straight to her voicemail. "Call me back when you get a chance," I said and hung up.

Turning my attention back to the file propped against my steering wheel, I picked up my reading where I'd left off.

The standoff between Alisha and her mother culminated on April twenty-eighth, Dustin's second birthday. When Alisha dodged requests to let Patty visit, she confronted her daughter. During the heated argument, Alisha finally confessed that CFC had taken custody of the boy in early January because of her ongoing drug use, and she had been too embarrassed to say so. But when Patty called the agency to verify the claim and see if she could visit Dustin at his foster home, she was told that Dustin was not in their custody and as far as they knew he was still with his mother. The authorities were brought in.

And all hell had broken loose.

Media quickly reported that in mid-December Alisha had been fired from her job at a local fast-food restaurant, and photos surfaced of Alisha's illicit drug use during the time frame Dustin had been missing. It was also revealed that over the past few months she'd taken in a number of questionable roommates.

All of which should have been red flags for the CFC. *If* they'd been paying attention.

It turned out that Dustin's caseworker had falsified reports of visiting Dustin—and hadn't actually seen him with her own eyes since early December. Her supervisor supposedly knew of the tampered reports and turned a blind eye. When that news broke, her job had been terminated immediately and the supervisor had been suspended. The CFC came under intense scrutiny. The commissioner vowed that this was an aberration, not the norm for their employees, but that the agency would crack down and make sure nothing like this ever happened again.

During the initial investigation, Alisha stuck to her story about the CFC taking Dustin. Then on advice from her court-appointed lawyer she clammed up altogether, refusing to cooperate or take a lie-detector test.

Before any charges could be filed against her, in early May Alisha McDaniel died of a drug overdose. She'd taken the secret of what happened to Dustin with her to the grave.

Closing the file, I looked at the building.

The last verified sighting of Dustin had been Christmas day. In missing persons cases, the first forty-eight hours were critical for recovery. For Dustin, it had been six months. Time was working against us.

Alisha's home and car had been processed by police and there was no sign a crime had taken place. Area searches had been completed with nothing found. The questionable roommates had moved in during the month of February and had been told the same story Patty heard: CFC had taken custody of Dustin in January. No one questioned that there hadn't been a guardianship hearing. No one in Alisha's immediate circle asked questions, period. Except Patty.

I flipped open the file again. Patty was now living in a hospice care center in Braintree and still called detectives on the case several times a week for an update. I made a mental note to pay her a visit.

Turning back to the photo of Dustin, I stared into his haunted eyes. A familiar feeling grew within me—the need to find out what happened to him. I'd do everything in my power to figure it out. To give him justice.

Letting out a breath, I checked my watch. I still had a few minutes.

I grabbed my phone and dialed a familiar number. When the call was answered, I quickly said, "Remember how happy you were to finally have a sister?"

"I never said that," Cutter denied, a smile in his voice.

"You must have thought it."

"Why do I think you want something?"

"Because you're a Valentine and brilliant?"

"You're starting to make me queasy."

"I need you to make sure Dovie and Preston keep away from the news. Far, far away."

There was a stretch of silence. "Why? What's this about, Lucy? Something with Dad? Did he get caught with another floozy?"

Dad. It warmed my heart to hear him finally calling him that regularly. "Not this time." A miracle, really.

"Then what?"

I gave him a quick rundown of the case.

He whistled. "Aiden has a kid?"

"*Shh.*"

"I'm at the store, Lucy, picking up approximately eighteen gallons of ice cream. I don't think they can hear me."

"Do not underestimate them."

He laughed. "I'll see what I can do. Dovie has a smartphone."

"Kill it. And hide yours."

"All right, but when she finds out...," he said.

"Enjoy my share of the inheritance, okay?"

Laughing again, he hung up. I decided to go inside, even though I was still early. I tucked Dustin's file into my bag and stepped out of the car, biting back a moan from my aches and pains. As I grabbed my crutches from the back seat, the clouds shifted, and I squinted against sudden sunlight. A commuter train rumbled from somewhere nearby.

Grass grew through the cracked cement walkway that led to the front door, which was flanked by two overgrown holly bushes. A prickly branch grabbed my dress as I passed and as I paused to untangle myself, I had the uneasy feeling the bush was trying to warn me about going into the building.

Nonsense, but nonetheless, I was suddenly spooked.

Inside, my eyes adjusted to the dim light in the reception area. A gum-chewing young woman sat behind a low curved counter. She glanced up at me but continued tapping away on a keyboard. There weren't many chairs in the reception area—only five or six and none of them were occupied.

I crutched up to the counter. "Hi, I'm Lucy Valentine. I have an appointment with Barb Manciello." I pulled out my state police ID.

The woman stopped typing. Her gaze narrowed on the cut on my cheek, but she didn't question it. She looked to be in her early twenties, and the way she chewed her gum was making me nauseous. *Smack, smack, smack.*

A charm bracelet jingled as she tucked a lock of thick dark hair behind her ear, and said, "I'm sorry, but she's not here."

"Not here? We had an appointment…"

An apology shone in pretty blue eyes heavily lined with liquid black liner. "Her daughter fell and had to go to the emergency room," she explained. "She said she called…"

"I didn't get a call."

She blinked at me repeatedly. *Smack, smack, smack.* "Sorry?"

The bracelet jingled again as she folded her hands on the counter. Her fingernails each had a crystal glued to the long tip. I didn't know how she got any work done with those—I'd be eternally distracted by the bling.

Even though her gaze held no sign of deception, I couldn't help but wonder if she was telling the truth. It seemed awfully coincidental that Barb was suddenly called away. And I didn't believe in coincidences.

I didn't want this whole trip to be a waste, so I said, "Do you know if Kira Fitzpatrick from Channel 3 news stopped by here recently?"

Recognition flashed in her eyes, and her gum-chewing slowed. I had the feeling she was debating how much she was allowed to tell me.

"When?" she asked, clearly stalling.

"Within the past two weeks?"

"I, uh—" She glanced over her shoulder. Dropping her voice a bit, she said, "She came in a few times, the last being on Wednesday. She said she was doing a story on the McDaniel case."

"Did she interview anyone here?"

She shook her head. "We're not allowed to speak to the press. I heard that she was missing. The reporter, I mean. Has she been found yet?"

"No," I said.

Smack, smack. Fear crept into her voice. "Do you think she's missing because of that case?"

Between the jingle jangle of the bracelet and the smack of the gum, I was pretty sure I would lose my mind if I worked with her.

"I don't know," I answered honestly. "I don't suppose you know someone named Jarvis, do you?" It was the name Trey Fisher had overheard. Who was Jarvis and what kind of information did he or she have regarding Dustin McDaniel?

Smack. "First or last name?"

"Either."

Looking at me like I had two heads, she said, "Doesn't ring a bell."

It had been a long shot. "Do you know when Ms. Manciello will be back?"

"No. Do you want to reschedule?" she asked, typing away again. *Jingle jangle.* "I can squeeze you in on Thursday. One p.m.?"

"That's fine," I said, knowing I'd ask Aiden to get involved before that.

The receptionist smiled, and I saw a bit of green gum peeking out from behind her teeth. *Ugh.*

"Okay, then," she said brightly. "Have a good day."

After stowing my crutches in the back seat, and turning on the car to get the air conditioning going, I dialed Aiden's cell phone.

"Surgery, Lucy," he said as he answered, his normally calm voice high. "They're talking surgery. I cannot have surgery. That's at least a week here in the hospital. I will lose my ever-loving mind. You might need to break me out of this place."

"Em would kill me." The sunbaked car was stifling, so I powered down the window until the car cooled off. A robin *chereeped* from a branch nearby.

"I don't think she would go that far, but it's a risk I'm willing to take."

"I understand perfectly." No one came nor went from the CFC building. I would have thought it would be busier. I said, "I hear there's a high infection rate with hospital surgeries these days. Did you hear that? It's been on the news a lot. Superbugs or some such."

"You're not funny."

"Or maybe I'm confusing superbugs with that flesh-eating disease…" I powered up the window and adjusted the air-conditioner's blowers to aim at my neck. "Or are they the same things?"

He groaned. "Fine. I'm sorry I said I'd let Em kill you."

"Apology accepted."

"Did you call just to torture me?" he asked.

"No, I think you're doing a fair job of that yourself. I called to see if you could get me the addresses of Dustin's CFC caseworker and her supervisor. I hit a dead end here at the office." I told him about my visit, Barb Manciello's sudden emergency, and also my meeting with Trey Fisher.

"What do you think the deal is with Kira and Fisher?" he asked. "It doesn't seem like they're well-suited."

"I don't know. Personally, I'd worry about STDs, but that's me."

"Now I'm nauseated on top of everything else."

"Sorry. I have Tova Fisher's number. If anyone can shed light on Trey and Kira's relationship, it's probably her." I poked a finger down the top of my boot, trying to scratch an itch that was out of reach. "I haven't met an ex yet who wasn't willing to sell the soul of their previous partner."

"That's a cheery thought."

"Sad but true."

"Have you set up a meeting with her yet?" he asked.

"Not yet. I'll let you know when I do."

"I'll get those CFC addresses for you within the hour."

"Thanks." I jabbed a pen down my boot and nearly sighed in relief. "I've been thinking about your predicament."

"Can you narrow it down? I've got a few going on."

"The surgery."

"Did you have to remind me?"

"Do you want me to call Orlinda?"

Orlinda Batista was my psychic mentor, a bit of a mystery herself, and a healer. I didn't know how she did it, but I'd been at the receiving end of her healing energy and knew it worked.

"Can she cure something like this?" he asked.

"I don't think it could hurt to try."

"Okay," he said. "I'm game. Give her a call. Thanks."

"I'll talk to you soon."

"Lucy?"

"Yeah?"

"Do you think you could bring Ava by the hospital tonight?"

"Is she allowed?" I asked. Most ICUs had rules against visitors so young.

"Not exactly."

"So you want me to sneak her in?"

"Yes."

It wasn't often straight-laced Aiden was willing to break the rules. "Fine," I said, "but if I get caught, I'm blaming you."

I heard the smile in his voice as he said, "It's a risk I'm willing to take."

12

"We're about as intimidating as Rocky and Bullwinkle," I said to Sean as clouds gathered on the horizon, dark and threatening. Afternoon pop-up storms were supposed to stay out at sea, but if the ominous thunderheads were any indication the forecast hadn't been accurate.

We were in the car, on our way to Stoughton to pay a visit to Elliman Bay, the supervisor who'd been suspended by CFC. Aiden had come through in a big way. By the time I arrived home from my wasted trip to the CFC office, I had the addresses I needed and was eager to visit them. To continue piecing together the timeline of Kira's last known whereabouts.

My mother suggested Sean go with me and had volunteered to watch Ava and the menagerie. I wanted to say no. I really did. Because Sean was still supposed to be taking it easy. And because I also suspected Mum only suggested he go with me so she could further plan my cottage's makeover.

But I'd taken one look in Sean's eyes and agreed.

I was weak where he was concerned.

We had several interviews to tackle. First with Elliman, then we planned to drop by Cat Bennett's (who wasn't answering her phone) house, then go to the hospice in Braintree to meet with Patty Keefe. Tonight, we'd sneak Ava into the hospital to see Aiden. I'd already called Orlinda to see if she could help him, and she had agreed to try. I hoped her healing magic worked. Aiden was going stir crazy.

I glanced at Sean. He had the passenger seat tipped back, a hat over his face as he rested. As much as he might deny being worn out, he was. I suspected, too, that being cooped up for so long was taking its toll.

But it wasn't only that. It was this case.

Instead of finding Kira's flash drive while searching Ava's things, he'd found a small keychain-sized GPS tracker beneath the pad of her car seat. Although we'd already dropped the unit off at the state police barracks to get it tested for fingerprints, neither of us could shake the feeling that we were dealing with something bigger than anyone imagined. Except, maybe, Kira.

Nya said Kira had called her investigation a shocker.

She had certainly uncovered something big…something that caused someone to track her whereabouts via Ava's car seat.

"Are you Rocky or Bullwinkle?" Sean asked, lifting a black-banded fedora from his face to give me a sideways look.

"What do you think?"

He laughed. "Oh no. I'm not falling into that trap."

"Smart man. We're here," I said pulling up in front of a two-story colonial. White-stained cedar shingles, red shutters, brick walkway. A dark sedan was parked in the driveway, and a dog barked from an upstairs window. A man appeared behind a screen door, his hands in his pockets.

Sean held out my crutches to me. He'd removed his head bandages and with the hat on it barely looked like anything was wrong with him at all. Just a few scratches on his face, which were mostly covered by his facial hair.

I, on the other hand, looked a complete mess.

Elliman Bay was expecting us—thanks to Aiden running interference, someone from the state police had called ahead.

At fifty-eight, Elliman had worked with the CFC since its inception and had worked for the DCF before that. Becoming a social worker had been a second career. His first had been in journalism, but his job as an editor at a local paper had been downsized. He'd gone back to school ten years ago to get a social work degree.

Tall with dark skin, keen black eyes, a rounded stomach, and a cleft chin, he met us at the juncture of the driveway and walkway, which was lined with pretty pink petunias.

Sean introduced us, and I gripped my crutches and smiled a hello in order to avoid having to shake hands.

"Let's sit out back," he said in a firm booming voice. He guided us around the side of the house, through a trellised gateway draped in green vines, and onto a back patio surrounded by lush plants and shrubs.

He held out a patio chair for me, one of five that encircled a teak table, and Sean took my crutches and leaned them against a bench. Inside the house, the dog still barked, one of the neighbors down the block was mowing his lawn, and birds chirped loudly. A suburban symphony.

"Something to drink?" he offered as Sean sat next to me.

"No thank you," I said. My stomach was still unsettled from my brunch of cookies and coffee—and possibly from being grossed out by Trey Fisher.

Elliman sat down and looked at us expectantly.

I used my outdoor voice as I said, "Thanks for meeting with us on such short notice."

He gave a curt nod. "I'll do anything in my power to see that Kira is found safe and sound."

Sean said, "Do you know her personally?"

It had certainly sounded that way.

"Kira and I worked together briefly a lifetime ago," Elliman explained. "She's a gifted journalist with intelligence and integrity—rare attributes in a generation fixated on sensationalism. I'm honored to call her a friend. Have there been any leads on her case?"

"Leads, yes," I said, "but none that are panning out quite yet."

"Her daughter?" he asked, his intense gaze locked on mine.

Sean said, "She's safe with a family member."

A bee buzzed by his ear and he swatted it away. "Good."

"We know Kira was working on a story about Dustin McDaniel," I said, noting the way he stiffened at the name. "Did she contact you for an interview?"

"No." His chin jutted. "I called her."

My head came up at his admission. "You did? When?"

"Two weeks ago."

Two weeks. Nya, Kira's boss, said that it was two weeks ago that Kira received a call about this case and had been engrossed ever since. I met his gaze. "You're Kira's anonymous source for this case?"

Elliman leaned in and clasped his hands on top of the table. "Yes. I'd had enough of the department's lies and wanted the truth to come out. I knew Kira would do justice to the exposé, however, I never for one moment thought she'd be in danger. If I had known…"

Sean said, "There's been some speculation that she planned her own disappearance in order to heighten interest in her story."

"Speculation?" Elliman scoffed. "Try pure fiction. Kira would never do such a thing, and for someone to suggest it makes me question not only that person's motives but also their intelligence."

From what I'd learned of Kira, I agreed, and I also questioned Trey Fisher's motives and intelligence, but there were those ATM charges... I hoped video surveillance would come through soon to verify if it had been Kira making those withdrawals.

"You mentioned you'd had enough of the CFC's lies. What in particular?" I asked.

"For one thing, I never condoned Cat Bennett's falsification of her case reports. Did I err in taking her reports as truth? Perhaps, but it wasn't in my job description to play babysitter for my staff."

I couldn't help but question what would have happened if she'd simply done her job and checked in on Dustin McDaniel. It was those kinds of thoughts that gnawed at my stomach, eating at me.

Elliman added, "My superiors felt the need to have another scapegoat to cover up the department's inadequacies, so I was suspended indefinitely. I became a social worker to try and right the injustices of the world, to make a difference, and in turn I was singled out for using my voice to do the right thing."

I could feel his anger from clear across the table. There were so many nuggets of information in his statement that it was hard to decide which one to focus on first. "What kind of inadequacies? I thought that the CFC was flourishing."

"You're not the only one who has fallen victim to the PR smokescreen. It doesn't matter that the state has added agencies, because there still remains a distressing number of at-risk families—a number that keeps growing instead of declining. It's all but impossible to keep up so the same problems that have plagued the DCF now plague the CFC." He let out a frustrated sigh.

For years there had been a debate on how to overhaul the system, with the culmination of those talks being the creation of the CFC. But now I was starting to think that the solution wasn't within child-protection agencies at all, but with preventative education and programs for the parents and families. Or perhaps a combination of both. I recognized that I was reaching for answers, but I hated thinking that this problem was getting worse not better.

"It's a broken system, and I cannot foresee any change," Elliman said. "Within the CFC, there's a profound lack of training. We're overworked—often off the clock. Underpaid. Only two years out of college, Cat Bennett oversaw twenty-eight families." His hands clenched into fists, then released. "Do you know the national average?"

Sean and I shook our heads.

"Fifteen. Fifteen families. I witnessed her exhaustion day in and day out and mentioned to my superiors that her workload should be cut back until she could catch her breath, but my request was denied. There wasn't enough manpower to cover her cases. I myself have—had—thirty-two families. Colleagues have the same numbers."

It seemed the complete antithesis of why the CFC had been created in the first place.

"It sounds as though you have sympathy for Cat," Sean said.

"Absolutely," he said, not denying it. "She worked sixty hours a week and couldn't put a dent in her workload—she hadn't had enough time to learn proper time management skills. I'm not surprised that she succumbed to doctoring reports, as heinous as that sounds. She was a committed worker who couldn't handle the pressure, and for that I blame not only her but myself and everyone else in the office who failed her."

"Do you know if Kira interviewed her?" Sean asked.

"The last I heard, Cat was ignoring Kira's requests," Elliman said, "but if I know Kira, that wouldn't deter her."

In the distance, thunder rumbled. "When did you last speak with Kira?"

"Wednesday afternoon." He looked at the dark sky as though wondering if the clouds were going to break right over us. "She called to ask me if anyone at the CFC drove a cobalt-blue four-door sedan with a smiley face ball stuck on the antenna."

Wednesday afternoon—right after she met with the mysterious Jarvis. "That's pretty specific. Did she say why she wanted to know?"

"She wouldn't say," he answered. "She rarely shared information during ongoing investigations."

It was becoming a familiar phrase.

"Do you know someone who drives a car like that?" Sean asked. The wind kicked up, and he grabbed his hat and tugged it low.

"Cat does." Elliman's jaw jutted again.

As if daring us to make some sort of connection.

He needn't have worried. There were no connections to make. Not yet. Not until we knew why Kira had asked the question in the first place.

"After I told her so, she asked if I could find out if Cat had been working on January third." He held up a hand as I opened my mouth. "Before you ask, I don't know the answer as to why she asked. I have a call into a friend at the agency who's agreed to check the date out for me. When I hear, I'll let you know."

January third. Why that date?

"Do you know anyone named Jarvis?" Sean asked. "We're not sure whether it's a first or last name or if it's a man or woman."

Elliman thought about it for a second then said, "No. Why?"

Thunder cracked again, this time closer. Goosebumps rose on my arms as I said, "It's a name that's come up in our investigation. A loose thread." There were lots of those with this investigation.

"From your questions, I presume you have not yet spoken to Cat," Elliman said.

I tucked a piece of loose hair behind my ear. "Not yet."

"A forewarning… When I last spoke to her, she wasn't in the best frame of mind." Elliman's tone hinted at something as dark and ominous as the clouds above. "I'm not sure how helpful she'll be."

"Depressed?" Sean asked.

"Yes. And drinking. She's distraught over what has happened and also blames herself for what happened to me."

"You two were that close?" I asked.

He shot me an annoyed look. "No, she is that kindhearted. She was upset that I, as her mentor, was suspended for voicing my opinion that she shouldn't have been fired, only suspended, until a complete investigation was undertaken."

Thunder clapped again, but no rain fell as Sean said, "You didn't think she should have been fired?"

I echoed the incredulousness I heard in his voice. If ever there was a case for someone being fired… "Dustin McDaniel's well-being was her responsibility, and she failed him. Of course she should have been fired."

"Maybe so," Elliman shot back, "but my argument is that if Cat was fired, then so should two other employees, because I suspect that Dustin is not the only child missing."

Thunder rolled, shaking the ground. Or maybe that had been from Elliman's statement. Stunned, I asked, "Not the only one? What do you mean?"

"When Dustin's case came to light," he explained, "I began hearing whispers around the office about other missing children. Apparently Cat wasn't the only one doctoring paperwork. From what I overheard, there are two other children currently unaccounted for, Ms. Valentine."

Sean looked at me. This case had just hit the fan, so to speak.

"Two girls between one and two years old who fell off the radar over the past eighteen months. I went to my superiors, who vowed to look into it."

"Do you have proof that the girls are missing?" I asked. "Names? Addresses?"

"No," he said. "I tried to go through the files, but there were too many. I do know the names of the two employees I overheard."

He listed them off, and I quickly wrote them down.

"In the weeks following the news of Dustin's disappearance," Elliman explained, "I waited for news of the other missing children to be released by my superiors, but it never was. I'm assuming they're keeping it classified because it would reveal the deep level of turmoil within the department, but I believe that information should not be suppressed. Lives are at stake. I couldn't go to the media myself. No one would believe me. That is why I called Kira."

No wonder she'd been consumed with this story. Three children.

I thought about the baby doll that had been left in Kira's car and the attached note.

A shiver slid down my spine.

"What about the girls' families?" Sean asked. "Why don't they come forward?"

Elliman shook his head. "Unfortunately, these children are probably missing because of one of their parents. Think about what you know of Dustin McDaniel's case. His disappearance came to light only because of his grandmother."

My heart ached for the cruelties of this world, and for the little babies who suffered because of them.

Elliman glanced up at the sky again, at the cloud ceiling that kept sinking lower and lower. "The blood of these children is on the hands of the CFC." His troubled gaze shifted to me. "I pray Kira's blood isn't as well."

13

The dark swirling clouds followed us to Braintree but the rain still refused to fall. Neither Sean nor I had much to say since leaving Elliman Bay's house. There just weren't words.

Three little ones missing.

Three children who had slipped through the cracks.

It was…incomprehensible. How could something like this have happened? How had it not been reported to the police? I'd already called Aiden to let him know this latest development. Detectives would soon be on their way to the CFC to investigate the allegations. Would they be bulldozed? Or would the agency 'fess up to misdeeds and reveal the names of the missing children?

Sucking in a deep breath, I let it out slowly.

Sean said, "You okay?"

"I'm…disgusted with mankind right now."

"Yeah." He stared out his window.

My GPS was programmed to find the hospice care center so Sean and I could speak with Patty Keefe, but as we drove along, I realized we weren't that far from where Dustin McDaniel had lived.

"Side trip?" I asked Sean.

"Sure."

I threw him a look. "You didn't even ask me where."

"We're not far from where Dustin lived. You want to go to his house to see if any of his belongings remain there so you can give them the sniff test, and you want to ask around to see if anyone knows Jarvis. From the timing of her call to Elliman, we have to assume that Jarvis is the one who told Kira about the blue car. Which means he or she probably saw that car near Dustin's house to have any relevance to this case."

"Actually, I was thinking about stopping for an iced coffee."

He laughed and the sound washed over me, chasing away the coldness of this case and filling me with warmth. "Lies, Ms. Valentine, lies."

I couldn't help but smile. He'd been right, of course. We were so close to where Dustin had been living that it seemed a shame to waste a perfectly good opportunity to stop by.

Five minutes later, we pulled into a visitor space in front of a low-income apartment complex. There were six three-story buildings in total on the street, three on each side. Despite the threat of imminent rain, several children ran around a playground, seemingly without a care in the world. I hoped that was true. Their squeals carried easily through the air, and it was all too easy to imagine Dustin McDaniel sitting in the toddler swing, his toothy smile wide as he sailed into the air.

At the corner, not fifty feet from the playground, I noticed a trio of men loitering near a lamppost—a buzz-cut blond with ghostly pale skin dressed in black from head to toe, a tall Latino covered in tattoos, and a short brown-haired guy who couldn't tear his gaze from his smartphone. Could one of them possibly be the mysterious Jarvis?

I kept staring at the blond. There was something about him that seemed familiar, but I couldn't quite place it. "We don't know him, do we? The blond?"

Cigarette smoke wafted above the guy's head as he puffed away. Sean squinted. "I don't recognize him."

"Something about the way he's standing..." I shrugged.

As I watched, two more men, one black, one white, came out of the woods across the street and approached the group. Money and a small bag of *something* were exchanged with the blond guy. The whole transaction took less than thirty seconds, and the two men from the woods wandered off again. It made me feel ill to see the trio operating their little business so close to the little kids. Ill and mad as hell.

My anger rose and rose until I couldn't take it anymore. I shoved open the door.

Sean clamped my arm, stopping me from getting out. "What're you doing?" he asked.

"Someone has to say something to them. Get them to move along. There are little kids right there. It's sickening."

"You're not that person."

Frustration stung my throat. "If not me, then who?"

"I don't have an answer to that, Lucy, but all three are carrying guns in their waistbands. You are not going over there."

I squinted. "I don't see any guns."

"Lucy."

I recognized that tone—I'd used it on him yesterday morning.

"Fine," I said, eyeing the three. My blood pressure continued to creep up. "We should call the police."

"No need." He pointed. "Look."

A Randolph police cruiser rolled slowly down the street and the trio quickly darted into the woods. They were gone for now, but how soon until they were back?

I squeezed my keys until I yelped, realizing I'd broken the skin on my palm.

Compassion filled Sean's expression. "Hating mankind again?" he asked, carefully lifting my hand.

"Yes."

He brought my palm to his lips and gave it a kiss. "Better?"

"Maybe a little. I..." I shook my head. "They're going to come back. How soon before they're selling to these little kids?"

"As the saying goes, not your circus, not your monkeys, Lucy. You can't fix everything and everyone."

"But I want to," I said.

He gave my hand another kiss, sending little zaps up my arm. "I know. It's one of the reasons why I love you so much."

Some of the anger dissolved. Some. Not all. "Yeah, yeah." I managed a small smile as I pushed open the door. "Let's do this. I think the sooner we get out of here the better for my peace of mind."

"Start with Dustin's old address?" he asked as a wind gust caused a sapling to bend like a limber yoga teacher.

"Sure." The building had twelve apartments, four on each floor, and each had its own separate entrance. The cloud cover cast the stairwells in creepy shadows, sending a shiver down my spine. But fortunately for me, the apartment we were looking for was on the first floor.

Still, I couldn't stop thinking about that trio, and as I fished my crutches out of the backseat, I threw a glance toward the woods. "But..."

"No," Sean said, following my gaze.

"Party pooper."

He crossed to the front of the car. "Come on, Bullwinkle."

I crutched over to him. "You did not just call me a moose."

Shrugging innocently, he said, "Did you ever watch that cartoon? You have to admit that he wasn't the most graceful moose around."

I poked him with my crutch. "What are you getting at?"

With a smirk, he led the way up a cracked walkway leading to Dustin's last-known address, an end unit that had a cranberry-colored door and a pot of wilting geraniums on the front step. Three shiny pinwheels had been stuck in the ground and were spinning crazily as the wind whipped them into a frenzy.

I clumsily followed him, trying desperately to think of a snappy joke about squirrels and nuts, but, by the time I did, Sean had already knocked on the weathered door and a young woman had yelled, "Who is it?" through the sidelight to the right of the door.

A window air conditioner screeched above us as Sean said, "We're investigating the disappearance of Dustin McDaniel," he said, flashing his PI identification.

I held up my state police ID, too.

Locks clicked as the woman released them and pulled open the door only enough to wedge her thin body into the opening. "I need to put a sign on the door."

"Sign?" I asked.

"I moved in the first of this month, and you're like the tenth person to ask. Newspaper reporters, TV reporters. It's annoying. I need to put out a sign saying I don't know anything about that little boy." In her mid-twenties, she had pale red hair streaked with pink stripes that framed a heart-shaped face. Freckles dotted a hooked nose, and thin lips pursed with frustration. She wore a nametag from a local department store, and I heard the sound of cartoons in the background.

"Did Kira Fitzpatrick stop by? The reporter from Channel 3?" I asked.

"Talked to her last week," she said. "Told her the same thing I'm telling you. I don't know anything. Now, if you don't mind, I've got to get my kids down for naps."

"Wait," Sean said as she went to close the door. "A couple of questions, that's all."

"Like what?" she asked. "I told you, I just moved here. I don't know anything or anyone that has to do with that little boy." Under her breath, she muttered something about knowing she should have moved to Quincy instead.

"Were there any belongings left in the apartment when you moved in?" I asked.

She stared at me derisively. "No. It had been cleaned out. Not so much as a nail hole."

"I don't suppose you know where they took the previous resident's belongings?" Sean asked.

Full of scorn, she said, "Are you joking? I gotta go." Backing up, she started closing the door again.

Deflated, I let out a breath, then suddenly jammed my crutch in the door so it wouldn't shut. "One more question."

"Don't make me call the cops on you," she warned, color flaring in her cheeks.

I wouldn't mind the cops coming. I knew a section of woods they could search... "Do you know anyone named Jarvis?"

Pale eyebrows shot up to her hairline. "Jarvis Kinson?"

Adrenaline shot through my veins. "Yes," I said, having no idea if that was the Jarvis I was looking for or not. I wanted to keep her talking, to give us a lead. How many Jarvises could there be? It was an unusual name.

"Why do you want to talk to him?" Concern filled her eyes, widening them. "He doesn't have anything to do with that missing boy, does he? Because he babysits my boys from time to time, and I always thought he was a good kid."

Kid. Jarvis was a kid?

"We don't know that he's not," Sean said, trying to reassure her. "His name has come up in our investigation, and we need to talk with him. Do you know where we can find him?"

"Right across the street." She motioned with her chin. "Directly opposite here, but on the second floor."

When Sean and I turned to look, the door slammed behind us.

"I think she liked us," he said dryly.

"You do have a way with women," I said as we headed for the apartments across the street.

Frowning, he said, "It's the hat."

"Maybe so," I said, trying not to laugh. "It's not nearly as sexy as your shower cap."

Dimples popped as he slid me a smile, and I was suddenly so grateful that he was here with me. If he hadn't been, I might have done something supremely stupid like chasing that trio into the woods.

As we approached the stairs, he said, "Do you want me to give you a piggyback up?"

"As fun as that sounds, I think I'll hop." The truth was if he hadn't been injured, I'd have taken that offer in a hot second.

The apartment was easy to find and, the same as across the street, a woman yelled out asking what we wanted. There were no sidelights here, so Sean and I held up our IDs to the peephole.

Sean said, "We'd like to speak with Jarvis."

The landing had a railing that overlooked the street, and as I stood there, I realized that all the front-facing windows of this apartment would have an unfettered view of where Dustin had lived.

Had he seen Cat on January third? If so, it was a huge lead, because supposedly the last time she'd come here was in December.

Locks tumbled, and an angry-looking black woman, late twenties, filled the doorway. Beautiful brown eyes dotted with flecks of gold shifted from Sean to me and back again.

"What do you want with Jarvis?" she asked, her tone sharp. Short black hair had been gelled into stylish spikes and it suddenly made me think of raised hackles. A mama protecting her young.

"We believe he may be a witness in the disappearance of Dustin McDaniel," I said.

"No." She shook her head. "He didn't see anything."

"Ma'am...," Sean said.

She wagged a finger at him. "Don't even start. The answer is no."

"But there's a little boy missing," I said.

"And my heart goes out to him, but my son is staying out of it."

Sean gave her his best innocent face. "We only have a few questions."

"No."

I almost smiled. I had a feeling he was going to ditch that hat as soon as possible.

"You don't have a warrant or something like that, right?" she asked.

"No," I said.

"Then we're done here." She crossed her arms over a large chest.

I handed her a business card. "Unfortunately, he'll have to talk to someone, us or the police detectives. How old is he?"

"Thirteen," she said, staring at my card. "And I guess we'll be talking with the detectives because he isn't speaking with you."

As much as it frustrated me, I understood her desire to protect her son. "You might want to consider talking with an attorney."

"You think if I had money for a lawyer that I'd be living here?" She snorted. "It's time for you to leave."

Sean tipped his hat. "Sorry to bother you."

"Look," she said, her tone softening a bit. "I understand how frustrating it is not to know where that sweet little boy is, but it isn't any of our business. You might want to ask his father a few questions."

"Jarvis's father?" Sean asked.

"No." She shook her head as though he was dense. "*Dustin's* father."

Corey McDaniel? "You think he had something to do with it from prison?"

"He's not in prison anymore," she said. An eyebrow rose and smugly she added, "I guess you two weren't at the top of your detecting classes."

I couldn't quite argue with her on that. We should have known Corey McDaniel had been released. "When did he get out?"

"You expect me to know everything? All I know is that he's been hanging around here at least three weeks now. I saw him not ten minutes ago at that corner." She pointed to the same corner where the trio had been hanging out. "Sad to say he's back to his old ways, doping and dealing."

I peeked over the railing. The corner was empty. "The blond guy?"

"That's him," she said. "Some people are just born bad. He's one of them."

With that, she stepped back and closed the door in our faces.

I was reminded of Danny Beckley and his parting words yesterday, about the world being an evil place.

I didn't want to believe people were born bad or that the world was evil.

But right now it was hard to argue.

Sean said, "We're still not going in those woods."

I'd call Aiden and get him on it—he had resources I didn't. Corey would need to be formally questioned. As would Jarvis, no matter how much his mother didn't want him to be.

I stared at that empty corner. "I just realized why I thought I might know him. I do."

"You do?"

Gripping my crutches tightly, I looked at him, held his gaze. "Yeah. I saw him on video yesterday in the Channel 3 garage. He's the guy who left the doll in Kira's SUV."

14

A half hour later, Sean and I were sitting across from Patty Keefe. The walls of the hospice care center were painted in neutral shades, but artwork burst with color, bringing a sense of light and joy. I fully expected a somber mood, but I found most everyone we'd come across to have a smile on their face. It was a relaxed atmosphere, and I suspected that came from the employees who strived to ensure their patients were surrounded by happiness during their final days.

It was humbling to say the least, and made me feel extra appreciative for all I had. But it didn't change the sad facts of this case—or that we'd brought up a painful topic to discuss with Patty.

Dressed in a loose floral-printed dressing gown, she was propped up in an armchair. A heating pad peeked out from an elaborately-crocheted blanket on her lap. An oxygen machine's narrow tubing snaked upward, branching at her neck to wrap around her ears. It then looped down to her nose where a nasal cannula delivered the supplemental breathing help. A support pillow cushioned her head that looked like it held the weight of the world.

Short blond hair had been clipped behind her ears with double bobby pins. Although her thin face and sunken eyes told the story of her terminal diagnosis, she still wore full makeup complete with fake eyelashes and perfectly-applied lip liner and lipstick. Her nails had been painted a bright pink as well. It brought a lump to my throat to see her attempting normality despite the abnormality of her situation.

"I knew Corey was trouble from the start," Patty said softly, barely able to shake her head.

On the way here, I'd spoken with Aiden, who'd gone momentarily silent after I told him my suspicion about Corey and that doll. Aiden promised to contact his superior and attain the reinforcements we needed to not only track Corey down but to pull Jarvis in for questioning. Then he cursed a blue streak about being stuck in the hospital and Em took his phone away.

"But," Patty said, her blue eyes suddenly flashing with a spark of life, "there was nothing I could say to sway Alisha from marrying him. *Love.*" She brought a trembling hand upward, stuck a finger in her mouth, and made a gagging noise. "I did my best to keep my mouth shut and be a part of her life, especially when Corey went to prison and she found out she was pregnant. It took everything in me to swallow that 'I told you so.'" She inhaled deeply as though trying to catch her breath. "It's hard to hate Corey, however. Because of him, I had Dustin. He was the sweetest baby. But unfortunately he didn't hold the power to keep Alisha from slipping back into her old ways."

"Old ways?" I asked for clarification.

With her lower lip jutting, her fingers worked tirelessly, rolling the edge of the colorful afghan between her thumb and forefinger. "Alisha started using drugs her senior year of high school, at first recreationally." She drew in a deep breath. "It snowballed after graduation. A year later, she was arrested and sent to a rehab facility. That's where she met Corey."

Patty glanced down at her hands, her fingers finally stilling for a moment.

"Did they get married straight off?" I asked, trying to keep her talking.

"They waited a year," she said, looking up again. Her fingers went back to rolling the crocheted yarn. "Then came news that Alisha was pregnant. She quit the drugs cold turkey—or so she told me. But Dustin was born with marijuana in his system. Alisha said she'd only smoked it because of nausea from the pregnancy...I don't think that's true. Anyway, that's how she came to the attention of the DCF and CFC."

I recalled reading that he'd been taken away at that point and only given back after Alisha completed a court-ordered drug program.

"Dustin was removed from her home once more after that, wasn't he?" Sean asked.

"Yes. Alisha was partying and got carried away. Forgot he was outside in his playpen. She was arrested again, and the CFC took custody of Dustin. I couldn't take him in because I was going through chemo at the time, so he went to a foster home. After rehab, Alisha got him back and vowed to change her ways. And she did. For a while. Until I got the news right before Thanksgiving that the chemo hadn't worked." She looked off to the side, her eyes unfocused. "Apparently, she went back to drugs instead of dealing with her emotions, and I didn't see it because I was too busy taking care of myself. I accepted her excuses as to why I couldn't see him because it was easier on me emotionally and physically than to investigate." Her fingers grabbed the afghan, squeezing it tightly. "Maybe Dustin would still be here..."

I struggled to find something to say that didn't sound trite. All I could manage was, "I'm sorry."

Looking haunted, she blinked back tears. "Do you think you can really find out what happened to him?"

"We're going to do our best," I said. Someone laughed in the hallway, completely at odds with the tension in this room.

Patty's eyebrows lifted. "That's what that reporter said, too, and look what happened to her."

"You spoke with Kira Fitzpatrick?" I asked.

Patty let go of the afghan and adjusted the heating pad. "She was here on Thursday morning, all excited that she was close to cracking the case. Do you think she's dead?"

Her words knocked me backward, as though she had physically shoved me. Even though it was a possibility I'd thought about a hundred times since Aiden and Ava appeared on my doorstep, hearing it said aloud seemed so harsh. "We don't know," I answered honestly.

I learned from Aiden that detectives from across the state were following up on tips about Kira's whereabouts. Supposedly there had been various sightings between the Cape all the way up to Portland, Maine. I hoped one of them proved accurate. I wanted to believe that Kira was alive and well and simply hiding.

"Do you know what happened to Dustin's belongings?" I asked. "His toys, his clothes, that kind of thing?"

"I assume the apartment manager threw it all away after Alisha died." She swallowed hard.

"She never..." I bit my lip. "She never confessed anything to you, did she?"

"No." Patty looked up at the ceiling before turning her attention back to us. "Until the day she died, she swore up and down that the CFC had taken him away. She begged me to believe her. I wanted to...so badly. I still want to." Her eyes glistened. "But I have to face reality. The CFC didn't take him."

My stomach ached. "Was Alisha violent? Had she ever hurt him that you knew about?"

"No!" she said emphatically. "If I thought for a moment that she'd hurt him, I'd have called the CFC myself. Maybe she left him outside again and someone took him? Maybe he wandered away? There's that pond near the apartments... Maybe one of her lowlife roommates did something? Or maybe," she swallowed hard, "maybe..."

She couldn't finish the thought. There were a lot of maybes. All of them tragic.

"Do you have anything of Dustin's?" Sean asked, his voice low. Solemn. "Something he may have left at your house at some point? Clothing? A stuffed animal? A blanket?"

Her eyes lit again. "I had a blanket." Motioning to the throw blanket on her lap, she added, "I made it for him. His was blue with a white border. It was the only thing of his I brought with me when I moved here. Everything else was donated."

"Had?" I asked, latching onto the idea of that blanket for dear life. "What happened to it?"

"I gave it to Ms. Fitzpatrick," she said. "On Thursday."

Sean leaned in. "Why?"

"As a favor to me. If she found out what happened to him, if I'm gone... If he's gone..." She paused, biting her lip. "I wanted him to be buried with it, to have something familiar with him, so he wouldn't be...alone. A part of me would be with him, too."

The ache in her tone tore at my heart. "You made the blanket for him?"

"Every stitch."

Glancing at Sean, I smiled, hope blooming. "If I find the blanket, not only might we find Kira but Dustin as well."

"I don't understand," Patty said.

I explained how I could locate items through touch and scent. Before I even finished talking, she'd lifted her hands, offering them up to me.

"Think about that blanket, Ms. Keefe." Sucking in a deep breath, I took hold of her chilled, frail, and nearly lifeless hands and closed my eyes.

Within seconds, a scene played out in my mind, taking me on a dizzying journey. I tried to focus on what I was seeing, the bits and blurs. It appeared as though the blanket was in a cardboard box in the back of a moving SUV. Concentrating as hard as I could, I tried to see a landmark and who was driving. I was taken aback to see two grade-school-age kids sitting in the backseat, watching a video. A big dog, a retriever, had his nose stuck out the window.

Silently, I willed the driver to look up, so I could glimpse a reflection in the rearview mirror. And when she did, I let out the breath I'd been holding.

I released Patty's hands and fought off the wave of dizziness that always came with visions. "The good news is that I know who has the blanket."

"Kira?" Sean asked.

"No. It's with Nya Rodriguez."

"Who?" Patty asked.

The wooziness was subsiding. "She's Kira's producer at Channel 3."

Patty rolled the afghan between her fingers again. "Why does she have it?"

"It was in a box of pictures and awards, that kind of thing. My best guess is that when Kira was fired and rushed out of the building on Thursday, Nya boxed Kira's personal effects to give to her later. That box is still in the back of Nya's SUV."

"You said that was the good news...what's the bad?" Sean asked, watching me carefully.

"It looks like Nya's on vacation," I said. "There was luggage in the back of the SUV as well as that box, and she was driving north. I saw a sign for the Mount Washington cog railway." Which was in New Hampshire. She was already three hours away.

"That doesn't make sense," Sean said. "Kira's disappearance is the biggest story Channel 3 might ever have. Why would Nya up and leave now?"

He was right. It didn't make sense. "I don't know. I think the only person who can answer that is Nya. We need to find her."

15

Twenty minutes later, I'd added Nya to my list of missing people.

She wasn't answering her phone. I'd already left two voicemails to call me back as soon as possible and hoped she wasn't staying in the wilds of New Hampshire with no cell coverage. I'd called Channel 3 to see if anyone knew where she had gone but no one had any idea.

Sean adjusted his hat and stifled a yawn as we walked up the brick path to Cat Bennett's front door. The house was a well-tended split level with a neatly-tended front yard. There was a sporty black car in the driveway, but no sign of the blue car with the smiley face ball on its antenna.

The dark clouds had moved past without a drop of rain falling. Sunbeams poked through thin clouds, spotlighting beautiful yellow rosebushes lining the walk.

"After this, we'll head home for a while," I said, noting the growing darkness beneath his eyes. "Get something to eat, make sure my mother hasn't brought in a wrecking ball, make some calls, and rest a little bit before going to see Aiden at the hospital."

"I'm fine," he said.

"Didn't say you weren't." I crutched up to the concrete landing.

"I know you, Ms. Valentine. 'Rest' is code for 'naptime.'"

"If it is, why do you assume I'm talking about you? I'm exhausted. My stomach hurts, my armpits are chafed from these damn crutches, and I can't wait to get this boot off so I can scratch my calf to my heart's content."

His eyes narrowed, then his lip twitched.

"You don't believe me?" I lifted my arm. "Look, look at this chafing."

The front door flew open, and a man I recognized from news footage as Cat's husband, Ross Bennett, stood in the doorway, staring straight at my armpit.

Embarrassment flooded my cheeks as I quickly dropped my arm. "Hi."

He looked worse for the wear. Red-rimmed bronze-colored eyes. Thick stubble. Messy reddish-blond hair. Smudged eyeglasses. His shirt was stained, his jeans torn. Confusion flashed as he tipped his head. "Do I know you?"

Introducing myself, I quickly held out my ID. Sean added his to the mix. I said, "We're here to speak to Cat Bennett."

He folded his arms across a muscled chest. "You're kidding." He looked at Sean. "She's kidding, right?"

"No," Sean said.

Ross took off his glasses and pushed the heels of his hands into his eyes. "I cannot even freaking believe this."

Glancing at Sean, I raised my eyebrows in question. He shrugged. Finally, I said, "Is Cat here?"

As Ross put his glasses back on, I saw tears pooling on his lower lashes. "No, she's not here. I can't find her. Anywhere. I filed a report, and sure, the police came out and looked around and asked some questions, but they say she's an adult and can voluntarily leave anytime she wants. Only I know Cat. Cat wouldn't just leave. Even with all this stuff going on with her job. And definitely not without her medication—she's diabetic. When I saw your ID, I thought for a second that you were actually here to help me find her. How stupid of me to think someone might actually want to help. Why are you here? To pester her about that missing little boy again? She's already answered everyone's questions."

Elliman Bay's words echoed in my head. *"A forewarning... When I last spoke to her, she wasn't in the best frame of mind."*

I bit my lip. "Well, yes, but we might be able to help you find her. Can we come in?"

He tossed his hands in the air and spun around, leaving the door open behind him.

Sean said softly, "Kira, Dustin, two other little kids, Nya, and now Cat all missing? What in the hell is going on?"

At this point I wasn't sure I wanted to know. I had a bad feeling about it all, one that twisted and twined around my soul, squeezing it tight.

Sean closed the door behind us as we followed Ross into the living area. He sank into a leather recliner, and motioned for us to sit on the couch.

Behind him, a brick fireplace was stained with soot. The mantel was decorated with grapevine, candles, and several photos of Cat and Ross. In each, the couple mugged for the camera, looking happy and carefree. It was a far cry from the way he looked now.

"How long has Cat been missing?" I asked.

"Since Thursday afternoon. I got a call at work from her at eleven, completely hysterical. She asked me to come home. I cancelled my class—I'm a professor at Plymouth Bay College," he said by way of explanation. "But I hit traffic and by the time I made it home, she wasn't here. I haven't seen her since."

"Why was she upset?" Sean asked.

I noticed another photo on the mantel, a group shot that looked like it was taken at a Christmas party. Ross had his arm slung around Cat, who stood next to Elliman, two other women, and the receptionist I'd seen earlier today. Not long after that joyous picture, Dustin had gone missing.

It made me feel ill that an agency created to do so much good had messed up so badly.

Ross clenched his jaw. "Because that reporter cornered her in the grocery store parking lot, peppering her with questions about her car and her whereabouts and it freaked Cat out."

"Reporter? Kira Fitzpatrick?" I asked.

"Yeah, that's the one," he said. "She's been harassing Cat for a couple of weeks now. I'd like to give her a piece of my mind. I mean, no one blames Cat for what happened to that little boy more than Cat herself. It's eating her up. She doesn't need the reminder of her mistakes day in and day out. The phone calls. The drop-by visits. If anything's happened to Cat, I blame that woman and her badgering."

Sean's eyebrows dipped. "You do know Kira Fitzpatrick is missing, right?"

Ross's shoulders stiffened as Sean's words registered. "What?"

"She's missing," Sean said again. "Disappeared on Thursday night."

"Thursday?" Ross echoed.

"It's been on the news," I said, wondering if Cat could possibly have had anything to do with Kira's disappearance. Kira had been awfully interested in Cat's car, and we'd heard from several people that Kira claimed she'd been close to solving the case. Had talking with Cat on Thursday morning been the turning point for Kira?

Ross dragged a hand down his face. "I haven't been watching the news. I've been looking for my wife."

I waited for the moment he realized the two events might be related and saw it as the color drained from his face. He, however, said nothing, probably not wanting to implicate Cat.

"Do you know if Cat came home after the run-in with Kira Fitzpatrick?" Sean asked.

"I don't know," he said. "She called me from the grocery store lot. She said she was going home…"

"Is anything missing here? Like she packed a bag and left?" I asked. It was possible she'd run away. I'd give almost anything to know what she and Kira discussed.

"No clothes or anything like that," he said. "Her car is gone, her purse, her phone. That's it. The phone has been turned off—calls go straight to voicemail. Our bank account shows no new transactions."

Sean said, "Aside from being upset by the confrontation at the grocery store, how was Cat's frame of mind?"

I recognized his tactic. We knew from Elliman Bay that Cat had been depressed, but would her husband be honest with us?

Sighing, he leaned forward, propping his elbows on his knees. "Honestly, she was…fragile. Ever since she learned that little boy was missing, she's blamed herself. She's barely eating. Barely sleeping. She finally went to a doctor a week ago. He prescribed a depression medication."

"Does she have it with her?" I asked.

"It's sitting on her nightstand." His wrung his hands.

Sean said, "I hate to ask this, but do you think she'd harm herself?"

"I—" His voice cracked. "I don't know. I just don't know. She wasn't herself..." He gave himself a good shake as though he could slough off his uncertainty. "How can you help?" he asked. "The police said there's nothing they can do until we get some sort of lead. Her using a credit card or something like that."

I gave him my standard speech about my abilities, how they worked, and my role with the state police. "With Cat, our chances are really good that I can find her. I can usually get a reading from wedding rings, because in my world, they're gifts you give each other. I can probably smell an item of her clothing to get a scent reading to find out where she is, and is her car in both your names?"

"Yes. Why?"

"Then it belongs to you, too, so I can find where it is."

One of his eyebrows lifted in skepticism. "You can really do that?"

"I really can," I said. "Are you willing to do a reading?"

"Yeah, of course." He still sounded distrustful.

I was used to nonbelievers. It came with the job. I hopped over and sat on his chair's ottoman. "I need you to focus on that wedding ring, and I should be able to read its energy through your palm."

"Okay," he said under his breath.

His hands were clammy as I rested my palms on top of his. In a flash, I saw the platinum wedding band, sitting alongside a solitaire diamond ring. I drew my hands back and looked around. "Does Cat take her rings off when washing dishes?"

"Yeah. How'd you—"

"Her rings are sitting in a little dish next to the kitchen sink."

Ross jumped up and jogged into the kitchen. He came back a second later with the rings in his hand. "She must've forgotten to put them back on. That happens sometimes."

"Does she wear any other jewelry? Something you gave her as a gift?"

He shook his head.

"Well, let's try a reading on the car. It's blue, right? With a smiley ball on the antenna?"

He slowly sank back onto the chair. "How'd you know that?"

"Came up in our investigation." I said. "Do you know if Cat was working on January third?"

After a second, he said, "I can't recall exactly when she went back after the holiday. Why?"

Sean said, "Someone may have seen her at Dustin McDaniel's house that day."

"Impossible," he said, shaking his head. "She openly admits she hadn't seen him since December. Who's saying this? What's to gain from it?"

What was to gain? I hoped the truth, but I understood him trying to protect his wife. Tucking a piece of hair behind my ear, I tried to diffuse his growing unease. "It's just a loose end. Now, think about that car, okay?"

Faint wrinkles pulled at the corners of his downturned lips. He held out his hands. "All right."

I set my palms on top of his and closed my eyes. It took only a moment to see the blue car, and I easily recognized the location where it was parked. "It's at the Quincy Adams T station."

"I don't understand any of this," Ross said, shaking his head. "What's it doing there? Did you see Cat?"

"No. Do you have something with her scent on it? A pillow? A shirt?"

He jumped up. "I'll get them."

When he left the room, Sean whispered, "You think Cat had something to do with Kira's disappearance?"

"I don't like the timing," I whispered.

"Me either."

Ross came back, carrying a pillow, a shirt, and two sweaters. "I don't get it," he said. "If you can find things, why can't you find the little boy?"

"Just things," I said.

"Like the set of car keys Cat lost in December at the Christmas party?" he asked, a hint of a smile on his face. "We couldn't find them anywhere, and you'd think they'd be easy to find with the big yellow smiley face key fob, but no. I wish you'd been around then. It was an expensive taxi ride home."

I knew all about expensive taxi rides. "Yes, like that. If Cat were here, I could find the keys. We do have a lead on the little boy, though, through an item that belonged to him. We're waiting for its arrival."

"Incredible," he said, holding out the items he'd selected. "I know a lot of people, including Cat and I, want to know what really happened. It'll be nice to have some closure. Selfishly, I look forward to the day Cat and I can go back to living normally. First, I need to find her."

I took the bundle and hopped back to the couch as he sat back down, watching me closely.

I inhaled, exhaled, and tried to calm my jumping nerves. Closing my eyes, I brought the pillow up to my face and breathed deeply. Adrenaline surged through my veins as I saw nothing at all. I grabbed the shirt, repeating the process. Again, I saw nothing. The same happened with the sweaters.

"What?" Ross asked, leaning forward, hope etched in his features.

I glanced at Sean and said, "I don't see anything at all."

Ross jumped to his feet. "What's that mean?"

"Could be she's sleeping," Sean said quickly.

Right. I didn't want to voice the other option: That I couldn't see anything through Cat's eyes because she was dead.

16

A couple of hours later, I decided "home sweet home" was a fallacy.

Home crazy home, maybe.

It was a nuthouse around this place. Mum stood at the stove, making beef stroganoff for supper that smelled wonderful but had every pot and pan I owned either on the stovetop or the counter. A fresh batch of cookies had been plated and another cookie sheet was in the oven.

My mother stress cooked.

"Dovie's called my cell phone three times today," Mum said. "I think she knows something's going on. Do you think Mac tipped her off?"

So much for Cutter killing her phone. "No. I think she has an internal warning system for deception." It was uncanny, really. "What did you tell her?"

"Nothing! I didn't answer." She wiped her forehead with the back of her hand. "You know I have trouble lying."

I definitely did not get my fibbing skills from her. "She's probably wondering what's going on because you're not answering your phone." The two were partners in crime—sometimes literally. They often talked several times a day.

My mother transferred cookies from a baking sheet to a cooling rack. "I didn't think about that."

"Well," I said, "you've been busy. Baking, babysitting, building me a new house, and avoiding Dad. Why are you avoiding Dad?"

Popping a cookie in her mouth, she spoke around it. "He's a pain in my ass."

I threw a look at Ava, hoping she hadn't heard that, but she was busy playing with the farm animals that came with a Fisher-Price Little People farm. She was *mooing* to her heart's content. "Does this mean you two are separated again?"

I'd been expecting this day for a few months now. My parents' relationship had been off more than on, and this particular stretch had been on for longer than I ever imagined.

"No," she said, making a face at me. "It just means I don't want to look at him today. Tonight will be soon enough. I'm sure he appreciates the break from me as well."

Smiling, I shook my head. Only my parents.

My phone rang, and I reached over and grabbed it off the dining room table. It was Marisol. "Where are you?" I asked at the noise in the background.

"At a bar in Stockbridge."

"What are you doing there?"

"I'm on a date."

I drew my lip into my mouth.

"Don't you dare give me the silent treatment, Lucy!"

I imagined her dark eyes narrowing and her hands gesturing. "I'm not."

"Look, I tried a date with Mr. Mysterious and it's just not going to work out," she said.

"Why not?"

"I like guys who actually talk. Tell me about themselves. Where they grew up. Not guys who clam up. He's a clammer. Oh, he's sexy, I'll give you that. Those eyes? I could die. But no. It's not going to work."

Suddenly, I smiled. She was trying way too hard to convince me. "Maybe he's an oyster."

"A what?"

"An oyster," I repeated, making Ava's toy horse leap over her legs. "If you're patient enough, you get a pearl."

"What a load of shit."

I laughed, which made Ava laugh.

"What was that?" Marisol asked, instantly suspicious.

"A baby."

"Whose? Did Dovie buy you one from the black market?"

In any other circumstance it would have made me laugh, but the joke hit a little too close to home. "Long story."

"Related to the dog you tried to ditch with me?"

"Ditch is so harsh," I said. "He needed a place to stay. Which reminds me…why isn't he staying with you?"

"Clinic's closed for painting this week. If you still have him next Monday, bring him by."

"How long are you in Stockbridge?" I asked.

"Not much longer. The date sucks."

"A clammer?"

"A groper," she said dryly.

"Fun."

"Sometimes," she said, then said her goodbyes and hung up.

"Looks like we have the dog for another week at least," I said to Sean.

He looked over the back of the couch. "What's one more?"

Mum said, "You shouldn't be putting questions like that into the universe."

He frowned.

I wiped chocolate from the corners of Ava's mouth, and she grinned at me. "*Scow!*" she cried, thumping the dog's back with her tiny fist.

Scout didn't seem to mind as he lifted his eyebrows, gave her a side glance, then went back to pretending to snooze. It made me wonder what he was thinking… Then I realized I knew who could tell me. Also, if Scout had seen or heard anything unusual Thursday night, he'd be able to tell Jeremy. I made the call and left a message on his machine.

I set my phone aside and hoped he wasn't avoiding me. I needed his help.

Reaching over, I rubbed Scout's head. According to Mum, he hadn't left Ava's side all day, including when she napped. He slept under the crib.

Ebbie kept hissing at the newcomer every time she strutted by, and Grendel kept sniffing his dog bowl as though hoping it would be miraculously filled, and Thoreau was busily investigating Scout's basket of toys. He barked intermittently at the unfamiliar balls and bones.

Welcome to the family.

Sean hadn't napped—he was stubborn—but at least he was lying down on the sofa, his laptop propped on his belly. A quick search yielded the information that Corey McDaniel had been released from prison on parole three weeks ago, as Jarvis's mother had said. Had Kira known? Spoken with him? I hated not knowing how he was involved in all this. He couldn't have possibly had anything to do with Dustin's disappearance—he'd been in prison. Unless he'd somehow orchestrated it from behind bars...but why would he?

I sighed. Too many suppositions and not enough answers. Unfortunately it seemed as though the people with answers kept disappearing.

The state police had impounded Cat's car. On first glance, nothing hinted at anything amiss. But her purse and phone had been found under the driver's seat along with a wallet stuffed with cash, which didn't make sense if she was on the run. So where was she? And why couldn't I see out of her eyes?

Fortunately, Ross Bennett had allowed me to take one of Cat's sweaters home, and I'd sniffed that thing a hundred times already with the same result. I saw nothing.

I picked up the Little People sheep and *baaaed* as I had it gallop into the barnyard Ava had set up. She smiled and reached for it, giving me the horse instead.

I still hadn't had any luck getting in touch with Nya Rodriguez, but I had managed to contact Tova Dovell Fisher. We were meeting tomorrow morning. I couldn't yet rule out that she was using the CFC scandal as a cover-up for getting rid of her husband's new lover. It would be pretty ingenious, actually.

Scout's head suddenly came up. A growl rose in his throat. Leaping to his feet, he dashed to the door, barking like mad. Thoreau joined in the barking, even though I was pretty sure he had no idea why he was doing it.

A second later, a sharp knock sounded.

"I got it." Sean set his laptop on the coffee table and was at the door in two long strides. He grabbed Scout's collar to hold him back.

I leaned back so I could see who had arrived as the door opened.

"Found him coming up the driveway. He says he's here to see Ms. Valentine," one of the security ninjas said loudly, motioning to the young black man who stood on my welcome mat, his eyes the size of Rhode Island as another of the guards gripped the back of his striped T-shirt to keep him from running off.

Scout and Thoreau quieted as I slowly stood up, wincing at my protesting muscles, and grabbed one of my crutches. At the door I studied the teen, who looked afraid to blink. He looked oddly familiar with his gold-flecked eyes… I took a guess. "Are you Jarvis?"

He nodded quickly, like a bobblehead. With long arms and legs and a short torso, he hadn't quite grown into his height yet. Give him a year or two, and I bet he'd shoot to six feet from his current five foot five-ish.

"You have your mother's eyes," I said. To the security ninjas, I said, "He can come in."

Jarvis slumped in relief as he was released.

My mother elbowed her way to the doorway and said to the security team, "Are you boys hungry? I'm making beef stroganoff. There's plenty. And I have more cookies."

They looked at each other, huddled up, and traded whispers. Finally one said, "Can we get it to go?"

"Sure thing," Mum said. "Give me a minute to get it together."

"Thanks. Just leave it on the porch," he said. "We'll come back for it." With that, they turned and walked off.

"I'm Lucy." I made quick introductions of everyone and motioned for Jarvis to come inside. "Have a seat."

Tugging up loose jean shorts, he stumbled in, still not blinking. Sitting in an armchair, he glanced around, finally relaxing a bit. Sean let go of Scout, who raced over to Jarvis and sniffed.

He reached out to pet the dog. "Does he bite?"

"I don't know," I said, sitting on the couch. "He's new."

His eyes went wide again, and he pulled his hand back.

"*Baaa!*" Ava shouted, rising to her feet and rushing over to show Jarvis her sheep. "*Baaa!*"

Thoreau hopped right up next to Jarvis as my mother shoved a plate of cookies in his face. "Are you hungry, young man? Here have some cookies," she said without waiting for an answer.

He took the plate, said, "Uh, thanks" and stared down at Thoreau and then at me.

Welcome to the nuthouse, I wanted to say, but instead, I said. "How'd you get here?"

Thoreau sniffed his sternum as he said, "Bus."

"How'd you know where Lucy lived?" Sean asked as he sat next to me.

"Google." He dug in his pocket and pulled out the business card I had given his mother earlier. "You can find anything on Google."

Apparently.

"I thought she'd live in the big place up the hill. Is this really where you live?" he asked, looking around.

"Yes," I said defensively. "Why?"

"I read that you were rich. This here house is a shack. No offense, it's small."

"Told you so," my mother sang.

Jarvis continued, "I think my house is bigger than this place. We at least got two bedrooms."

My mother chuckled.

"I like it," I said. "That's why I live here."

He shrugged and looked at me like I was all kinds of crazy. "Okay."

Ava dropped the sheep in his lap and darted back to the farm yard to grab the toy cow. She brought that over and held her palm out to show off her treasure.

"*Moo?*" he said as though asking her a question.

"*Moo!*" she squealed, bouncing up and down. She took the cow and repossessed the sheep and went back to her spot on the floor. Scout followed her.

"Why come all the way out here and not just call?" Sean asked. "The number's on the card."

"Something to do?" Jarvis shrugged and bit into a cookie. Thoreau laid down next to him, resting his head on Jarvis's leg.

"Good?" Mum asked him from the kitchen.

"Yeah," he said, wiping crumbs.

"Need some milk?" she asked.

"Sure. Thanks."

Jarvis was going to move in at this rate. I said, "Were you home earlier when we spoke with your mom?"

"Yeah. She hadn't known I'd talked with that reporter. She's mad I did."

"Why?" I asked.

Jarvis lifted dark eyebrows. "When you live in my neighborhood, sometimes talking gets you hurt. Don't talk, mind your own business, and people mostly leave you alone." He stuck another cookie in his mouth.

Mostly. I let out a breath.

"But you talked with Ms. Fitzpatrick," Sean said. "Why?"

"The anonymous tip money. My mom lost her job as a secretary at an insurance company last month. She hasn't found another one yet. Money's tight."

My mother *tsk*ed as she set a glass of milk on a coaster. "That's terrible."

"I can't get a real job until I'm fourteen," Jarvis explained. "I babysit sometimes, but it's not a lot of cash. People can't afford much." He shrugged and set his empty cookie plate on the coffee table. "The money that reporter offered was too much to pass up."

"How much did she offer?" I asked.

"Two hundred dollars. That's a month of groceries if we stretch it out." He sipped the milk then backhanded his upper lip to wipe away the residue. "I felt kind of bad about not telling anyone what I saw anyway."

Grendel abandoned Scout's food bowl and hopped up on the coffee table to sniff the cookie remnants.

"Is that a cat?" he asked, his eyes squinting as though he was seeing things.

"Yes," I said.

"He's huge. You feeding him cookies, too?"

"Sometimes," I answered, not explaining about the breed.

"What did you tell the reporter?" Sean asked, trying to redirect the conversation.

Jarvis tore his gaze from Grendel and dipped his head. He looked over at us from lowered lashes. "I don't suppose you all are offering a reward, too?"

Aha. The real reason he'd come here instead of calling.

"No," Sean said, not playing his game.

"Sure." Mum pulled her wallet from her purse.

"Judie," Sean warned.

"Shush," she said, tucking several crisp bills into Jarvis's hand. "I was going to give it to him anyway."

Sean slowly shook his head, but I smiled. My mother was a giver—and I loved her for it. To be honest, I'd planned to send Jarvis off with a little something, too. I had the feeling he'd come knowing he could probably play to our sympathies, but I fully believed that if you had, you should give... That and I was a complete sucker.

"Thank you," Jarvis said, "but this is too much." He tried to give some back.

"Nonsense," Mum said, taking three plastic containers of food, forks, and napkins out to the porch.

"What'd you see?" Sean asked Jarvis again as he pocketed the money.

"It was January third," Jarvis said. "I remember exactly because it was the first day back to school after Christmas break. I was up early to help my mom deliver newspapers."

"I thought she worked at an insurance company?" Sean asked.

"The paper thing was her second job," Jarvis said. "She had to quit it in March because our car broke and we didn't have money to fix it."

It was probably good my mother hadn't heard that or he'd be taking a new car home with him, too.

After another sip of milk, he said, "We'd just gotten back from driving the route—it was about five in the morning. My bedroom looks out at the street, and I saw the blue car with that stupid ball thing on its antenna pull in. I recognized it because I'd seen it before. I thought it was strange because it was early for a visit, but I thought it might be some kind of surprise visit. Lady got out of the car and knocked on the door to the apartment. She went inside, and I got ready for school."

"But?" I asked, because I felt there was something he still hadn't said.

"I happened to see her when she came out again." He wiped his palms on his shorts. "She wasn't alone."

"What do you mean?" Sean asked. "Who was with her?"

Jarvis looked up, his eyes filled with uneasiness. "She had the kid with her."

17

"Okay, you mosey on up to the nurses' station and distract them with your charm," I instructed Sean as we stood in the hospital's stairwell. We were mere steps away from Aiden's room. Only a thick door, a short hallway, and six nurses who buzzed busily around a horseshoe-shaped desk stood in our way.

Catching his reflection in the door's glass, he said, "I should have left the hat at home."

"Just smile a lot. Your dimples trump the hat. Now stop teasing and go."

He turned to face me. "You sure you can carry her and crutch at the same time?"

"I have excellent crutching skills," I assured as I kept Ava pressed close to my chest. I used a cocked hip to keep her in place. It helped that I had only brought one crutch—and that Ava wasn't all that heavy. "Now go on." I shooed him.

"Bossy," he whispered with a smile and strode off.

"Sean, wait!"

He slowly turned.

I crutched over and kissed him soundly. "Thanks for coming with me." He hated hospitals. Utterly despised them.

"For you, Ms. Valentine, anything." In a flash he was out of sight, leaving me grinning like a love-struck fool at my reflection as I propped open the door with my foot. "He's a keeper," I whispered to Ava.

She blinked at me.

I took that as an agreement.

A second later, I heard him asking something about visiting hours. As quietly as I could, I zipped through the open door of Aiden's room, nearly running smack dab into the back of a nurse who was checking his blood pressure. In my quest to not knock her over, I skidded to a comedic stop and dropped my crutch, raising a clatter so loud it could rival Santa's Christmas Eve rooftop landing.

In hindsight, during the planning stages of sneaking Ava in unseen, I should have first ensured the room was empty of hospital personnel.

Damn that hindsight.

The nurse spun around at the commotion, looking ready to do battle.

"I, uh—Hi," I said. "Sorry. Didn't see you there. Dropped, uh, my crutch."

"Obviously." She eyed Ava.

Ava's curious gaze zeroed in on one of the machines that beeped intermittently before she shifted her head and spotted her father. Her hands opened and closed as she offered her version of a wave. "Hihihi!"

With a wide smile, Aiden looked…good. Sitting up in bed, he didn't look to be in much pain. It took only a second to see why as the nurse moved aside. Orlinda Batista sat in her wheelchair on the other side of Aiden's bed.

She grinned. "Fancy meeting you here."

Although they looked completely opposite, Orlinda reminded me a bit of my mother. Same down-to-earth, nature-loving way about them. Her brown hair curled in soft waves around her face, and her intelligent blue eyes sized me up.

I said, "You're the best. Truly. Look at him. No one would ever guess he was almost blown up yesterday."

"I know." She winked and smiled, her full cheeks plumping.

Smiling, I asked, "Where's Em?" I'd expected to see her glued to Aiden's side.

"She's at school, taking an exam for her night class," Aiden said.

"You talked her into going?" I asked. "How?"

"It was pretty easy once Orlinda showed up and fixed me up. She promised to stay with me, and told Em she'd be less stressed if she just went and got it over with. She'll be back soon."

I was glad she went. Em was Type A, and missing class had to be hard enough on her without missing an exam. I also knew she had been skeptical of Orlinda—her science mind has trouble wrapping her head around the paranormal—and I wondered if this visit had changed her opinion.

Sean came strolling through the door, his hat in his hand. He spotted my crutch on the floor, bent to retrieve it, and said, "You sure know how to make an entrance."

The nurse looked between us—focusing on Sean's gauzed head and my boot—and said to Aiden, "Interesting company you keep, Lieutenant."

"We're not usually this…bandaged," he said.

"Why do I doubt that?" she asked with a smirk. "Twenty minutes until visiting is over." She scooted around Sean and me and headed out the door, tugging it closed behind her.

"Did you bribe her to overlook the fact that Ava is here?" I asked him, incredulous that she hadn't said a word about it.

"Turns out visitors under eighteen are allowed in with an adult," he said.

"All that wasted subterfuge," I said mournfully.

"You call that subterfuge?" Sean asked. "I had to whip off my hat and show off my head wound to keep the nurses from running in here at the commotion."

I rolled my eyes as Aiden laughed.

Laughed.

Orlinda had worked more than magic. This was a miracle, and I told her so.

"Willing victims of my gift are my favorite kind," she said, her plump cheeks dimpling as she smiled broadly.

"Hihihi!" Squirming, Ava held out her hands toward Aiden. I carefully set her on the edge of the bed and she lunged forward. He caught her and lifted her in the air.

Afraid he was going to drop her or reinjure himself, I held my breath, but it turned out I had nothing to worry about. Aiden had everything perfectly under control.

"He won't be running a marathon anytime soon, but I believe any talk of surgery can now be squashed," Orlinda said, wheeling toward me.

"Forget a marathon, I'm happy to be able to walk down the hallway," he said, trying to keep wires and tubes away from Ava's quick fingers.

I glanced at my boot, wondering if Orlinda could speed up the healing of my broken foot, but then I remembered she once told me she couldn't fix broken bones. Plus, I'd already used my allotted favors for the day.

Sean and I sat in matching armchairs, the fabric worn and faded and the seat cushions lumpy. Orlinda reached for my hand, holding it loosely in her own. "Aiden's been kind enough to update me on the case. It's become quite complex."

"An understatement," I said, flicking a glance at Aiden and Ava.

When I called to tell him about Jarvis Kinson's

statement, he'd shared his own news. That Corey McDaniel's fingerprints had been on the doll found in Kira's SUV. Police were tracking Dustin's father but so far hadn't been able to locate him.

Orlinda studied me closely. "How are you holding up?"

"I'm fine."

Where her skin touched mine, warmth flowed through my hand and up my fingers. One of her eyebrows dipped low and she tipped her head to the side, assessing. She was reading my energy. "Good, good," she murmured, sounding as though she didn't believe me.

It was nearly impossible to lie to her. Beyond her psychic gifts, she was a psychologist and trained to detect deception.

The truth was I was stressed out. It had been a rough couple of weeks—mentally and physically. My mind was tired. My body was achy and tired. And I had a long way to go in learning how to juggle my personal life and my work. There had to be a balance. I just needed to find it. Until I did, I didn't particularly want to talk about it. Especially not here. Aiden and Sean were also dealing with much the same issues.

"The little boy," she said. "The witness who came forward claiming to see him was reliable?"

Sean said, "We believe so. He provided details that verified Dustin McDaniel's mother's version of events. The social worker came to the home on January third and took custody of the boy."

"The witness should have come forward earlier," Aiden said, his tone hard and unyielding.

"Remember," I said, "he didn't know anything untoward had happened until Patty Keefe raised alarms in April. None of us did."

Although my heart ached for the situation Patty was in, I also grieved for Alisha McDaniel, for what she had lost to her addiction. She had to have been so far gone in a haze of narcotics not to raise hell—or seemingly care—when Dustin had been taken away. I admit it made me angry as well. How had she let this happen to herself? Why hadn't she fought harder? Why hadn't she been stronger to resist the lure of the drugs? But then I had to remember that her drug use had caused her to lose absolutely everything, including her life. It seemed like that should be punishment enough, but I still struggled not to judge her choices.

"Then at that time he should have come forward." Aiden had given Ava an empty cup to play with. She was having a grand time banging it against the bed's railing.

"Should have, could have, but didn't," Orlinda said. She pinned me with a meaningful glare. "There's no use in dwelling on what cannot be changed."

Her message to me was clear. However, I had no idea how not to dwell.

I was a dweller.

Fortunately, not a bottom dweller.

At least not yet. There was still time.

"Aiden mentioned the little boy has a blanket?" Orlinda asked. "Any luck finding it yet?"

"Not yet. I'm waiting for a return call from the woman who has it." I explained the situation. "If she's camping or something like that, she might not have cell coverage."

"You could do another reading," Orlinda suggested. "If the blanket is in the car, and the car is now parked at a cabin or wherever, then you might be able to see the location. Someone could be sent to retrieve the blanket."

"Good idea," I said. "I'll set up another meeting with Patty Keefe."

"What I don't understand," Sean said, "is why the CFC has no idea where Dustin McDaniel is. If Cat Bennett took custody of him, then there should be paperwork..."

I rubbed my temples. "Maybe the CFC is keeping it under wraps. There have been numerous discrepancies on case reports. This could be another one. Cat brought him in and placed him with a foster family, and the agency lost the information..." It sounded like a stretch to my own ears.

"If that's the case, why didn't Cat admit to taking custody of him?" Sean asked. "It would have made her life easier to put the blame on the CFC, that's for sure."

It would have. She'd been under fire since his disappearance became public. "I don't know," I said. "Maybe she had a confidentiality agreement? We should ask Elliman Bay. Her boss," I explained to Orlinda.

"It also doesn't explain the other two missing children," Sean added. "I'm curious if those families also say that the CFC took custody of their children. We could be looking at something much bigger, like black market adoption, or God forbid, that they were sold to the highest bidder in a trafficking scheme."

Nausea rolled through my stomach at the thought. Though I knew it was an all-too-frequent occurrence, it made me feel ill to think too much about it, especially when small children were involved. I watched Ava and wanted to burst into tears.

Orlinda set her hand on my arm, and again I felt that strange warmth radiating to all my pulse points.

There's no use in dwelling on what cannot be changed.

Taking a deep breath, I tried to focus on that message, to embrace it. But I couldn't quite let go of feeling like things like this should never happen. Ever.

"Have you checked the caseworker's bank account?" Orlinda asked.

"When Lucy called earlier to tell me about her meeting with the witness who saw Dustin being taken away, I had my team run a report. There was nothing unusual on her bank statements," Aiden said. "Two joint accounts with her husband, checking and savings. Lots of debt—school loans, a mortgage, car payments. They were mostly living month to month but managed to build a small savings, a few thousand dollars. Unemployment benefits had just kicked in, supplementing her loss of income, but no big deposits. No red flags. The only way to find out why she took Dustin is to ask her. We need to find her."

"I'm working on it." I explained to Orlinda about the scent readings I'd done and how they'd yet to reveal anything.

"Don't lose hope yet, Lucy," she said. "Sometimes scents can fade or comingle with other scents and dilute the energy. If you continue to see nothing from the pieces you have, inquire for more items."

"And if I still don't see anything?" I asked softly.

Her lips flattened into a grim line. "Then it is undoubtedly because the woman in question is seeing nothing at all."

Aiden said, "That's not an option. Cat Bennett holds the keys to this case."

I didn't point out to him that we might not have a say in the matter. He knew.

"Especially in light of this." Reaching over, he grabbed a folio from the bedside table and handed it off to me.

Frowning, I opened the folder, almost afraid of what I was going to find.

"My team sent that over along with her bank records," Aiden said.

"What is it?" Sean asked, leaning over my shoulder.

Aiden replaced Ava's cup with a pen and notebook. She happily scribbled nonsense on the paper. "Phone records for the Bennetts."

"What am I looking at?" I asked. "It's just a bunch of numbers."

Aiden said, "See the call made from their landline at eight fifty-three on Thursday night?"

Thursday night. My adrenaline kicked up a notch. "Yeah?"

"That was to Kira's cell phone," he said. "The conversation lasted over a minute."

I glanced up. "Ross Bennett didn't mention anything about speaking with Kira."

"That's because he didn't." Aiden's tone was hard. Rock solid. "At eight fifty-three, he was at the local police station filing a missing persons report on his wife."

"Then who made the call?" Orlinda asked. "Cat Bennett?"

"Don't know," Aiden said.

"What about Cat's cell phone?" I asked. "Any strange calls made on that?"

"Last call was to her husband's cell phone Thursday morning. As you know, her phone was found along with her purse and wallet in her car at the T station."

Sean said, "Why would Cat be missing all day, then go home to call Kira, only to disappear again? Was she setting up a meeting? Why not call her on her cell phone?"

Ava leaned over the bed and waved the pen at us. "Hi!"

"Hi there." Orlinda reached out and took Ava's hand.

I watched Orlinda's face carefully to see if she was reading the girl's energy, but she gave absolutely nothing away. A trait I needed to learn.

Aiden said, "Again, there's no way to know right now, but it makes me wonder."

"Wonder what?" I asked.

"If Cat Bennett is being framed," he said, his tone dark. "For what happened to Dustin McDaniel and what likely has happened to Kira."

We were all silent for moment, letting that sink in. The pieces, no matter how I tried to shove them together, didn't quite make sense. "Kira might be hiding out," I said, clinging to that hope. "Her bank account…"

Aiden nodded, but he didn't seem to have the same hopes I did.

"If Cat Bennett is being framed, by whom?" Sean asked.

"My gut says someone inside the CFC," he said. "A search warrant request is before a judge right now."

The nurse I almost knocked over tapped on the door. "Time's almost up."

"I need to get going anyway." Orlinda looked at me. "Walk me to the elevator?"

"Absolutely." I grabbed my crutch.

"I can't thank you enough for coming, Orlinda," Aiden said.

Really, she'd gone above and beyond. "Me, either," I added.

"Is there anything I can do?" Aiden asked. "A donation or something?"

"No, no." She waved him off. "But..."

"What?" he asked.

"I do like that hat..." She motioned to Sean's hand—to the fedora.

Apparently more than happy to see the thing go, he thrust it at her. "It's yours."

Putting it on, she jauntily tipped her head. "Perfect." With a wave, she wheeled out of the room.

Sean looked up at me. "You think she knew I hated it and was doing me a favor taking it off my hands?"

"Undoubtedly. I'll be right back." I crutched quickly to catch up with her.

She'd already punched the elevator call button. "You know you can contact Dr. Paul. He would be able to tell if the mother's spirit surrounds the little girl."

I bit the inside of my cheek. "I will if I have to."

"Your call."

I said, "I need a little time away from the other Whiners right now."

She nodded. "Understandable."

The group came with a lot of emotional baggage. Stuff I hadn't quite worked through yet. I was glad Orlinda understood.

She looked up at me, studying my face. "You need to take better care of yourself."

"I'm trying," I said. "But I keep getting in the way of psychopaths."

Her lips curved in a half smile. "Take care of yourself up here," she clarified, tapping her head. "You're not a superhero. You cannot save the world. You shouldn't condemn yourself for not being able to."

"You're crushing my dreams. I'd really like a cape."

"Lucy."

I sighed. "I'm trying."

"Try harder. One case at a time, okay? And learn to appreciate all those you have been able to help."

The elevator dinged and the door slid open. A shiver went down my spine at the sound, but I stepped forward and held the door open with my body as she rolled forward. "Be careful, Lucy Valentine."

She smiled as the doors closed.

You cannot save the world. You shouldn't condemn yourself for not being able to.

Catching a glimpse of my reflection in the stainless steel elevator doors, I saw the determination flaring in my eyes.

I might not be able to save the world, but I could find Kira and bring closure to little Ava, who'd need it to fully heal. And I could find Dustin to set his grandmother's heart at ease.

Uncovering the truth on what matters.

It had been Kira's tagline.

But it had just become mine.

As I spun around to head back to Aiden's room, I could practically see my superhero cape flying out behind me...

18

Blinking drowsily, Sean twisted his torso to look at the clock on the nightstand. "It's three in the morning, Lucy."

At the sound of Sean's voice, Odysseus suddenly stopped running on his wheel as though he was disturbed by noise in his usually-quiet nocturnal environment. The two cats, twined at the foot of the bed, lifted their heads in curiosity, deemed us unworthy of further attention, then went back to sleep. Thoreau had opted to sleep with Scout in the dining room under Ava's crib, the traitor.

"In every photo since May, she's wearing a watch," I said, tapping the screen of my iPad. I couldn't sleep, so I'd been watching news footage of Kira again.

Lamplight fell across his puzzled face. "What?"

"She started wearing this watch last month. It's Gucci. Not inexpensive."

"It's three in the morning, Lucy."

"I did a little research. Her birthday is in May. So is Mother's Day. I'm guessing it was a gift."

"I don't think Ava would have enough money in her piggy bank."

I nudged him. "If you were dating me, and I had a kid, you'd buy me a gift for Mother's Day from the baby."

"Gee, I'm a pretty nice guy, aren't I?"

Ignoring his teasing, I added, "Especially if her father wasn't in her life. Either way, I'm guessing it was a gift from Trey."

"Did you drink coffee before bed?"

"Yes."

Odysseus went back to running as Sean yawned, stretching his arms over his head. I tried not to be distracted by his muscled chest.

"I think you're reading more into it than what's there," he said. "She got a new watch. It's not a big deal."

"It is a big deal. I know these things. I'm the psychic one, remember?"

"You're the crazy one," he countered. "You know your abilities had nothing to do with this theory of yours."

"Intuition plays a big role in being a psychic, you know. I'm intuit…ing."

"And making up new words. How many cups of coffee did you have?"

I tried to remember. "One. Or two. Or three."

He laughed. "How long have you been up?"

"Not long," I lied. I hadn't really slept. Just tossed and turned until the sheet had twisted into an uncomfortable knotted lump. I couldn't seem to shut off my thoughts.

Em had called earlier—she was going to spend the night in the cot next to Aiden's bed. He was hoping to be released in the morning. I was actually feeling badly about not speaking with Preston or Dovie today, a bad case of the guilts. I knew it was best for them to stay out of this case, but...I missed them. Then there was this case. This complicated case.

Plumping the pillow under his head, Sean rolled to face me. "I thought you already went through the list of gifts Fish gave Kira. He didn't mention a watch."

"Maybe he forgot."

"Maybe you're reaching."

I rubbed my eyes. "Maybe. I just want to find her."

"You will."

"How? If she had on that watch, and it was a gift, yes... Otherwise, I'm not sure. Her house burned to the ground. I've already tried sniffing Ava—that didn't work, though she does smell good. There's something about that baby shampoo scent..."

His eyebrows went up. "You sniffed Ava?"

I smiled at his incredulous tone. "I figured it couldn't hurt to try."

"What about those awards you saw in that box with the blanket? Someone gave those to her..."

It was an interesting idea. "It's worth a try. If Nya ever turns up."

"She'll turn up."

"You're placating me."

"It's three in the morning. You need to get up early. Now turn off the light and try to get some sleep."

Turned out Jeremy Cross wasn't avoiding me (yet) and had called back earlier. He was due here at a little after seven to read Scout's energy. After that I needed to make a quick trip into the city to see Tova Dovell Fisher. When we were through, I was hoping to sneak in another visit with Patty Keefe. Aiden believed it was Cat Bennett holding the keys to this case, but to me it seemed that Nya Rodriguez was proving to be the key-keeper.

I set my iPad aside, and before I turned out the light, I drew in another deep breath of Cat's sweater, and again saw darkness. My hopes of finding her alive were dwindling.

I shut off the lamp and rolled to face Sean. His fingers slid up and down my arm, keeping far from my palm to avoid those little zaps of electricity that happened when our palms touched.

Moonlight seeped in under the lowered shades, and the air conditioner hummed white noise that usually helped me drift off. But try as I might, I was wide awake.

It might have been four cups of coffee that I'd had before bed.

"I've been thinking," he began.

"Oh?" There was just enough light to make out his somber expression. Reaching up, I ran my fingers through the hair behind his ear. "About?"

"Us."

"Oh?" I repeated, going still. Why was he so solemn all of a sudden?

Leaning in, he kissed my wrist, making my pulse jump against my skin. "I can't believe I'm about to say this..."

My nerves were shot. "What?"

Clearing his throat, he said, "I think I agree with your mother."

"I...what?"

Rising up on his elbow, he looked down at me. "Right now this place is fine. I mean, not right this minute, with Ava and Scout, but when it's just us and Thoreau and the cats and the hamster...it's perfect. But what about when we have kids?"

I leaned up on my elbow, too. I kind of loved that he was thinking about our babies.

"There's no place for them here," he added. "We could probably keep them in this room with us for a while, but even then it'll get claustrophobic fast. You don't handle claustrophobia well."

I knew. "I always thought we'd get a new place when we have kids."

"You love this place."

I did. "But do you?"

"I'm happy here."

It was the best thing he could have said. Sean had lived in many places—most of them unhappily. "Well," I teased. "That could be because of me."

"Or the view."

I shoved him, and he laughed. I said, "My mother is going to gloat."

"I know. We don't have to tell her right away," he said. "Get some more cookies out of it."

"I'm shocked, Mr. Donahue. Shocked. And I like the way you think."

"So?" he asked. "Renovations?"

"I'm in. We may have to listen to gloating and endless talk about baby nurseries, but on the plus side, we could make the shower bigger."

"I like that idea." He grinned.

Pulling me close, he kissed me. It was a kiss of love, of happiness. It completely chased away all the anxiety I'd been feeling. For the first time all day I was completely at ease. But as his hand slid up my tank top, I pulled back. "Hey, I thought it was time to go to sleep."

"Did I say that?"

"Yes. Yes, you did."

Laughing as he leaned in for another kiss, he said, "I misspoke. I meant to say it was time for bed."

Jeremy Cross showed up at precisely seven thirty the next morning. I watched him from my perch on a stool at the breakfast bar as he sat on the floor near Scout, who lounged next to the couch. I doubted Jeremy had ever been tardy a day in his life. I bet he had been the kind of kid who arrived to grade school half an hour early to get a head start on his morning work, didn't participate in the senior prank in high school, and never skipped a single college class.

I was glad he was prompt. His arrival had been the catalyst I needed to turn off the morning news. Trey Fisher had been interviewed about Kira's disappearance and had managed to scrounge up a few crocodile tears while waxing on about missing her and begging the public for help.

It had been nauseating.

Ava sat with Sean on the couch, reading a book to him in a language I couldn't understand. Sean, however, kept up his end of the conversation just fine.

I thought of him doing the same with a child of ours, and warmth flooded my chest.

Jeremy kept throwing glances at Ava, and I couldn't help but feel for him, for his devastating loss. "Thanks again for coming by. You sure you don't want some coffee?"

"No thanks. I'm at my caffeine max," he said. Sunlight streamed through the window making the few threads of silver in his dark hair sparkle.

"What's your max?" I asked, curious.

"One mug."

"All day?"

"Yes."

"You're serious?"

"Yes."

"Is it a thirty-six ounce mug?" I questioned.

Sean chuckled. I had the feeling he was recalling my coffee binge before bed last night.

"No," Jeremy said. "Twelve ounces."

I'd already consumed twice that amount in the past hour. I needed it, too. My late night was catching up to me. The coffee-before-bed idea definitely hadn't been my wisest. I'd managed a couple of hours of sleep before I got up, showered, and dressed. As I went about my morning routine, I noticed that my body barely ached.

I'd been Orlinda-ed.

In Aiden's hospital room, I thought she'd only been reading my energy when I felt that warmth from her hand. I'd been wrong. She'd been at work, healing.

Jeremy had been sitting next to Scout for a good ten minutes now, letting the dog adjust to his presence. Sean and I had filled him in on the latest developments in both Dustin and Kira's disappearances, including the news that Dustin's father might be involved and that Cat Bennett was missing.

Reaching out to pet Scout, Jeremy said, "I've been assured that the surveillance footage for the ATMs where Kira's accounts were accessed will be available today."

"Thanks," I said. "It'll be nice to know if it is Kira. Because if it's not, then someone else is using her debit card. We need to figure how it was obtained."

"Yes," he said, agreeing.

"Do you have a theory?" I asked, probing. Although he now specialized in animal communication, he'd once been a leading behavioral profiler for the FBI. I suspected he had a wide range of psychic skills, but I had no clue exactly what kind. He *was* a man of mystery.

"No."

My probing skills were clearly inferior to his evasion tactics.

He rubbed a hand over Scout's head slowly, soothingly. Scout rolled onto his back and offered up his belly. His tail thumped gently.

"He's happy to be with Ava, but he despises the cats. Apparently Ebbie keeps hissing at him every time she walks by, and he's not pleased that Grendel keeps eyeing his food." Jeremy glanced at me. "Grendel also requests a new brand of cat food. He's grown tired of what you've been giving him."

I looked at Grendel, sitting oh-so-innocently in the bedroom doorway, his tail swishing. "You poor thing."

Ignoring me, his eyes drifted closed.

Scout whined.

"He's concerned for Kira," Jeremy said softly. "She was scared when she left him with the neighbor."

Spellbound, I watched the way Jeremy worked with Scout, gently touching, maintaining eye contact. It fascinated me.

"I asked him about the phone call she received," he said.

We'd told him about the phone records showing someone had called Kira from the Bennetts' house.

After a second, Jeremy said, "The call that sent Kira into a tailspin came from someone named Lillian."

"Lillian?" I repeated.

"That's who called. She made Kira very upset. She kept saying the name."

Sean looked over at me. "Have you come across anyone named Lillian?"

It didn't sound the least bit familiar. "No."

Jeremy's shoulders relaxed, and he roughhoused with the dog for a moment before saying, "That's all Scout knows."

Lillian? I was stumped. "I don't even know what to do with that information."

"Go back to the beginning," Jeremy said, "and question everyone you've come in contact with about Lillian. Someone has to know her."

I groaned. The last thing I wanted to do was backtrack. Going back to the beginning seemed counterproductive, but if it needed to be done, I'd do it. Because I couldn't help but feel that at this point in the investigation, time wasn't just working against us...it was rapidly running out.

19

The smell of smoke still stubbornly clung to the city streets, which had apparently also been bypassed by yesterday's storms. However, there was once again rain in the forecast, and I was hopeful that today would be the day rain cleansed the city...and my bad memories.

Because I was so early for my appointment with Tova Dovell Fisher, I decided to drop by the Porcupine and get a cup of coffee. I'd hit virtually no traffic on the way downtown, which was a miracle of epic proportions. I almost wanted to play the lottery to really test my luck.

The restaurant was jumping as usual, with almost every table full and waitstaff hurrying about. Raphael looked up from wiping the counter and smiled. "Look at you with only one crutch."

"I'm downsizing," I said, leaning across the counter to kiss his cheek. "I'll be roller-skating in no time."

"I've seen the way you roller-skate. You'll end up with another broken foot."

"I'll keep the crutches handy." I slid onto a stool, dropping my tote bag on the stool next to mine. "I'll have room to store them soon. Did you hear about my mother's plans to expand my cottage?"

"Ah, yes. She and your father were discussing it here the other day."

"By discussing do you mean fighting?"

"Debating," he countered, setting a coffee mug in front of me.

"That explains why she was avoiding him yesterday."

Grabbing the coffee carafe, he filled my cup and smiled. "Time apart isn't necessarily a bad thing. Let the dust settle."

Aside from me, no one was more aware of the nuances of my parents' relationship than Raphael. "Let Dad transfer money into his secret account?"

He laughed, then his eyes sobered as he examined my face. "You're doing okay?"

"I'm good." As good as I could be, I supposed. My mind was a mess, trying to make sense of the insensible. Who in the world was Lillian? Why had she called Kira on Thursday night?

But I didn't want to worry Raphael too much, so I said, "Healing quickly." Thanks to Orlinda.

"My trips to the hospital to visit you are becoming alarmingly common."

I agreed. "I think I should get frequent patient points."

"Or at least speak with your father about a better health care plan."

I smiled. "Or hazard pay."

Laughing, he said, "Imagine that conversation."

I sipped my coffee. Dad would surely have another heart attack. Money and women were his downfalls.

"How's Aiden? Sean?" Raphael asked.

"Much better. Aiden's to be released this morning, and Sean did a little work with me yesterday."

"No luck with finding the reporter?"

"Not yet. I have a meeting in a little bit, another lead." I explained how complicated the case had become.

A group of four entered the restaurant and Raphael said, "Be right back."

My phone rang, and I dug inside my tote bag. A shiver of uneasiness rippled through me as I answered.

"I dropped Dovie's phone in the pool," Cutter said. "She has it sitting in a bag of rice, so you have two, maybe three days, before she has access to the Internet again. She's pissed."

"Are you sure that's from the phone and not from Preston's attitude?"

"No."

I laughed. "I owe you."

"I know."

I smiled. I rather liked having a little brother.

"Oh, and for God's sake, have your mother call Dovie on the house line. She's suspecting something's up because she can't reach Judie. I can only do so much."

He took after my father in more ways than one. "I'll tell her."

"How're things up there?" he asked.

"Frustrating. Lots of leads, mostly dead ends." I winced at the phrase.

"I have faith in you."

Feeling sappy, I smiled. "Thanks, Cutter."

"Gotta go," he said and hung up quickly.

I dropped my phone in my bag. The sleeve of Cat's sweater stuck out, and I reached over to tuck it back, but on a whim, I pulled it out to try yet another reading.

Lifting it to my nose, I breathed in, fully expecting to see nothing at all. I nearly fell off my stool when an image came into focus.

I blinked, trying to decipher what I was seeing. There wasn't much light, only a single bulb dangling from a bare beam and a few shafts of sunlight coming through a small dusty window. A blue hydrangea bush, its limbs sagging from the weight of the blooms, sat directly in front of the window, blocking any further views.

As I could only see through Cat's eyes, I silently begged her to look around, to give me more information.

She was lying in bed. Nearby a washer and dryer sat side by side. There was a tiny windowless bathroom in the far corner. Duct work and pipes ran through joists above her head.

The space, I realized, was an unfinished cellar.

"Lucy?" Raphael asked.

I held up a wait-a-sec finger and tried to stay in the moment with Cat.

But, her eyes closed, and all I saw was darkness once again.

Feeling like a bloodhound, I sniffed the sweater again and again.

"Lucy?" Raphael asked, reaching out to touch my hand.

I blinked. "She's alive."

"Who?" he asked. "The reporter?"

"No. I mean, I don't know if she is, but this is someone else. I have to go. I need to call Aiden."

"Do you need me to do anything?" he asked.

I reached for my crutch. "No, but thank you." I grabbed my wallet to pay for the coffee and he waved me off.

"Go on. I've got this covered."

I gave his cheek another kiss. "Thanks."

"Try to stay out of the hospital," he called after me as I rushed to the door.

Over my shoulder, I said, "I'll do my best."

In the distance, thunder rumbled as I leaned against the outside wall and dialed Aiden's cell phone.

Cat Bennett was alive. If we could find her, we could possibly find out what happened to Kira.

And to Dustin.

If.

A half hour later, dark clouds hovered overhead as a stern-looking housekeeper opened the door at a Back Bay brownstone, its front stoop decked out in vertical planters overflowing with lush flowers and dripping with ivy.

"I'm Lucy Valentine," I said, sneaking a peek behind her into the expansive foyer. "I have an appointment with Tova." I hoped the housekeeper didn't leave me out here to verify the meeting because I didn't want to get caught in a rainstorm. The city needed a good soaking—I didn't.

I'd spoken with Aiden, but even though we knew Cat was alive, we still had no idea of knowing where. I kept sniffing her sweater, but she was still asleep, giving me no more clues.

I kept thinking about her in that basement. Had she been locked in? Or was she hiding out?

"This way," the woman said in a heavy accent I couldn't quite place. Something from Central Europe. Polish, maybe.

Moving noiselessly on thick-soled shoes, she led me through the stunning interior of the home, which looked like a hybrid of a gentleman's study and a French country drawing room. Dark woods and masculine furniture mixed with toile and lace fabrics. It was an interesting combination, and I liked it.

The noise of my crutch hitting the wooden floor seemed to echo like a jackhammer. I winced as the sound reverberated upward to the wood-beamed rafters.

"I'll take it from here, Serafina," a masculine voice said. Trey Fisher trotted down a mahogany staircase wearing nothing but a pair of gym shorts.

The housekeeper nodded and turned in the opposite direction that we'd been walking.

"Couldn't stay away from me, eh?" he asked, his eyes widening. "I get a lot of that."

"People staying away?" I asked as innocently as I could manage.

His eyebrows dipped. "*Not* staying away."

"Oh." I hid a smile as I turned to look around. "I'm actually here to see Tova, but I'm glad I ran into you."

"I knew it." He motioned for me to follow him into the kitchen. "Something to drink?"

"No thanks." The kitchen was the size of my whole cottage. Beautiful ivory-colored custom cabinets filled the wall space, some with clear glass panels to show off sparkling crystal. A long island was topped with a stunning pale green glass countertop that reminded me of sea glass.

He pulled a juicer out of a cabinet and gathered green leafy veggies, a beet, and two carrots from the cavernous fridge. "Did you find Kira yet?"

"Not yet." I eyed him. "You haven't heard from her, have you?"

"Nope." He grabbed a pear from a fruit basket and a glass from a cabinet.

"You still think she's hiding out?"

Dropping the beet into the juicer, he used the plunger to push it through. Vibrant red liquid spilled down the chute into the glass. He followed it up with one of the leafy green veggies—some sort of lettuce—and the carrots. "You don't?"

"No."

"Then where is she?" he asked.

He fed the pear into the machine, followed by another leafy veg. "You sure you don't want some of this?" he asked, lifting the glass.

I tried not to gag. "No."

"It does a body good."

As much as I hated to admit it—and I did—his body was just shy of spectacular, what with those perfectly-chiseled muscles and all. That, however, didn't change the fact he was a jerk. "I'm still full from the Froot Loops I had for breakfast. Oh, and the two lemon-filled donuts." I hadn't had any such thing—but only because there weren't any in the house. I'd had peanut butter on toast, but he didn't need to know that.

He choked a bit as he stared at me over the rim of his glass. "Froot Loops? Do you know what's in those?"

"Fruit?" I blinked at him.

He shuddered.

I think any attraction he had for me just went out the window. Thank goodness. Maybe now he would drop the macho act and answer me straight.

Light spilled in from double doors leading onto the back deck. "I was watching video clips of Kira and noticed she started wearing a Gucci watch in May. Did you give that to her? A birthday present? Or a Mother's Day present?"

Gulping down the rest of his drink, he wiped his lips with the back of his hand. "She's not my mother."

4 x 4 is 16.

480/2 is 240.

"Her birthday present?" I asked.

"I got her a car."

Whoa. Seemed a little excessive for a new relationship. "So you didn't give her a watch?"

"No."

Damn.

He set his glass in the sink and leaned on the counter. "I've been thinking about what you said yesterday, about jewelry. She sometimes wore a necklace I gave her."

"Really?"

"Yeah. It had this little silver coin thing that dangled." He shrugged. "She liked it, so I bought it for her for birthday."

"Are you willing to do a reading?" I asked.

"Sure. I mean, if it helps find her."

He still didn't seem all that upset she was missing, and I couldn't figure out why other than he truly believed she was hiding out to boost interest in her story.

Coming around the island, he leaned a hip against the countertop and held out his hands.

I *really* didn't want to touch him.

15-3 is 12. "Think about that necklace."

"Did you really have Froot Loops?" he asked, holding out his hands.

"Yes." I rested my palms on top of his and closed my eyes.

"Despite your questionable diet, you have nice skin. I mean, not where it's all cut up, but the rest of it."

I opened one eye. "Concentrate on the necklace."

Coughing, he said, "Okay. Concentrating." He *ohhhmed*.

Pulling my hands away, I said, "You're not even trying."

With a grin, he said, "I will. I promise. You're just so beautiful when you're worked up. And you smell good, too. What is that?"

"Lemon. From the donuts."

Disapproval crept into his eyes. "Why do you eat that stuff?"

"It's delicious."

"The sugar alone…" He made a disgusted face.

"The necklace?" I reminded.

He shoved his hands toward me. "Fine."

I took hold of them, but after a moment, I knew it was pointless. "I don't see anything." I didn't know if it was because he wasn't concentrating or if there was another reason—like he hadn't really given her a necklace.

He kept holding his hands out. "Try the earrings. It was a matching set."

Exhaling, I pressed my palms to his, letting my eyes drift close. Almost immediately, his fingers closed around my hands tightly, and he gave me a yank, pulling me close to his chest. Pivoting, he pinned me against the island in one smooth move.

"Now, isn't this nice?" he said, his breath hot in my face.

Angry, repulsed, and a tiny bit scared, I glanced up at him. Through clenched teeth, I said, "You have two seconds to let me go before I knee you so hard you'll think you put nuts in that juice you just drank."

My eyes must have told him that I wasn't the least bit kidding because he immediately released me and took a big step backward.

The sound of womanly laughter filled the kitchen.

I spun around. Tova Dovell Fisher stepped into the kitchen, smiling broadly. Heat flooded my cheeks from pure rage. I wondered how long she'd been listening in. Wondered, too, if she had planned to stop Trey if he'd dared take things further.

"Nuts. That's a good one," she said, crossing her arms.

Her "that's" sounded like "dat's." Normally I might find her accent charming, as I adored accents, but right now my patience level had bottomed out.

"Yes," Trey said. "Hysterical. I will leave you two to your warped senses of humor. I have somewhere to be."

He grabbed his glass and strode off.

"I wasn't joking," I said to her.

"He knows. Personally, I wish you'd done it." Her bare feet made no sound on the wooden floor as she crossed the kitchen to fill a tea kettle. "Would you like some?"

"No thanks."

"Something else?"

I shook my head. My stomach churned after that encounter with Trey, and I could still feel his hot breath on my face. Phantom breath.

A long colorful maxi dress swished around her long legs as she moved gracefully, setting out a teacup, a saucer, and a canister of tea leaves before waving for me to follow her. "You're Lucy?"

I tucked my crutch beneath my arm and followed her. "Yes." I didn't verify her name—we both knew who she was. Her face had been plastered across billboards, magazines, and TV commercials for years.

She led me to a cozy sun room, filled with bright light, overstuffed furniture, and lots of muted colors, from the blue-green walls and lavender throw pillows to the yellow rug. It was a welcoming space—one I might have enjoyed under any other circumstance.

Air conditioning hummed as she moved aside textbooks and notebooks. "Please sit. Also, excuse the mess. I'm studying for my citizenship test."

Her ice-blond hair had been pulled up atop her head in a sloppy knot that she managed to make stylish. Clear bright blue eyes assessed me as I hobbled in.

"When is it?" I asked.

"Next week." She sat in a ray of sunshine that made her look like an angel.

Fortunately, I knew better than most that looks could be deceiving. "Good luck."

"Thanks." Her gaze swept over me. "Looks like you've had a time of it lately."

"One too many psychopaths in my life." One of whom, I suspected, she was married to. I set my crutch on the rug and sat in a floral rocking armchair that I immediately wanted to take home with me. Some of my anger seeped away. "Thanks for agreeing to meet up."

"No problem. I've been reading up on you. Your ability is quite fascinating."

Absently, I rubbed my cheek, trying to get rid of that feeling of Trey's hot breath. "It is that."

She shifted on the sofa, pulling her legs up onto the cushions. "Have you located Kira Fitzpatrick yet?"

"Not yet."

Three tall white bookshelves stuffed full of books occupied the wall space next to the sofa. Everything from Diana Gabaldon to Homer to Maya Angelou. A basketful of magazines sat on the floor. The *New Yorker* and *Time* mingled with *Vogue* and *Allure*. A paperback of *The Princess Bride* was cracked open and face down on the side table, its spine broken.

"I suppose you want to know about my relationship with her," Tova said.

I liked her directness. "Your name has come up, especially in regard to social media."

Glossy lips pursed. "You're looking at the wrong person in that regard."

Her "the" came out as "da." "What do you mean?"

"I don't use social media. I don't Twit or Facebook or anything. My assistant handles that."

Twit. I tried not to smile at the bumble. I rocked slowly. "I heard otherwise."

The kettle whistled in the kitchen and was immediately silenced. She said, "I suggest you consider your source."

Currently, I wished bad things on my source. "Is it possible your assistant posted hateful things about Kira on your behalf?"

"No. Most likely your source is also the source of most malicious gossip about me: my dearly unbeloved husband. If you have not figured it out, he is not the most trustworthy."

I glanced toward the doorway, wondering about the suddenly-silent kettle. "Yet you married him."

"Tequila," she said, shaking her head.

"That's what he said."

"Another lie. He brought me to Vegas with the sole intention of matrimony. I, on the other hand, shouldn't have drunk so much."

"Why?" I asked. "I mean, why would he lie about it?" I knew why she'd turned to the tequila. I'd have done the same in the company of Trey for an extended period of time.

"He's an opportunist, that's why. He wanted headlines to keep his name in the limelight. Marrying me gave them to him. It took me nearly a month to realize his scam."

I recalled the tabloid blast. "Why not an annulment?"

She smiled, a sly devious smile. "Oh, he's asked. *Begged.*" Her eyes glittered with satisfaction. "I wasn't in the mood to comply after being duped by him. Now he's paying the price with this lengthy divorce. I don't even care if it costs me money in the end."

If she was willing to stay married to Trey this long, she took her revenge seriously. How had Kira factored into her plans? "Were you upset about him dating Kira?"

"Not the least bit. I felt badly for her, actually."

"Why's that?"

Looking toward the garden, she seemed lost in thought for a moment. Finally, she said, "As I mentioned, he's an opportunist. And a narcissist. He doesn't care for anyone but himself. *His* wants, *his* needs, *his* desires. I knew what he wanted from her, and it pained me to see him defraud another woman, especially when there was a child involved. I told her my suspicions, but..." She trailed off.

"But?" I prompted.

"It seemed she knew."

"She knew?"

Leaning forward, she sighed. "She told me she appreciated my concern, but she knew what she was doing. What could I do? I washed my hands of it."

"You said you knew what he wanted from her. What was that?"

"He'd been freelancing as a sportscaster for the TV station a long time. He wanted to be the lead sports anchor. From there he wants to go national. She is a stepping stone for him, as I was."

Putting pieces together, I tipped my head. "He was promoted last week."

Serafina came in, carrying a tray with the teacup and saucer Tova had set out earlier. The case of the silenced tea kettle had been solved. She set the cup and saucer on the side table.

"Thank you, Sera," Tova said, smiling warmly at the housekeeper, who quickly ducked out of the room. She picked up our conversation. "Yes, he was promoted. Thanks to his girlfriend pulling strings. I predicted a few more weeks before he broke it off with her. Except now she's missing…and he's reveling in being a free man without a messy breakup."

I didn't doubt a word Tova had said. It all rang true. So, if Kira had known he was using her, what game was she playing? It made no sense to me. Had she been blinded by Trey's sexy eyes and six-pack abs? I hated thinking so—she seemed too smart to be fooled by him.

I said, "I have to ask where you were last Thursday night."

"I've been out of town all week. I left last Sunday and landed last night from a photo shoot in Tahiti."

Unless she had minions to carry out her dirty work, then I'd say that was a fairly solid alibi.

"Also," she said, "we were on a remote island with no cell phone or Internet coverage. I'll have my assistant email you the details so the police can verify everything."

There went my scorned-woman theory.

Still, she could have minions... "If you're not making the online comments, then who?" I asked.

"Who do you think likes all the attention? Who wants this case to drag on and on because it will get him more screen time? Who's acting like *he* was the victim?"

I recalled Trey sniveling on TV this morning, and how his readings had all been dismal failures. No wonder he wanted this case to drag out.

He didn't want Kira to be found.

My anger rose again, and I found myself clenching my fists.

"He lied to you earlier," she said, sipping her tea. "I overheard him telling you he knew nothing about the watch she wore, but he knows."

"Did he give it to her?" I asked.

She shook her head. "No. He's too cheap. Even the car he supposedly bought for her is one he borrowed from our home fleet. It's leased in my name as well as his. My lawyer has been fighting that one for a while now."

"Wait, wait," I said, scooting to the edge of my chair. "The car isn't hers?"

"No."

This explained why Aiden was having a hard time tracking down a registration. My head spun with all this new information. "Okay, first things first, the watch. What do you know about it?"

"They had a big fight about it. I overheard the whole thing."

"When?" I asked.

"Last weekend."

Ah, so this was the fight Morgan had heard about.

Tova said, "Trey didn't like that she was wearing a gift from another man, and she yelled that he was only angry because another man was more thoughtful than he was. He accused her of sleeping with him, and she yelled that he was just insecure because she was waiting to sleep with him."

"Trey? She wasn't sleeping with him?"

Eyes wide with mirth, she shook her head. "Nope. Holding out."

Well, color me shocked. I wanted to laugh. Morgan had said Kira was particular, and it seemed as though she put her boyfriends to the test before letting them fully into her life.

"I had the feeling she wore that watch to make him angry," Tova added. "I liked that about her."

"Do you know who gave it to her?"

"I don't know his name, but he lives next door to her. Trey hated the guy because he was always around."

Morgan Creighton.

I wanted to do a happy dance right there in the sunroom, broken foot and all. A reading from Morgan could lead me straight to Kira.

I said, "Would you be willing to do a reading on Kira's car?"

"Will it help find her?"

"Possibly."

She set her tea down. "Trey would hate it."

"Yes."

Smiling, she said, "Let's do it."

I wasn't above using her revenge to suit my needs. She made room on the sofa, and I hopped over to sit next to her. I gave her a quick rundown on how readings worked.

With curious eyes, she watched me carefully as she held out her hands, palms up.

Sucking in a deep breath, I met her gaze, then placed my hands on top of hers. If what she said was true—about the car being in both her and his names, then I should be able to get a reading on it from Tova. Closing my eyes, I braced myself as images flew at me, taking me along highways, through a suburban area, and finally deep into the Blue Hills where I saw Kira's missing SUV.

Or, rather, what was left of it.

Concealed by overhead foliage, the SUV rested at the bottom of a deep ravine, crushed nearly flat. I swallowed a lump in my throat.

No one could survive such a crash.

20

The beautiful Blue Hills Reservation, a state park, was located south of the city. Its area was so big it extended into several towns. With hills (appropriately), ponds, marshes, and swamps, it was a great place to hike, bike, or spend a day splashing in the ponds.

It had a bit of a dark side, too. Many dead bodies had been found in these woods over the years. I couldn't help but wonder if Kira would become one of the statistics.

On my drive, I'd called Morgan Creighton only to get his voicemail. I'd left him a message, told him to call me, that it was urgent, and hung up, feeling a spark of hope.

The pieces were coming together.

By the time I made it to the Blue Hills—more than an hour later because my traffic luck had run out—the place was crawling with emergency personnel. State and local police milled about, and there was an abundant number of fire vehicles. I found a parking spot along the side of the road and made my way toward the scene.

Black clouds rolled overhead, dark wisps dipping low. A young trooper tried to stop me at a blockade, but he quickly let me by after I flashed my ID.

Police scoured the roadways, marking areas to be examined further. At the top of the hill, I wasn't the least bit surprised to see Aiden in the thick of things. When he spotted me, he broke away from the madness.

"It's down there," he said, motioning me to the side of the roadway.

There was no guardrail and only a four-foot strip of land before it gave way to a steep drop. From up here, I couldn't see the wreckage through the thick canopy of leaves.

Thunder cracked and everyone looked upward at the same time. There was a shout for tents.

"Is Kira...?" I asked, my heart thumping.

"Don't know yet," he said, fussing with the collar of his polo shirt. "Crews are down there now."

It was strange to see him in jeans and not a suit. When I called him from the Fisher house he'd been about to check out of the hospital and didn't have time to run home and change. Fortunately, he'd had his badge with him, which was now clipped at his waist. He'd sent Em home and caught a ride here with a hospital security guard.

"I'm not sure we would have ever found it, Lucy. Even when the leaves fell... It's such a remote area."

Aiden and I moved out of the way as a wrecker chugged up the hill, its orange rooftop light flashing. It was going to be quite an ordeal to get the SUV removed from its resting spot.

"Any sign of where it went over?" I asked. "Was it an accident?"

"We haven't found any broken glass to indicate a collision," he said, leading me farther up the hill, to an area that seemed to be the main focus of the investigators.

Thunder rumbled and a bolt of lightning flashed in the distance.

"Damn it," Aiden said, glancing skyward. "We're going to have to suspend the search if the storm gets much closer."

As much as I hated that idea, it was dangerous out here, being this high up with all these trees around.

"The car went over here," he said.

I noted the tree damage and flattened brush that was already bouncing back. I only noticed because I was looking for it. A normal observer could pass on by without knowing anything was amiss.

I studied the ground. "No skid marks." Kira hadn't braked before going over.

"No." His jaw worked back and forth.

"It was dark," I theorized. "If she wasn't familiar with this road she could have easily missed the curve…"

"Why would she be out here?"

I didn't know. There was nothing here. Trees. Trails. Wilderness.

I wanted to believe it was an accident. The most likely supposition was too hard to swallow.

That someone had orchestrated this outcome.

It was easy enough to do. Simply angle the car at the right position, put the car in drive, and get the hell out of the way as it rolled forward, letting physics take care of the rest.

The wind kicked up, whipping my hair against my cheek. A drop of rain fell. Another.

Lightning flashed brightly and thunder rocked the ground, shaking it like an earthquake.

"Get them up here," someone shouted as people scurried.

I stood next to an unmoving Aiden. Two statues in the midst of chaos.

It seemed like an endless wait before the first bucket of firefighters was winched to safety. Aiden burst forward as others unbuckled the group.

I stood back, watching and waiting, as Aiden conversed with the crew. Lightning cracked, raising the hair on my arms. It took everything in me not to turn and run as fast as I could with this stupid crutch to the safety of my car.

I hated lightning. It brought back painful memories of the day I'd lost the ability to see the colorful world I'd grown up with.

For Aiden, I stayed put. Rain spit from the sky, quickly darkening the color of the road beneath my feet, turning it from slate gray to charcoal to black.

After a moment, Aiden came back to me, despair etched in his eyes.

"Kira?" I asked, my mouth dry—the only part of me that was.

"Nothing," he said so low I had to strain to hear him.

Raindrops splattered my face. "What's that mean?"

"The SUV is empty. No sign of an occupant. No blood or anything that would indicate there was ever anyone in the vehicle." As he looked over the vast expanse of woods, the sky fully opened and a pouring rain soaked everything in sight.

I was glad the city was finally getting the cleansing it needed, but I couldn't help but feel as though the heavens were crying.

Water streamed down Aiden's face as he looked over the expansive forest. "She could be anywhere, Lucy. Absolutely anywhere."

"We'll find her," I said to Aiden as I turned up the driveway of Aerie. Finally home. I was missing it after the day I'd had. Missing Sean. Missing my critters. Right now I'd be happy to take a hot shower, slip into my pjs and just spend some quality time with all of them for the rest of the night. But that was a pipe dream.

There was still too much to do with this case. And being alone with Sean wasn't going to happen anytime soon.

Right now Em was out doing more shopping, planning to add an air mattress to my dining room décor. Aiden wanted to be near Ava and wasn't comfortable moving her from my place—where she'd become accustomed—to Dovie's. So, Em and Aiden were moving in with Sean and me until this case was solved.

"Yeah," he said, staring out the window. The rain had gone as fast as it had come, leaving behind cloudy skies and an unsettled feeling.

We'd waited in the Blue Hills long enough for Kira's SUV to be hauled out of the ravine, to verify that there wasn't a body trapped underneath the wreckage.

There hadn't been.

I'd been sure finding Kira's car would answer some questions, but it had proven only to elicit more of them.

Why had her car crashed? Who'd crashed it? Where was Kira?

The tires of my car splashed through rivulets of rain water that snaked down Dovie's driveway. As I crested the hill at the top of the drive, I glanced at Dovie's house, so stately yet welcoming, and wondered how I was going to explain everything to her.

There was going to be hell to pay. Guilt tugged at my conscience, but I knew Dovie, and I knew Preston. It was best they didn't know, I reminded myself, and tried to believe it.

At the top of the drive, I turned to the right, my gaze focused on my cottage. I tried to picture it after a renovation and couldn't even conjure an image in my head. Taking a breath, I told myself I'd get used to it. I'd adjust. I'd—

"Lucy, look out!" Aiden shouted.

I jammed on my brakes and jerked backward as my seatbelt tightened. A man dressed in black slid across the hood of my car. Three security ninjas, hot on his heels, gave pursuit.

"What the hell?" Aiden asked, his mouth agape.

I watched as the man in black zig-zagged across the property. At one point, his hood slipped off, and I recognized the buzz cut.

"It's Corey McDaniel."

Aiden threw open the door, pulled his gun from his holster, and ran into the fray.

I noticed the front door of my cottage open, a brown and white blur came racing out. Scout. Thoreau, I noticed, followed the bigger dog, yapping his head off the whole way. The front door slammed closed again, and I could easily picture Sean going for his gun to protect Ava.

I sat there, behind the wheel of my car, unsure what to do. I couldn't very well give chase. Not with this clunky boot.

Corey veered off, heading for the bluff, and I suddenly wondered if this wasn't his first time on the property. The security team had thwarted an intruder the other night—one who'd jumped into the ocean to escape. Had that been Corey?

Scout dashed ahead of Corey, blocking him from making a leap. Teeth bared, he snarled, and Thoreau nipped at Corey's ankles. He spun right, circling around the cottage and reappearing on the wooded side.

I eased off the brake and zoomed forward. If he reached those woods he might get away. My tires spun on the crushed gravel drive, and mud spit as I drove off-road, onto the immaculately-manicured lawns. I winced at the ruts I left behind.

Corey looked up as he heard the engine, his eyes widening. He didn't slow down, however, as he bolted for cover. I swerved right, straightened, and stomped on the gas pedal, pushing it to the floorboard.

He was forced to slow down to avoid running into me, and in a blink, Scout was on him, his teeth sunk into black running pants. Yelping, Corey spun around, trying to loosen the dog, and before I could even open the car door, one of the security guys had tackled him.

"Scout," I called. "Come."

The dog gave me an are-you-serious glare, and continued to pull at Corey's pants. It took some serious convincing from Aiden to get Scout to release.

I left the car on the grass and hobbled over. Thoreau barked and bounced his way toward me, obviously proud to be involved in the takedown. I scooped him up, and gave him some loving for his good work.

Corey was quickly cuffed, pulled into a sitting position on the wet ground. His mouth was set in a flat line and resignation filled his eyes.

Aiden had stepped off to the side to make a phone call, and his voice carried as he called for backup.

The security team stood side by side, menacing with their weapons and angry expressions. Scout sat at my feet, panting hard. I patted his head, too. "Good boy."

After ending his call, Aiden said, "Your parole officer's not going to be happy with you, Corey."

Corey's eyes flared. "How'd you know my name?"

Aiden crouched down. "I'll tell you if you tell me why you're here."

I bit my lip as Corey contemplated an answer in silence. He looked so young sitting there that I suddenly felt sorry for him.

Then I reminded myself that I couldn't fix everyone or everything.

Finally, he said, "I got a job offer I couldn't refuse."

Aiden said, "We know your name because we're investigating the disappearance of a TV reporter. You put a doll in her SUV last week. There's video surveillance and your prints were on the doll."

He mentioned nothing of looking into Dustin's disappearance, and I wondered why. I wanted to know if Corey knew anything about it.

"A TV reporter? I didn't know whose car it was," Corey said. "It was just a job."

"Who hired you?" Aiden asked.

Corey said, "You'll help me get a deal?"

A plea deal.

I could only imagine the time he was going to have to serve now.

Jaw clenched, Aiden nodded.

I wasn't surprised he agreed—he needed information and right now Corey was the only one who could give it to us.

"A lady," Corey said. "Never gave me a name, and I never met her."

A lady. Who? Kira? Cat? I was consumed with wanting to know.

"How'd she get in touch with you?"

"Called my phone."

Aiden pressed. "How'd she know your number?"

Confusion crossed Corey's eyes as though he never wondered. "No idea."

"How'd the transactions work?"

Gulls flew overhead. "She'd call, tell me the job, and leave the money at a specific site."

"You never questioned any of this?" Aiden asked.

"Money's money. I've been having trouble finding employment." Corey deadpanned.

Seemed to me he'd been working yesterday, selling drugs.

"How much money?" Aiden kept his voice low, in control.

"A thousand dollars for each job." Aiden whistled. Corey said, "I know. It was too good to pass up. And I didn't see no harm. Dropping off a doll. Easy stuff."

"What about today?" Aiden questioned. "Why are you here?"

"Supposed to break in and look for a flash drive." He shrugged. "Like I said, easy stuff, except for the Rambos."

Kira's flash drive. Someone was going to great lengths to make sure it never surfaced.

"Did you try to break in the other night, too? And jumped in the ocean?" Aiden asked.

I noticed that Sean watched from the doorway of the cottage. It was probably killing him to stay away, but I knew he was in protector mode. He wouldn't leave Ava alone, despite the threat being neutralized.

"Yeah," Corey said. "Almost drowned. The lady didn't care—she just wanted the job done. Threw in hazard pay for the guards."

I nearly laughed at the fact that he had received hazard pay. If I ever brought it up with my father, I was using Corey McDaniel as an example.

"What other jobs did she have you do? Planting the doll. Breaking in here. Anything else?"

"Calling the lady with a death threat," Corey said.

Had he broken into the Bennetts' house and called Kira from their phone? Was his call what set this all in motion?

"What lady?" Aiden stiffened.

Corey closed his eyes and screwed up his face. "I'm trying to remember her name."

"Kira?" Aiden supplied.

"Nah." He shook his head. "Nina. No. Nala?"

Wait a sec… "Nya?" I asked.

"Yeah, that's it." His gaze snapped from me back to Aiden. "Nya."

Well, that explained Nya's sudden departure for the wilds of New Hampshire—and why she wasn't returning my calls.

"Anything else?" Aiden asked.

"Don't think so. You'll be able to get me a plea deal?"

"I'll see what I can do," Aiden said, standing up as a siren grew closer.

A few minutes later, Corey was tucked into the back of a cruiser and on his way to the state police barracks to be questioned at length later on.

I thanked the security guys, and Aiden and I made our way to the cottage, the dogs racing ahead of us. "Why didn't you ask about Dustin?"

"He'd have clammed up. Too personal. I needed the information on Kira first." He rubbed a hand over his head. "I'll ask him about Dustin later."

I understood but was still disappointed. In my mind, finding Dustin had become almost as important as locating Kira.

I hobbled onto the porch and Sean, who still stood in the doorway said, "Nice parking job."

Laughing, I gave him a quick kiss as I walked past. Aiden looked around and said, "Where's Ava?"

Sean said, "Sleeping in the bedroom. I don't know how she slept through all that noise, but she did."

Aiden headed that way.

"What's that?" I asked, motioning to the TV screen. A black and white image was paused.

"ATM footage. Jeremy sent it over earlier."

"Is it Kira?" I asked.

"No. I don't recognize her. She only uses walk-up ATMs, not drive-through." Sean hit the play button on the TV remote. For a surveillance video, the images were of good quality.

I squinted at the screen, at the woman wearing a large-brimmed straw hat that covered most of her face. I couldn't see any features other than plump lips and a well-defined jawline. She knew how to dodge the camera to avoid face time. "Is it the same woman making every withdrawal?"

"Yep. Same woman. Same hat."

How'd she get Kira's debit card? Had she found her purse? Stolen it?

Aiden came out of the bedroom, quietly closing the door behind him. "ATM surveillance?" he asked, glancing at the screen.

"The woman using Kira's debit card," Sean explained.

Approaching the TV, he said, "It's not Kira."

Sean sat on the arm of the couch. "We don't know who she is."

The woman punched in a PIN, and I did a double-take. "Rewind that part," I said, rushing up to the TV set for a closer look.

Sean rewound, and again I watched the woman poke buttons. Adrenaline shot through my veins as I pointed at the screen. "I know who she is." I spun around. "And how to find her."

21

The man answered the phone on the third ring. "Do you read minds in addition to finding objects, Ms. Valentine?"

I paced the living room, my steps uneven and clunky because of the boot. Thoreau trotted beside me. Sean and Aiden watched my every move. "No, why?"

"I was just about to call you," Elliman Bay said, his deep voice resonating through the room—I had him on speakerphone. "Any updates finding Kira? News sources aren't saying much."

I thought again of Trey's tearful plea this morning, and it made my stomach turn. He was bound to take advantage of her car being found—especially since he was the one who'd loaned it to her.

"A few things," I said. "And one requires another favor from you, which was why I was calling."

"Name it."

I glanced at Sean then Aiden and swallowed hard. "There's a woman who works at the CFC. Blond, gum-chewing. She was wearing a charm bracelet and has fancy fingernails. Do you know her name?"

She had been the woman in the video. I recognized her fingernails as she punched numbers, and had seen the charms on her bracelet swaying as she grabbed the cash spit out by the machine.

He laughed. "I know exactly who you're talking about. Her name is Lillian Moore."

Freezing in place, I nearly dropped the phone. "Lillian?" I repeated, recalling what Jeremy Cross had said earlier.

The call that sent Kira into a tailspin came from someone named Lillian.

"She's not," I swallowed hard, "not your contact at the CFC, is she?"

"No, no. My contact is Barb Manciello."

The assistant director? The one who skipped out on my meeting the other day? "Really?"

"Between us, she wants this case solved more than anyone. She's aiming to take the director spot once the dust settles. She's actually why I was going to call you," he said. "She did me a huge favor by looking into Cat's schedule on January third. I'm very pleased to report that Cat Bennett wasn't in town. Kira must have been mistaken in believing so."

"She wasn't?" This seemed to completely contradict what Jarvis Kinson had told us.

"Cat was out of town at a conference in Houston. She'd left the day before and didn't return until several days later. In addition, her car was at Logan the whole time."

The airport? How had it gotten to Dustin's house?

This made no sense. Then I recalled Ross Bennett mentioning that Cat had lost a set of keys at the office Christmas party, and it suddenly hit me who it had been driving that car, who'd taken Dustin McDaniel. I felt sick to my stomach. More pieces fell into place, and there was no doubt in my mind that Lillian Moore was in trouble up to her eyebrows.

She knew Cat was out of town. Knew where to find the car. Knew she could borrow it without raising any alarms whatsoever. It was rather…ingenious.

Exactly how much trouble Lillian was in remained to be seen. Kira and Cat and Dustin were still missing. Until we found them, we wouldn't know the extent of Lillian's deviousness.

"If you'd like," Elliman continued, "I can track down the conference coordinator to nail down a specific timeline."

Aiden nodded that he wanted the information.

"That'd be great." As I turned and hobbled in the other direction, I noticed that Ava had piled all her toy animals into the bassinet along with a handful of Cheerios and two dog toys. "Thank you. Do you happen to know where Lillian Moore lives?" We had to find her.

"Hanover, I believe. I have the exact address on my computer. Do you want it?"

"Yes," I said. "I do."

"Do you want to hold on," he asked, "or do you want me to call you back?"

"I'll hold." I resumed pacing. Nerves twisted my stomach into knots.

Elliman's voice dropped. "Ms. Valentine, may I ask how Lillian Moore factors into your investigation of Kira's disappearance?"

"Mr. Bay," I replied in all honesty, "I wish I knew."

Lillian Moore lived in a quaint neighborhood of classic older homes, on a quintessentially New England road dotted with mature trees. The modified gambrel looked in need of a little TLC, with faded siding and missing shingles. The stonework that ran along the foundation appeared sturdy enough, but rotted wood trim needed replacing around a large bay window that overlooked a lawn in desperate need of mowing. Despite the dark skies, no lights glowed in the windows. The cracked blacktop driveway led to the closed door of a two-car garage. It didn't appear as though Lillian was home.

A lot had happened in the couple of hours since Corey McDaniel's arrest and me seeing the ATM footage of Lillian. The search was on for Nya Rodriguez to let her know that there was no longer a threat to her family.

Aiden had gone home to shower, change, and pack a bag. He'd also stopped by the barracks to pull info on Lillian.

I had continued to try to reach Morgan Creighton with no luck and attempt another reading on Cat's sweater that revealed no new visions. I was beginning to worry about how much she was sleeping—it was unnatural. Was she ill from not having her diabetes medication? Or drugged?

From what we now knew, Lillian Elizabeth Moore, twenty-three years old, had moved to this home a year ago. There was currently a two-hundred-thousand-dollar mortgage taken out in her name after she'd dropped a hefty down payment of one hundred and twenty-five thousand. She had an associate's degree in business administration. Her annual income at the CFC was thirty-four thousand dollars a year.

Uneasiness swept over me as I wondered how in the hell she had afforded this house. I tried to convince myself she came from money or had received an inheritance. That it had nothing to do with stolen debit cards and missing children.

8 x 2 is 16.

I couldn't do it. The money had come from some black market baby deal. Rubbing my temples, I tried not to jump to conclusions about Kira's fate. But I could easily picture Lillian gaining access to the Bennetts' house with those stolen keys on Thursday night and calling Kira, luring her out of her home under false pretenses. They'd already met at the CFC, so Kira undoubtedly considered her a reliable contact. Perhaps Lillian had promised details on Dustin's disappearance. It didn't explain why Kira had left Scout with her neighbor or Ava with Aiden—unless Kira had also pieced together what had happened and went willingly into danger...

The fact that Lillian called from the Bennett home told me that she had a plan in place to frame Cat for the crimes. She'd purposely left that trail.

So, where was Cat? After meeting with Kira in the grocery store parking lot, she must have—at some point—figured out that someone had been driving her car while she was out of town. Did she put it together that Lillian was behind it? Had she confronted her? Lillian would have been desperate to cover her tracks.

Or, was it possible that Cat was her partner in crime? Had they orchestrated this devious plan together?

I didn't know, and I hated that I didn't know. But the one thing I was sure of, was that Cat was alive. But was she hiding out...or being kept captive?

I kept thinking about how much she was sleeping, and it just felt wrong. Something was off. She obviously wasn't well...

Glancing in my rearview mirror, I saw Aiden pulling into the driveway, his gray unmarked cruiser matching the steely color of the sky—and my mood. We'd driven separate cars so he could take Lillian in for formal questioning if need be.

I thought it was entirely needed, but Aiden reminded me that there was no *proof* Lillian had done anything wrong. That it was possible Cat had let Lillian borrow her car, and she might be involved with the baby stealing as well. Or that Kira had *given* Lillian the debit card to use on her behalf. That the two were somehow friends or something...

I didn't think he believed his theories any more than I did, but I supposed that's what made him an excellent detective—he waited for facts whereas I was ready to throw Lillian into the clink. It was clear to me that she was involved, but I recognized that he had to play by the book.

As I hobbled to meet Aiden, my phone rang. I glanced at the screen and immediately took the call.

It was Morgan Creighton.

"Any news?" he asked. "Did you find her? I heard about her car on the news, but nothing was said about a...body."

I tried to ignore the way his breath hitched as he tried to keep his emotions in check. "We haven't found her yet. It's actually why I've been trying to reach you. I think you might be able to help."

Tapping his foot impatiently, Aiden's eyebrows were furrowed deeply as he scanned the house, from chimney cap to the rose bushes hugging the foundation. Touching his sleeve to get his attention, I waved for him to go on without me.

"How?" Morgan asked in my ear.

"Did you gift Kira a watch?" I asked. "Gucci?"

"Yeah, for Mother's Day. Why?"

Ha! I couldn't wait to let Sean know I'd been right. I bit my lip and watched a squirrel scamper across the yard. "I noticed in recent video footage that she wore it often. There's a chance she had it on when she disappeared."

"I don't understand," he said, then quickly added, "Hold up. Is this about you doing a reading on me?"

Apparently, he'd done some research on me while recuperating. "Yes. If you gave it to her, and she has it on...I should be able to find it."

"When? Where?" he asked eagerly.

I watched Aiden pound on the front door and press the buzzer. I wasn't sure how long we'd be here. "How about tonight?" I asked, playing it safe. "My place, eight o'clock?"

I gave him directions, and told him I'd call if plans changed. I tucked my phone back into my tote and wondered why Kira had bypassed a man who clearly adored her for someone like...Trey. I couldn't fathom it, and I couldn't even imagine how that had made Morgan feel.

Aiden came back down the driveway, his hands on his hips. He'd changed clothes before picking up his car, and he looked more himself in a button-down and khakis. His gun and badge were clipped to his belt.

"Not answering," he said, pinching the bridge of his nose as though to ward off a headache.

I heard a noise behind me and looked back to see an older man, eighty-ish, striding toward us. He wore a pair of loose trousers and a green bowling shirt with GUY embroidered on the pocket.

"You looking for Lil?" he asked in raspy voice. Behind rectangular-rimmed glasses, he eyed Aiden's gun and badge. He held out a hand for a shake. "Guy Lester."

Aiden made introductions, and I was grateful Guy didn't offer to shake my hand, too. My stress levels were already high enough without possibly seeing any visions of Guy's lost objects. I immediately pegged him as the neighborhood lookout, the person who watched for strangers, weird happenings, and who didn't mind getting in someone else's business. I liked that about him. Especially right now when we needed to find out as much information about Lillian as we could.

"State police, eh? You here about the accident?" Guy asked, resting his hands atop a big belly.

"What accident?" Aiden asked.

"Lil's accident," Guy said. "Last night."

Shit. I leaned on the push bumper guard on the front of Aiden's car. "What happened?"

"Car accident on Route 53. Local police came around this morning, looking for her family," Guy explained. He sucked in plump cheeks as he inhaled, then whistled low. "Said she crossed the median and hit another car head-on."

"Is she…" I couldn't bring myself to say the word dead.

"She's at South Shore Hospital. Critical," he said. "They're not sure she'll make it. Too bad. Sweet girl. The other driver is critical, too. Damn shame."

"Does anyone live here with her?" Aiden asked, looking back at the house. "Family? A roommate? Boyfriend?"

Guy's lips puckered as he shook his head. "Lives alone, not that she's antisocial. Always has people coming and going. Friends and the like. There's an on-off boyfriend that drives a small black car, but I don't know his name. I don't think it's anything serious. She has no family that I know of."

"Did you ever see a blue four-door sedan here? Has a smiley face ball on its antenna?" I asked.

"Yeah, I've seen that car a few times," he said.

"Recently?" Aiden asked.

Looking upward, Guy appeared lost in thought for a moment. "Thursday afternoon. I recall I saw it as I was on my way to my weekly golf game."

Cat had been here, but where did she go afterward? The car had been found in the T station, after all. She could be anywhere by now.

"Actually," he snapped his fingers, "on my way home, I saw Lil driving that car. Going a little fast, too. I'd been meaning to talk to her about it." White bristly eyebrows dipped. "Did she do something wrong?"

"That remains to be seen," Aiden said.

My pulse jumped. Cat had arrived…but didn't leave? I glanced at the house again. What secrets did it hold? My gaze fell on that big bay window again, and I gasped. "Aiden, look."

He spun around. "What?"

"There's a vase in the window," I said, excited. "Full of blue hydrangea."

"Oh, yes," Guy said. "Fresh-picked from Lil's back yard. Gorgeous flowers."

I was striding toward the back yard before he finished his sentence. Aiden jogged to catch up with me, and Guy was hot on his heels.

Sure enough, there was a hedge of hydrangea bushes, divided by back steps. I started pushing full branches aside, trying to see the foundation.

"What're you looking for?" Guy asked.

"A window," I answered.

"Here, Lucy," Aiden called out from the other side of the stairs.

I limped over and crouched next to him. "See anything?"

"It's too dark," he said.

I stood up. "We need to go in. I think she's really sick."

As I brushed past Guy, heading for the steps to see if the back door was unlocked, he said, "What's going on here?"

I was reaching for the handle when Aiden suddenly grabbed my arm, his grip tight and unyielding. "Lucy, stop! Don't touch the door."

Heart pounding, I snatched my hand back.

He examined the door frame. "We need to call the bomb squad. Just in case."

"But—" I sighed.

It was safer to wait. I knew he was right, but it didn't make it any easier to accept.

As I stepped down, I threw a look toward the window. Hopefully by the time we made it inside it wouldn't be too late to save Cat.

22

The wait for the bomb squad to arrive, set up, and begin the search process felt interminable. Houses had been evacuated. The street had been cordoned off with yellow tape, and dozens of police officers, troopers, firefighters and EMTs lurked on the fringes. Despite the size of the crowd, it was deathly quiet. It was as though we were all collectively holding our breath.

Three bomb techs and an explosive-sniffing Labrador had already cleared the doors of the house. They had gone inside only moments before. We'd know soon enough if Cat was inside.

If she was alive or dead.

A squawking crow swooped by, breaking the utter silence and startling me. I instinctively ducked and then had to laugh at my reaction. Clearly I was on edge.

Aiden and I stood back from a group of uniformed troopers at the rear of a command truck. Unmoving, he had his arms folded on his chest, his jaw lifted, and a don't-mess-with-me look on his face. He didn't even so much as blink—at least not while I was watching.

I wanted to say something, anything, to ease some of his strain, but I couldn't think of a damn thing. It had been one hell of a day.

One of the troopers at the command truck turned and gave Aiden a thumb's up. A minute later, two EMTs, escorted by two police officers, dashed through the crowd carrying big medical bags.

Aiden sprinted toward the front of the house, and I limped after him. We were followed by a swarm of emergency personnel. A bomb tech met us at the door.

In full protective gear, the trooper was imposing. "Female located in the cellar as you suspected, Lieutenant."

"Alive?" Aiden asked.

"Unconscious, but yes," the tech answered. "She'd been locked down there. No way out, not that she could have attempted escape in the condition she's in. She's in rough shape."

Two more EMTs arrived with a stretcher. As they tried to maneuver around us, I reached out and grabbed one's arm. "She has diabetes and hasn't had insulin in days."

"Thanks," she said and kept on going. They shouldered past us, heading for a set of stairs in the kitchen.

The bomb tech said, "You'll want to check out the guest bedroom upstairs." He walked off.

The living room had been decorated in cool colors and expensive furniture. I noted, however, that there were no photos on the walls. Wooden floors creaked as we cut through, hurriedly headed for the stairs.

Aiden took hold of my elbow as we climbed, and at the top of the steps, he took a right into a narrow hallway. "In here."

As soon as I entered the room, it felt as though I'd been sucker-punched. Breath whooshed out, and I leaned against the door jamb until I caught my bearings.

"Don't touch anything," Aiden said. "I'll be right back."

I didn't want to touch anything. It all felt so…evil.

The room had been cleared of all furniture except a long dining table. One wall was completely devoted to large photos of six children in various candid shots. Playgrounds, daycares, grocery stores. I recognized Dustin's face right away—and also Ava's.

Kira had been rightfully concerned for Ava's welfare—someone had been stalking the little girl.

My gaze zipped from face to face, smile to smile. I had no idea who the other children were, but all of them, I noted, were white with blond hair and blue eyes. All looked under three years old.

I felt sick to my stomach. How many of these kids were victims versus targets? Elliman Bay spoke of three missing children. Had there been more that he just hadn't heard about?

Aiden came back in, slipping on a pair of disposable gloves. He handed me a pair. His lips were smashed together as he poked around the table.

He pulled a wallet from a purse and flipped it open. "Kira's."

I wished I'd been more surprised. I wasn't. My heart broke for Ava.

My steps were heavy as I walked over to him. A destroyed laptop sat on the table, and I figured that was Kira's, too. It looked as though someone had taken a jackhammer to it. There was a set of car keys that had a smiley face key fob—Cat's keys. Underneath a printed packet on how to make a homemade explosive, there was a photo of Corey McDaniel, a phone number written on it.

The lady.

Aiden shoved his hands into his hair and turned to face the wall of children. After a long minute, he crossed to the window and stared out.

I let him be and picked up Kira's purse. I sniffed it, but all I could smell was leather. It had been worth a try. I stepped back and scanned the table. Something was nagging at me, but I couldn't quite place what it was. Something out of place.

"I'm glad," Aiden finally said, his voice hard.

"Of what?"

"I'm glad Lillian Moore isn't here." He turned and faced me. Rage blazed in his eyes. "Because I might have killed her."

Fireflies flashed outside as I lay on the sofa, my head resting on Sean's thigh. He threaded his fingers through my hair. Across the room Ebbie and Grendel were curled together in the bassinet, and I had the feeling I'd have to fight off Dovie to keep the baby bed for them. They were getting attached.

Outside, the dogs barked and Ava squealed as Em blew bubbles on the porch.

"*Mo dubbles!*" Ava said, laughing.

More bubbles. I was getting better at deciphering her language.

She sounded so happy, so carefree. I didn't want her to lose that joy. Didn't want her to know about the cloud of evil that had been shadowing her.

It was still light out, and the night air was still, eerily so. The ocean was calm, the gulls were quiet. The windows were open wide, letting in the rain-cooled air.

The TV was on but muted, and I watched as news cameras captured Ross Bennett sprinting into South Shore Hospital. I felt for the couple and this test of "in sickness and in health." Word had come that Cat had been diagnosed with diabetic ketoacidosis from a lack of insulin, and was currently in a coma suffering from a multitude of problems related to the ailment, including brain swelling that, if she survived, could take months or years to fully recover.

If. The doctors were doing everything they could to save her, but it wasn't looking good.

In a twist of fate, Lillian was in the same ICU ward, in a medically-induced coma due to brain swelling from her car accident. Her prognosis had taken a turn for the better, however. Doctors now felt that in time she would recover fully.

It didn't seem right that Lillian would be fine while Cat was fighting for her life. Where was the karma?

Both were being watched over by police.

Neither would be interviewed any time soon.

Aiden had said he'd try to make it back in time for my reading on Morgan, but it was almost eight now, and there was no sign of his return. I wasn't surprised. He had a ton of work to do processing Lillian's house. Interviewing Corey. Pulling together evidence. Holding onto hope.

I worried for his health.

I worried for him.

Maybe it was better if he didn't make it back in time.

Flipping over, I looked up at Sean.

"Hey now," he said, swiping a tear from the corner of my eye.

"I hate this case."

"I know." He caressed my cheek. "I know."

Closing my eyes, I breathed deeply, soaking in the scent of him. It did more to calm my nerves than anything else in the world.

Em's voice came through the window. "Car coming."

Morgan. I hadn't needed to alert the security ninjas about his arrival. They'd said their good-byes earlier this evening. With Lillian's hospitalization, all threats against Ava had been neutralized.

Now we just needed closure.

I sat up and rubbed my eyes. Grendel leapt onto the couch, climbed into my lap, and plopped down. Curling him upward, I kissed his head and relocated him.

He *rreowed* at me.

"I completely understand," I said to him. "But Morgan's here."

Hopping off the couch, he stalked off, his tail in the air.

A car door slammed and Em shouted out a hello to the visitor. Scout's happy barks were punctuated by Ava's laughter.

I stood up, took a step, and was pulled to a stop as Sean grabbed onto the hem of my shirt. I glanced back at him.

"You okay, Ms. Valentine?"

Managing a smile, I bent and kissed him. "I will be."

He nodded. "Time."

"Lots of it," I said, heading for the door.

I opened it in time to see Ava running toward Morgan, a big smile on her face. He dropped a bag he was carrying and scooped her up, swinging her around.

Holding her close, he asked, "How's my girl?"

Scout jumped around, clearly happy to see someone he recognized. "Scout? What're you doing here?"

I said, "Slight change of plans. Don't ask."

He patted the dog's head. "I'm sure he's glad to be with Ava."

"Inseparable."

Ava placed her small hands on Morgan's cheeks. "Boo-boo?"

His face didn't look too bad—the lacerations were healing fast.

"Yeah," he said. "Boo-boo."

She made kissing noises until he bent down and let her smooch his forehead.

When he looked up again, there was moisture glistening in his eyes.

"*Dubbles.*" She pointed and wiggled.

"Bubbles? You don't say." Clearing his throat, he set her down. "Show me."

Scout followed her as she trundled off toward Em, who leaned against a porch column with a sappy look in her eye.

Picking up the bag from the ground, Morgan trailed Ava, making sure she made it up the steps okay. There was nothing but sadness etched in his features.

"Morgan," I said, "this is Em Baumbach."

She shook his hand. "Nice to meet you. I'm Aiden's fiancée. I think you met him the other day."

"Hard to forget that day. I'm Morgan Creighton. Ava's sometimes babysitter."

I thought he was much more than that.

"She's really happy to see you," Em said as she blew bubbles for Ava to chase.

"Not as much as I am to see her." He watched her for a moment before turning his attention to me. Holding out the bag he carried, he said, "I forgot to take this with me to the vet office the other day and thought you could get it to Scout... Looks like mission accomplished."

"Half a bag of dog food?"

"Special dog food." He shrugged. "Kira left it with me for a reason, so I wanted to make sure Scout had it."

Ah. This hadn't been about Scout at all. It had been about Kira. I took the bag. "Thanks. Come on in."

Em wrinkled her nose. "Ava and I will stay out here."

"Thanks, Em."

"You got it," she said, blowing more bubbles.

I introduced Morgan to Sean, who'd set out coffee and cookies. He was sitting in my favorite rocking glider and offering moral support. Thoreau hopped onto his lap and licked his chin, then settled next to him for a pre-bedtime nap.

Morgan eyed Sean's head but didn't mention anything about the injuries. Me? I would have made some sort of joke about explosions or dodging shrapnel or starting a club for the walking wounded. But I was inappropriate that way.

"Have a seat," I said. "Cookies?"

"They look great, but I couldn't eat. My stomach is...in knots," he said, sitting on the sofa. "I've been glued to the TV this afternoon. What's with the house in Hanover? Everyone's talking in circles. I saw you and the lieutenant there in the crowd."

"It's complicated," I said, hoping Cutter was still keeping Dovie and Preston away from the news. I was pushing my luck where they were concerned.

"Does it involve Kira's case?" he asked softly.

"Yes." I sat next to him on the couch. "But I can't say much more because of the ongoing investigation."

Scout barked outside, and it was followed by Ava saying his name over and over as though she were having a conversation with the dog.

Morgan examined his hands, slowly curling them into fists. "Part of me doesn't want to do this. The reading. Because if we don't know where Kira is, there's still hope that she's alive."

I could understand that.

"But," he went on, "if I don't do it, there's always going to be this empty aching questioning hole, not only in my life but also Ava's, too."

It was a hard choice, I knew, but most of the people I worked with wanted closure. The day-in and day-out of living a life of uncertainty took a toll, mentally and physically.

Scout playfully barked again and Thoreau's head came up but apparently he decided he preferred naptime as he curled against Sean's leg.

Em said, "Ava, slow down. Slow!"

Ava laughed, and next to me, Morgan look visibly pained at the sound.

"The overriding factor comes down to this," he said. "If someone hurt Kira...I want that person to pay. Dearly."

I could easily hear Aiden's words ringing in my ears.

I'm glad Lillian Moore isn't here. Because I might have killed her.

"Let's do this." He held out his hands.

They were trembling.

"Think about the watch." Inhaling deeply, I picked up the scent of the salty sea air, a hint of chocolate from the cookies, and a touch of strawberries—Ava had been snacking on them earlier. I glanced at Sean, and the compassion in his eyes nearly did me in. With another fortifying breath, I met Morgan's terrified gaze, reached for his hands, and closed my eyes.

The vision took me across Hingham, up Route 3, northward where it joined with 93 and brought me back to the Blue Hills. On the other side of the park, far from where Kira's SUV had been found, I followed a dirt road and caught glimpses of water through the trees.

Deep in the woods, down a trail, to a remote shore of a large pond. The vision took me to the edge of the water, and I squeezed my eyes tighter at the image of woman floating lifelessly, her body snagged in a tangle of brush and branches.

I drew my hands back, pressing them to my chest, and opened my eyes to find everything blurry because they were filled with tears. Dizzy, the room spun.

Focusing, I looked at Sean and a stricken Morgan and shook my head. Forcing the words out, I whispered, "She's...dead. Water. Pond." My breath hitched, and I started shaking.

Outside, Scout was still barking, and Ava was laughing until she suddenly let out a cry. There was a pause, then she started sobbing full force.

Footsteps pounded on the porch as Em loudly said, "It's okay, it's okay. It's only a little scrape."

Ava quieted. Hiccupped.

"There, there," Em soothed. "It's okay."

"Boo-boo?" Ava asked, sniffling loudly.

"Yes, boo-boo," Em answered.

I heard the sound of noisy kisses, much like the kind Ava had given Morgan minutes ago. "There," Em said. "You're going to be just fine."

A tear slid down my cheek, and I hoped with every bit of my soul that what Em said was true.

23

"Do you want the good news or the better news or the best news; or the bad news or the worst news?" Sean asked me, his eyebrows raised. Ebbie sat on the counter, her tail curled around her paws.

It was Thursday morning, just two days since I'd read Morgan's energy.

Two days since a dive team pulled Kira Fitzpatrick's body from Houghton's Pond.

Two days since a little girl's life was forever changed.

"Is that a trick question?" I asked, crutching to the coffee pot. I stopped to tighten the sash of my robe, gave Ebbie some loving, and grabbed the mug Sean had set out. "I was only in the shower for ten minutes."

My damp hair tickled my neck as I filled my mug.

"Ten minutes was plenty," he said.

I wasn't sure I could deal with more bad news. It had been a hellish week.

Ava sat on the floor, zooming a toy car along the rug. She and Scout and Em and Aiden were moving out tomorrow. Em was at Aiden's house right now, painting one of Aiden's guest rooms a pretty purple and getting it ready for Ava. Aiden was at the funeral home, finishing up arrangements for Kira's services. After that, he was off to see his attorney, to make sure he had all legal rights to keep Ava because Trey Fisher had been making statements to the press about possibly filing to adopt her.

It made me hate him more than I already did, and that was saying something.

I figured it was nothing more than a ploy for public support on his part, but man-oh-man, what I wouldn't do to take him down a notch. Or twelve.

I pulled open the fridge door, looking to forage for breakfast. "Is the bad news that we're out of just about everything?" I needed to make a run to the grocery store. Not only were we almost out of food, but the pets were running low, too. I was even out of Grendel's favorite cheese slices. No one wanted to experience a hungry Grendel. It was like the term "hangry" had been invented with him in mind.

Currently, he was giving me the silent treatment from atop the fridge because I'd had no canned food for him this morning, only kibble. Which he'd gobbled up without complaint, I might add.

"No." Sean sipped his coffee, looking cool and calm as could be for someone delivering upsetting news.

Bracing myself with a cookie from the dwindling supply, I said, "Well, hit me with the bad news first."

"Aiden called. Cat Bennett's taken a turn for the worse."

Damn. She'd been fighting so hard. "That's not the worst news?"

He shook his head.

"Don't tell me Lillian broke out of the hospital."

"No," he said. "She's still in the ICU."

Aiden had verified through phone records that she'd been the one to hire Corey McDaniel and figured it had been part of a backup plan to frame him if framing Cat hadn't worked out. We wouldn't know for certain until she woke up fully, as she was still coming to after her accident. The doctors were slowly bringing her out of the coma, but it would be quite awhile before the police could formally question her. At some point down the line she'd be charged with murder.

I winced. "What's the worst then?"

"Dovie called."

I choked on a chocolate chip, finally coughing it up. "Oh no."

Sean thumped me on the back. "Oh yes. Someone or another she knows down there asked how you were faring after the explosion… They'd seen it on the news."

I was glad I'd been in the shower and missed the call. "How mad is she?"

"On a scale of one to ten?" he asked, talking louder to be heard over Ava's vociferous *vrooming*.

I nodded.

"Ninety-four and a half. I heard swear words I've only heard in the firehouse."

This wasn't good. "Does Preston know?"

"She was the one doing the swearing. Speakerphone. They're on their way back."

Dovie was going to make me pay for this for a long time, and I wasn't going to hear the end of it from Preston...ever. "I might need to hire the security ninjas again."

"Maybe they'll start giving you a discount. Ready for the good news?"

I swiped crumbs from the counter and dropped them in the sink. "Lay it on me."

"You got a package from Orlinda. Arrived a few minutes ago, special delivery."

I perked up. "Really?"

He grabbed the box off the sofa and handed it to me. I used a steak knife to slice through the packaging and laughed as I lifted the item out of the box.

"What in the—?" Sean asked.

With a flourish, I tied the satin cape around my shoulders. It was bright pink and embroidered with a giant cursive L. A note said: *Because I suspect you might have a bit of superhero in you after all.*

Sean peeked in the box. "I want a cape."

Smiling, I said, "We'll work on that. What's the better news?"

"Your orthopedic doctor returned your call. Said you could stop using the crutches and just use the boot."

I let out a whoop, and Ava mimicked me. I whooped again, drawing the noise out in a song as I hopped around the kitchen.

Ebbie leaped off the counter and ran for the bedroom, and Thoreau dashed to the front door and scratched to get out.

"Jeez," I said, watching them scatter. "Is my singing that bad?"

Sean wisely ignored the question and said, "The *best* news is that Aiden also mentioned that Nya Rodriguez was located. She's headed back. You'll have Dustin's blanket by tonight."

I grabbed his shirt and looked into his eyes. "Really?"

"Really." He wrapped his arms around me and pulled me close.

I listened to his heart thump for a moment, before planting a big kiss on his lips.

Ava copied the noise and Scout barked.

"I'm going to get dressed and head to the store. I'll take Ava with me to give you a little peace and quiet."

"What's that?" he asked, grinning.

"Don't get used to it. My mother's bringing the contractor here tomorrow to go over plans and timelines for the renovation."

"What did we get ourselves into?"

I pulled back to look into his eyes. "Having a change of heart?"

"No," he said softly, tugging me close again. "My heart is quite happy right here with you."

I barely noticed as Ava started making kissy noises again.

An hour and a half later, Ava and I were in the checkout lane at Shaw's, and she was crying because she wanted the woman's keychain in front of us. It had a dog on it, and Ava was fixated. She wanted it, wanted it now, and nothing else would do.

I tried shushing. That didn't work.

I tried giving her my own keys that had a heart-shaped key fob, but she didn't want anything to do with that.

I finally started handing her groceries to put on the conveyor belt, and she tossed them on there like she was pitching for the Sox. The grapes went flying. The can of whipped cream. Grendel's cheese. The box of Cheerios.

By the time I paid, she was crying again, and I couldn't wait to get back for naptime.

I was hoping Ava would sleep, too.

As I approached the car, I clicked the remote to unlock the door, and the car beeped.

Ava silenced, her watery blue eyes focused on the keychain. I clicked the unlock button again, and the car chirped. She smiled through her tears.

Aha. Music soothed the savage beast.

Grabbing the remote, she went to town, pressing the lock/unlock buttons as I lifted the trunk and started loading in groceries. She was happy as could be until she accidentally hit the alarm button, which set the car to honking obnoxiously.

Frightened, she stared at me, started crying again, and dropped the keys.

I quickly bent to grab them so I could silence the alarm. As I picked the keys up, I paused, staring at them in my palm. I had the nagging feeling my subconscious was trying to tell me something—it was the same sensation I'd had yesterday at Lillian Moore's house.

I tried to focus on capturing that elusive crumb, but Ava's crying was too distracting.

"*Shh, shh*," I consoled, unbuckling her from the grocery carriage. I picked her up and held her close, swaying until she calmed down.

Using the back of her hand, she rubbed wildly at her nose and eyes as I tugged the carriage to the corral. It took a couple of minutes to wrangle her into her car seat—how parents did this quickly I'd never know—and by the time I turned the keys in the ignition, I was completely exhausted.

Ava, too. Her eyelids drifted closed as soon as I backed out of the parking spot, and her face went slack with sleep.

Relief. I took a deep breath and headed for home.

However, I'd driven only a few feet when the car started to vibrate and wobble. Great. A flat tire. I pulled into a space at the back of the lot, grateful it wasn't crowded. Glancing in the rearview mirror, I smiled at the peacefully oblivious look on Ava's face.

I set the car in park and got out. Sure enough, the front driver's side tire was dead flat. I got back into the car while I tried to decide what to do. I had two options. Call for roadside assistance or haul the groceries out of the trunk, unearth the spare, and get to work.

Thanks to Raphael's many tutorials, I could have the tire changed in ten minutes, and it would probably take the auto club a half hour, at least. With that decided, I rolled down all the windows and shut off the car. Pulling the keys out, I studied my key fob, feeling that unreachable memory tease again.

My phone rang as I pushed the button to pop the trunk. I grabbed my cell before it woke Ava.

"Hello," I whispered.

"I'm heading into the lawyer's office and called to check on Ava," Aiden said. "Why're you whispering?"

"She's sleeping, and I prefer her to stay that way."

"Why?"

I lifted the trunk lid and took out a bag, setting it on the ground. "Grocery stores and tired toddlers don't mix."

He laughed. "I see. Where are you now?"

"Still at Shaw's. Well, in the parking lot." I grabbed the huge bag of dog kibble, and my keys slipped out of my pocket. "I have a flat tire. We'll be back on the road as soon as I get this tire changed."

"Need me to send help?" he asked.

Bending to pick up the keys, I stared at the key fob again, and suddenly the memory I'd been searching for popped into place. It was the video I'd watched of Cat Bennett coming out of the district attorney's office. She'd been walking with her husband, and he'd dropped the keys as he unlocked the car. A set of keys with a yellow smiley-face fob.

Just like the set of keys in Lillian's house yesterday.

"Lucy?" Aiden asked. "You still there?"

Which would have made perfect sense, especially seeing as how we believed Lillian had stolen the keys from Cat at the office Christmas party... Because Ross Bennett had told us that was what had happened. That they had been stolen.

Yet, he was holding those same exact keys in that news footage two weeks ago.

Two. Weeks. Ago. Not months.

"Lucy!" Aiden shouted.

"I'm here." I didn't know quite how, but Ross Bennett was involved in what happened to Dustin. What happened to Kira. Maybe he'd framed Lillian, but most likely they'd been working together. Together stealing kids and selling them. I'd bet my last Twinkie he was the mastermind of the whole thing.

"What happened?" he asked. "Are you okay?"

"We need to look into Ross Bennett, Aiden," I said, my voice high, my words coming out in a rush. "He's involved. He's—" I looked at my flat tire. Adrenaline set my heart to pounding. "Oh my God. He's coming here."

I casually walked around the car and noted that my other tires were close to flat as well. It took everything in me not to look around, to see if I was right. If I did, Ross would know I was onto him. I quickly dug through my trunk, looking for some sort of weapon. Right now I had the element of surprise on my side.

"I don't understand, Lucy," Aiden said.

"It's exactly like Danny Beckley theorized about Kira's nearly-flat tire. Ross let the air out of my tire so I couldn't get away." And he had to be desperate to do it in the middle of the day. Why would he take such a risk? Then it hit me, and it hit me hard. Barely breathing, I said, "He's coming for Ava."

There was a moment of silence on the line before Aiden's voice came through, loud, clear, and in command. "Lucy, sweet Jesus. Get Ava and go back in the store!"

"I don't think there's time." The car seat alone would take me three minutes...

I heard him talking to someone else, telling them to get 911 on the line. "Then get in the car. Lock the doors. Can you drive on the flat?"

"I could, but I don't think I'd get far." Especially not with my other tires low on air as well. I had to think fast. How would Ross approach this? He'd probably offer to help me out, right? Offer to assist with the tire? Would he have a gun? A knife? How was I going to disarm him?

All I knew was that he wanted Ava. And I could not let that happen.

I knew what I had to do. My hands shook as I quickly arranged a few items in the trunk, getting them ready, and left the lid open. Quickly, I got back into the car and started it, turning on the air conditioning.

"I called for help, and I'm on my way," Aiden said. "Keep talking to me. Don't hang u—"

I hung up on him, dialed 911, told the dispatcher where I was, that I was being attacked, and to send police and EMTs and firefighters and anyone who could help. Leaving my phone on, I set it in the cup holder.

Taking a deep breath, I looked back at Ava, and felt a bolstering of courage. I had to do this. For her. I opened my door, hit the lock button, and slammed it behind me.

Ava was locked in.

My hands were sweating as I limped back to the trunk. I just had to stall. The police would be here soon. Three minutes. Maybe less. The station wasn't that far.

I went about the business of pretending to change my flat. It took only a minute before a small black car pulled up in an adjacent spot. Ross had arrived.

My throat was dry, and I could barely hear my own thoughts because of the pounding of my heartbeat.

The window powered down. "Ms. Valentine?" Ross said. "I thought that was you. Small world."

I forced a smile. "Ross? It is a small world. How're you doing? How's Cat?"

I listened for the sounds of sirens, pleaded silently to hear them. But I only heard regular traffic noise.

Dark circles colored the skin under his eyes. He shook his head. "It's not looking good."

"I'm so sorry." *You lying, psychopathic monster.* My mind spun, trying to figure out what had happened to his wife. My best guess was that Cat had called him on Thursday morning after Kira confronted her. Probably because she was on to the truth. That he had to be involved because she'd been out of town when Dustin was taken… It made my stomach ache, thinking about how he'd left his wife in that basement to die.

"You have a flat?" he asked, even though he was parked on the passenger side of my car and couldn't possibly see the tire.

"Yeah, I called my auto club, but it's going to be half an hour before they can get here, and well, I have a little one in the car and don't want to wait that long. Thought I'd tackle it myself."

"Need help?"

"You don't have to do that. I'm sure you need to get back to the hospital."

"I don't mind," he said, getting out of his car.

I noticed he left it running. It felt as though my heart was going to pound straight out of my chest. Where were the damn sirens?

"Did you say you had a little one?" he asked, rolling up his sleeves as he walked over. He cupped his hands and looked into the backseat. "She's cute." He tried the door. "It's locked?"

"Oh, it's set so that only the driver's door unlocks when I put the car in park," I explained. "You can never be too safe with carjackers and stuff. But the spare tire is back here."

I played dumb pretty well, I thought.

He came over to me, stood close. His eyes looked so kind behind his glasses. If I hadn't known better, I'd truly believe he was a Good Samaritan.

I knew better.

When I reached into the trunk as though I was going after the spare, I suddenly felt a sharp jab in my stomach. I looked over. He held a gun under my ribcage.

"You're going to get the girl and get in my car."

My gaze flew to his. "What's going on?"

His eyes hardened into snake-like slits. "For a psychic, you're kind of lame."

Now he was taking things too far. I feigned confusion. "Ross, I don't underst—"

"Shut up. Get the girl and get in the car." He jerked my arm.

In a flash, I brought my hand up and sprayed whipped cream into his face. Surprised, he let out a cry, frantically wiping his eyes. I took advantage of his distress and grabbed the tire iron. I hit his arm that held the gun as hard as I could, wincing as I heard bone crack.

He let out a howl of pain, dropped the gun and grabbed his wrist. I kicked the gun under the car just as I heard a siren in the distance. His head jerked up at the plaintive wail, and he spun around to jump back into his car. I stuck my boot out and tripped him. He went sprawling, hitting his head on his bumper.

Moaning, he writhed on the ground.

The sound of sirens grew louder and louder as I rushed over to his car, reached in, and grabbed the keys. I chucked them as far as I could.

Feet apart, I held the tire iron out in front of me like a sword, ready to gut him if I had to. That was the way I was standing when the first police car showed up. And the second, third, and fourth.

As officers jumped out of their cruisers, guns drawn, I glanced into my backseat.

Ava was still sound asleep.

24

Almost two weeks later, life was almost back to normal as I sat on a bench overlooking a crowded Connecticut beach.

Well, as normal as my life could be. After all, I was due back at my place this evening for a groundbreaking celebration, to kick off the renovations of my cottage, which were set to begin bright and ungodly early on Monday morning.

Even though I didn't think the remodel party worthy, Dovie insisted, and I was in no position to tell her no after deceiving her. Or so she told me repeatedly—every chance she got.

Normal would have to wait, too, until the last few loose ends were wrapped up in Kira's case. Then I could put it behind me for good. Examine my scars, mental and physical, and tuck it away as another case solved. Another bad guy brought to justice.

It was a hot Saturday afternoon, the sun was shining, the ocean sparkling. Wind sent my hair into my face, and I kept pushing it back as I watched a family of three build a sandcastle. Today was a day to tackle one of those loose ends.

Patty Keefe gripped my hand tightly, and I didn't even mind. I'd signed her out of the hospice for the trip down here, a three-hour drive, round trip.

Worth every second to bring a little closure.

She sat next to me on the bench, a rolling oxygen tank next to her. "He looks...so happy," she said, watching her grandson shovel sand into a neon-green bucket.

"He does." Happy and healthy.

A floppy hat shaded his face, and his fish-printed bathing shorts were sagging, even though he'd put on some weight. He didn't look scrawny and underfed anymore. A woman kept applying sunscreen to his pale skin, and he wiggled, trying to get back to playing.

The woman was Cecelia Wright. Her husband Neil was nearby, busy hauling buckets of water from the ocean. Cecelia tied the little boy's shorts more tightly, and he ran off, trotting alongside his father, his toothy smile flashing as he laughed.

Almost six months ago, Cecelia, a graphic designer, and Neil, a dentist, adopted a bright-eyed, light-haired little boy through a Boston baby broker, who charged them a small fortune. A price they were more than willing to pay after years of failed infertility treatments.

That broker had been Ross Bennett, using an assumed name.

The Wrights had no idea their little boy, Brandon, was Dustin McDaniel, a stolen child. I wouldn't say they were entirely guilt-free as they didn't seem to do much digging into Ross's background, but they were too overjoyed at the possibility of having a family to question where the child had truly come from.

Desperation often wore blinders.

Because I could only see images through Dustin's eyes, it had taken me nearly a week of scent readings on the baby blanket Patty had crocheted to locate the town where he was living. Another three days of investigating his new family. A day to drive down here and scope out the situation. And one day to get enough courage up to broach Patty with my suggestion.

Now here we were, sitting on a bench, watching Neil scoop up Dustin and buzz him around like an airplane. Dustin screamed with happiness.

Patty squeezed my hand. Tears welled in her eyes.

I blinked and looked away, watching the white-capped surf slam against the shore. The water was dotted with swimmers.

My phone rang, and I checked the readout. Aiden.

To Patty, I said, "I'll be right back."

She patted my hand. "Take your time. I'm happy right here."

I stood and answered the call, limping a little farther down the sandy boardwalk, searching for privacy.

"Where are you?" Aiden asked.

"The beach," I said, glad I didn't have to lie. "How'd it go?"

"Strange. Shocking."

I glanced at Dustin, who was back to shoveling sand. He crouched, focused on the task at hand, oblivious to all around him. I looked at Patty, whose skin was so thin it was nearly translucent. Her heart was in her eyes as she watched his every move.

I'd found Dustin only because of the blanket that Patty had crocheted. After the showdown with me in the Shaw's parking lot, and being arrested on a multitude of charges ranging from attempted kidnapping to murder, Ross Bennett hired a fancy lawyer and clammed up. Way up. He absolutely refused to talk. Not about Kira's murder. And certainly not about the missing children.

However, Lillian Moore had finally come out of her coma and was more than willing to spill her guts. Her attorney cut a deal with the district attorney's office in exchange for her testimony.

Her interview was today. I wasn't invited—it was a meeting reserved for detectives and attorneys only.

Sea oats swayed in the stiff breeze. "How so?"

"First shocker was that she and Ross were a couple. Started seeing each other on the sly after meeting at the CFC office Christmas party, a year and a half ago."

I recalled the photo on the mantel at the Bennetts' house. I wondered if Ross smirked at it every time he walked by.

"He reeled her in hook, line, and sinker with his big plans to save the world," Aiden explained. "Threw around a lot of sociology terminology as to why the majority of the kids in the system would continue the cycle and never make anything of themselves."

"That's not true."

"We know that, but Lillian was smitten and believed everything that came out of his mouth, including that he planned to eventually leave Cat. When he first brought up the idea of rescuing," he emphasized the word, "at-risk children to make sure they went to good homes, she readily agreed. She wanted to save the kids, and if they made a few dollars on the deal, all the better. By the way, they have a secret account set up that has several hundred thousand dollars in it."

I thought of all the babies that represented and my stomach turned.

Aiden said, "Between him wheedling information from Cat about her case files, and Lillian's access to databases and office gossip…it was a match ripe for baby brokering. I think Ross had this plan in place for years, Lucy. He just needed a willing accomplice."

"Did they set out to frame Cat?" They'd used her car in the kidnappings, after all. If it had been identified sooner…

"I don't think so. She was an easy scapegoat if they happened to get caught. Oh, and the first couple of kids they bought. Paid willing parents a few thousand dollars. Then they decided it would be easy enough to take some of the kids..."

It was all so twisted. A couple brushed past me, carrying a cooler, towels, and chairs. I turned and walked back toward Patty and threw another glance at Dustin. "Was Ross really trying to save the kids?"

"No." There was a pause before he added, "It was money all along, something Lillian discovered only when he set his sights on kidnapping Ava. Lillian couldn't understand why Ross wanted Ava, because Kira was a more-than-competent parent, but she went along with it even though it seemed dangerous, because Kira was a public persona. But he claimed that with the sale of Ava, he'd have enough money to leave Cat. The going rate for blond-haired, blue-eyed babies, by the way, is one hundred thousand dollars."

I knew. It was how much the Wrights paid for Dustin.

"Ross proclaimed with the sale of Ava, he could leave academia behind and he and Lillian could move somewhere tropical."

"Sick," I said.

"Yes. Lillian went along with it because she loved him, but doubts were setting in, especially when he had her bring Corey McDaniel into the fold to do some of the dirty work and take some blame if caught."

Corey McDaniel, who was now back in jail for parole violations, also had new charges pending. Even with the plea deal Aiden helped him get, it would be another five or ten years before he'd be released from jail. I looked at Dustin, running circles as Neil dug a moat, and my throat tightened.

I coughed. "How'd Cat end up in her basement?"

"Ross brought her over. After her chat with Kira at the grocery store, Cat figured out Ross was somehow involved with Dustin's kidnapping and threatened to go to the police. He knocked her out, put her in the trunk, drove her to Hanover and left her in Lillian's cellar."

"Without her insulin."

"He wanted her death to appear natural. When she died, he planned to relocate her body to a highway underpass so it would be found. Because she had been depressed he counted on the cause of death being believed accidental."

"Bastard."

"That's putting it mildly."

I swatted a fly intent on inspecting every pore of my face. "Yet, he let me do scent readings. Why?"

"He figured you wouldn't be able to see much through Cat's eyes. Nothing identifiable as to her location. No harm, no foul, and it made it look like he was cooperating."

I thought about what a good actor he was—something I needed to keep in mind for future cases.

"But bringing Cat to Lillian's freaked Lillian out. The more she thought about it the more concerned she grew. She drove to his house to confront him. He kept trying to reassure her it was the only way. That he had it all under control and that soon they would be well on their way to a new life. First he needed Ava...and to get rid of Kira. It's when she drew the line."

"She called Kira to warn her."

"Exactly. She claims she didn't want anyone else harmed. So when Ross went to the police station to file a missing persons report, she called Kira and told her to get herself and Ava to safety—and to ditch her car as soon as possible, because it had a tracker on it."

I kicked a pebble, sending it skittering down the boardwalk. I didn't know what to think of this information. That she had tried to save Kira, yet she had a dying Cat locked in her basement.

"According to Lillian," Aiden went on, "Kira did ditch the tracker on her car."

Obviously neither Lillian nor Kira had known about the one in Ava's car seat. Smart criminals like Ross Bennett were the scariest kind. Always seeming to be one step ahead.

"However," Aiden said, "Kira didn't take Lillian's advice in its entirety."

"What's that mean?" I asked.

"Lillian said that after dropping Ava off with me, Kira drove straight to the Bennetts' house."

A jet roared overhead, and I waited for it to go by before I said, "Why in the hell would she do that?"

"Lillian is sketchy on these details, because she'd already left, but Ross told her enough to put it together. An enraged Kira had shown up, knocked on the door, and demanded to speak with Cat or she was going to call the police.... Kira hadn't quite figured out that Cat wasn't in on the scheme. Ross was puzzled by her behavior, because," Aiden explained, "he didn't know she'd gotten a call that Caller ID identified as coming from his house, but then he took advantage of the situation." Aiden paused. "Ross let Lillian know the next morning that Kira would no longer be a problem. He'd dumped the body and the car and was hell-bent on getting Ava and getting out of town as soon as possible."

I took a moment to send cosmic thanks to Jeremy Cross and his security team. Without them, I wasn't sure if we would have been able to keep Ava safe.

"Why would Kira go there? And why alone if she'd been warned?" It was so bittersweet that Lillian's plan to save Kira had backfired terribly, luring her to her death.

"I don't know, Lucy." I heard the rattle of a Tic Tac box. "I can only imagine that she was still chasing the story. Maybe she figured she could get a confession out of Cat. I don't think she had any idea the level of danger she was in."

Over the next few minutes, Aiden filled me in on other particulars. Like when Ross went looking for the flash drive at Kira's and couldn't find it. He rigged the explosives so no one would. He'd hacked Kira's laptop and found her passcodes, including the PIN of her debit card. He wanted the police to think Kira was alive and using her bank accounts. It seemed he'd thought of just about everything.

Except, perhaps, Lillian's betrayal. It wasn't until he learned about Lillian's phone call when told about the phone records that he put it together. That was the night he tried to kill her. She'd been at his place when he attacked her. She somehow managed to escape him, but she'd been woozy, and had crashed her car trying to get home.

The accident had probably saved her life. Otherwise he would have tracked her down to finish the job.

"There's another thing, too," he said, sounding hesitant.

"What?" I leaned against a fence post, feeling the need to brace myself. I watched a small sailboat skim across crests.

"Lillian claims..." He broke off.

"Just spit it out, Aiden."

Finally, he said, "Ross wasn't only after Ava in that Shaw's parking lot. He planned to get rid of you, too. He didn't want you to be able to find Dustin or any of the other kids and figure out what he'd done. You spooked him when you proved your abilities."

I tucked a strand of hair behind my ear. It wasn't the first time someone had wanted to kill me, and it most likely wouldn't be the last.

"Lucy?" Aiden asked. "You okay?"

"Yeah. Just wishing I'd hit him a few more times with that tire iron."

I heard the Tic Tac box again as he said, "Me, too."

"What happens now?" I asked.

"Lillian will stay in the hospital until she's well enough to be locked up. With her plea deal she'll serve five years before being eligible for parole."

Hesitantly, I asked, "Does she know where the kids are?"

"No. Ross handled finding families for the kids. Other than pretending to be the mother giving the kids up for adoption, she didn't know anything about the couples."

I let out the breath I'd been holding.

"We'll start tracing the money," he continued, "and hope it leads back to the adoptive families, but Ross is clever and it's not going to be easy. And you'll keep working on trying to find the kids. It's a shame you couldn't get a reading from Dustin's blanket."

"It is." The heat of a guilty flush crept up my neck, and I was glad he couldn't see me.

The truth was that I'd found a couple of the kids already. They, like Dustin, had been placed with decent, loving families, who just happened to be wealthy and unable to have kids of their own.

It made me think that Ross Bennett might possess the tiniest bit of human decency. He'd done a good job of screening potential parents before taking their money.

It left me with a big moral dilemma. I could leave well enough alone and let the kids stay where they were...or return them to the lives they led before. If I did the latter, most would go straight back into the system, into foster care, especially the ones Ross had bought from parents willing to sell their children... And then there was Dustin.

His mother was dead.

His grandmother was dying.

His father was in prison.

There were no other relatives to take him in.

Dustin would become a ward of the state... Sure, he'd probably be adopted again, but when? How long would it take? How traumatized would he be after being pulled from a family he clearly loved after living with them for six months?

Tears stung my eyes, and I blinked them away.

If I told Aiden I'd found the kids, he'd be bound by law to do the right thing, to return them to the state.

I couldn't do that to this little boy. Even though it was legally wrong, I fully believed it was the morally right decision.

"I've got to go," Aiden said. "I'll see you tonight?"

"Definitely. Dovie wouldn't have it any other way."

He laughed and hung up.

"Something wrong?" Patty asked as I sat down next to her again. "You looked mighty concerned at the end of that conversation."

"Just wrestling with right and wrong," I said honestly.

She patted my hand. "You're speaking of Dustin's situation?"

"Yes," I said, not elaborating about the other children. I'd tackle those cases one at a time. Let my moral compass guide me.

Patty and Sean were the only people who knew I'd found Dustin. I'd gone to her with my findings and recommendation to keep Dustin with his adoptive family—and she agreed on one condition. She wanted to see him again and give him his blanket. We'd concocted a lame plan to get him the afghan, deciding to approach the family and randomly gift the blanket to the little boy…

"Look at him," she said, her voice catching.

He'd fallen asleep on Cecelia, their bodies shaded by a large umbrella. The wind ruffled his blond hair, and his full cheeks were flushed pink. Cecelia rubbed his back, soothing him even in sleep.

"He's loved." A tear slipped from Patty's eye. "He's had that taken away from him once. It would be a travesty to allow it to happen again."

My heart felt like it was breaking with the weight of my decision, but I knew she was right.

"Come on," Patty said, standing up and clutching the handle of her oxygen tank. "We should go. I'm tired, and it's a long drive. I've seen enough here to last me…forever." Shuffling, she headed for my car.

"What about the blanket?" I asked. It was draped over her arm.

She lifted her chin. "I've decided to keep it. So I'll always have a piece of him with *me*."

I reached out and touched her arm. "You're sure?"

"Very."

Letting out a breath, I looked back at the little boy one last time. He stirred in his sleep, and his arms flopped to his sides. He was completely relaxed. At peace. Safe.

It was how all children should feel.

The weight on my chest lifted.

I linked arms with Patty and helped her to the car. I'd just turned the key in the ignition when my phone rang.

It was Sean.

When I answered, he said, "You're not going to believe what I found, Ms. Valentine."

"What?" I asked, intrigued by the smug tone.

"Kira's flash drive."

25

Later that night, long after the ceremonial shovel of dirt had been pitched, the party was still going strong. My garden looked fantastic. Tents housed tables of food (much too much), and twinkle lights stretched from one outdoor light to another, giving off a whimsical vibe. A portable dance floor had been set up, the scent of flowers and music filled the air. Dovie and Mac were doing the Hustle.

There might be evil people in the world, but here tonight there were only good ones gathered. This...was joy.

A sky full of glittering stars and a full moon hanging low over the ocean only added to the fanciful ambiance as I carried a slice of cheesecake up the porch steps and sat in the swing, setting it swaying.

Preston stuck her foot out, dragging it against the floorboards. The swing stopped abruptly, nearly pitching me off it. "No swinging. I've been getting motion sick lately."

"Then a swing might not be the best place to sit."

She pursed her lips. "No one asked you."

I held up the plate. "I brought you cheesecake."

The look in her eye softened, but she shook her head. "No thanks."

"Are you sure? It's the last piece, and it has the most amazing strawberry drizzle…"

She grabbed the plate. "This doesn't mean I forgive you."

"You know I couldn't tell you. I couldn't risk your health. The baby's."

She forked the cake and stuffed a bite into her mouth. "Doesn't make me feel any less betrayed. Half the papers in town have already taken this story and run with it. Even if I did an article now, it certainly wouldn't be front page news."

I bit back a comment about how "half the papers" in town meant two. "I know."

Looking back on it all, I was extremely grateful Preston hadn't been part of this case. She was a damn good writer who probed her stories deeply. She might have figured out that I was keeping a big secret.

"What about those missing kids?" she asked. "There's still a story there."

My father had taken charge of the music for the night, which promised interesting selections. When "At Last" started playing, I had to smile as my father pulled my mother into a tight embrace. It appeared their doomed relationship had been given a reprieve.

I shrugged and tried to look innocent. "I'm working on it, but I don't think it's healthy for you to do a piece on missing kids. Do you?"

Preston glanced at Aiden, who danced closely with Em, whispering in her ear. She floated around the floor, a smile plastered to her face. "Do you think Aiden would let me do a story on him and Ava?"

"No."

She shoved another bite of cheesecake into her mouth.

Ava was sound asleep in Raphael's arms, and he looked quite pleased to have her there. Maggie was being twirled around the dance floor by Cutter.

"What about Jeremy Cross? Think Dr. Doolittle will throw me a bone?"

"No."

Across the lawn, a competitive game of horseshoes was being played. Jeremy versus Marisol. Both looked like they were playing to the death. I wasn't ready to give up on them.

Orlinda was deep in conversation with Suz Ruggieri, Valentine Inc.'s right-hand woman, and her husband, Teddy, was playing volleyball with Sean's brother Sam and his family.

Nearby, Sean was chucking a rubber chicken for Mac's dog Rufus, Scout, and Thoreau. So far, Thoreau had almost been trampled five times. Sean, eight.

"This sucks," Preston said. "It's the story of the year, and I have nothing. Nada. Zippo. It's your fault. I had been thinking about naming the baby after you and everything. But now? No way."

"The baby is a boy."

She took another bite. "So?"

"What were you going for? Lucifer?"

A smile tugged the corner of her mouth. "Maybe. And no fair making me smile. You owe me, Lucy Valentine. Big time."

"How big?" I asked.

"Huge. A cover story for the *Mad Blotter*. So keep working on that sniffing thing you do, and see something I can work with."

"Huge, you say."

"Enormous."

"I see."

She shifted to look at me and narrowed her eyes. "What?"

"What?" I echoed.

Her eyes widened. "What have you got? You've got something!"

"Maybe."

She jiggled my arm. "Come on."

"Promise not to name the baby Lucifer."

Crossing her heart, she said, "I promise."

I pulled a flash drive out of my pocket and held it up. "It's a copy of Kira's. I think you can do justice to the information on it." The original had already been handed over to Aiden. Sean had found it while feeding the dogs. It had been in the bag of dog food Morgan Creighton had brought over.

The flash drive I held out to Preston held only the information on the other story Kira had been investigating. A top-secret exposé.

About a certain former hockey player who was suspected of running a banned-substance ring. Kira's notes named names. Big names. Not just in hockey, but across all New England sports.

Kira had only been dating Trey to get an inside peek at his world, to get a story.

It made me feel so much better to know that they'd been using each other.

"What is it?" Preston asked, setting her empty plate on the porch railing and grabbing the flash drive.

"You'll see," I said coyly.

"I have to find a computer..." She glanced around.

"Not tonight," I said. "Tonight is for celebrating."

"Celebrating a big scoop!"

"Preston..."

"Fine," she grumped.

I stood up. "I'm going to get a piece of cheesecake."

Her pale brows dipped. "I thought you said that was the last piece."

"I fibbed." I motioned toward the house and smiled. "My laptop's on my bed."

She popped off the seat, looking healthier than I'd seen her in a long while. I moseyed to the dessert table, and was quickly cornered by my mother.

"Jeremy and Marisol, eh?" she bumped me with her elbow. "I'd say there was still hope."

I set a piece of cheesecake on a plate, and glanced over at the horseshoe pit. Marisol was up in Jeremy's face, arguing while pointing downward—some sort of horseshoe dispute. Her short black bob swung about her face as she gestured. He stood stock still, his arms folded, and kept shaking his head. The more he shook, the more animated she became. If he wasn't careful, she might toss him over the cliff. "Made for each other." I elbowed her. "You and Dad?"

She bit into a cream puff and tried to look uninterested. "He's not half bad."

It was the other half of him I worried about, but that was a concern for another day.

"I've been thinking, LucyD," Mum said, tucking a strand of hair behind my ear.

"My cottage doesn't need a solarium."

She laughed, and the sound filled me with happiness. "No, not that, but since you mentioned it…"

I smiled. "No."

Finishing off the cream puff, she said, "I've been thinking about that young man."

"Which one?"

"The one who was here the other day." She waved her hands—she was a hand talker. "You know, the one whose mother lost her job..."

"Jarvis."

"Right. Jarvis."

"What about him?" I asked.

"If it's not too meddlesome, I'd like to help his mother find a job. I have friends who are always hiring. Surely, we can find something to help them out."

"I don't think it's meddlesome at all, but she already found a job."

"Wonderful! Where?"

"At the CFC office."

Mum tipped her head. "Oh?"

I confessed to asking Elliman to pull some strings now that he was back on the job. Sue me.

"You get your meddling skills from me," she said. "You big softie."

"Yeah, yeah."

"Now, about this solarium," she said. "We could easily add it to the east side of the—"

"No."

Laughing, she walked off, accepting Dad's invitation for another dance.

I was about to join Sean and the dogs when I was shanghaied by Dovie.

"I've only mostly forgiven you," she said, her color high from dancing. Her green eyes were full of life, and her long snow-white hair cascaded down her back in beautiful waves. "After all, you were only trying to protect Preston…"

She was going somewhere with this. I needed to head her off at the pass. "Did you hear how I fought off that crazed killer in the Shaw's parking lot with only a can of whipped cream?"

Thin slivers of silvery eyebrows rose. "You're conveniently forgetting the tire iron, LucyD."

"Post-traumatic stress."

"Be that as it may," she said, "I feel as though there's only one way of making this up to me."

I sighed. I should have seen this coming. "Don't you have enough babies in your life? You have Lucifer and Ava…"

"Lucifer?"

"Preston and Cutter's son."

She looked flustered for a second, then snapped out of it. "Don't try to distract me. Besides, I'll barely see Ava now that Em is moving in with Aiden."

They'd made the announcement earlier, and also moved up the timeline of their wedding. She was going to take a semester off until everything settled down a bit. She and Aiden both wanted to forge a new kind of normal for Ava. It was strange how life worked out sometimes. A year ago Em had been working as a doctor and engaged to another man…

"Still, that's two whole babies," I said.

She cupped my chin and smiled sappily. "But they're not *your* babies, Lucy."

I looked at Sean, caught his eye. His head wound had healed nicely, and his hair had grown in enough to cover the scar. He was no longer a mess, but he was still gorgeous. And mine. "Maybe. Someday."

"Soon," she pressed. "You know what they say. New house, new baby."

"I don't think that counts for renovations."

"I think it does," she said stubbornly.

Desperate for rescue I looked around and found Sean still watching me. I mouthed, "Help me."

With a smile on his face, he quickly strode over and grabbed my hand. He whirled me away from Dovie and onto the dance floor.

Dovie yelled, "We'll revisit this conversation, LucyD!"

Sean said, "Do I want to know?"

"Babies."

"Ah. I should have known that."

"Yes. Dovie's nothing if not consistent."

"Strangely enough, it doesn't bother me anymore," he said.

"Dovie?"

Laughing, he said, "The thought of babies."

"Me, either." Heaven help us if Dovie found out.

Stars twinkled as Sean pulled me close. Holding me tightly, he led me around the dance floor. I'd skipped the boot altogether tonight and opted for flats but still felt clumsy and awkward as Frankie Valli's "Can't Take My Eyes Off Of You" came on.

I immediately glanced over at my father, the deejay. He winked at me, showing a rare glimpse of his tender side. He knew I loved this song. In fact, I often thought if Sean and I got married that it should be played for our first dance.

If. If we got married...

No, no, no. No *if.*

When.

I was going to start thinking positively.

As Frankie sang about love finally arriving at long last, I wanted to sing along at the top of my lungs but didn't want to scare anyone.

"How're you doing, Ms. Valentine?" Sean asked, the back of his hand sliding across my cheek.

"I'm...good." I looked into his eyes. Smiled. "Really good."

"I am, too."

After lifting me off the ground to spin me around, he dipped me low and kissed me. Em let out a wolf whistle, and everyone clapped.

The whistle distracted the big dogs, allowing Thoreau to snatch the rubber chicken and take off. Rufus and Scout gave chase—straight under the food table, knocking it over.

Inside the house, Preston yelled, "Hot damn!"

Marisol cursed Jeremy a blue streak.

Even as Mum rushed to clean up the dogs' mess, she was saying something about a solarium to Dovie.

I glanced around, suddenly filled with a happiness so powerful it almost brought me to tears. This might be a nuthouse, but it was *my* nuthouse, and I loved every single looney tune in it.

OTHER BOOKS BY HEATHER WEBBER

The Lucy Valentine Novels
Truly, Madly
Deeply, Desperately
Absolutely, Positively
Perfectly Matched
Undeniably Yours

The Nina Quinn Mystery Series
A Hoe Lot of Trouble
Trouble in Spades
Digging up Trouble
Trouble in Bloom
Weeding out Trouble
Trouble Under the Tree
The Root of all Trouble

WRITING AS HEATHER BLAKE

The Wishcraft Mystery Series
It Takes a Witch
A Witch Before Dying
The Good, the Bad, and the Witchy
The Goodbye Witch

The Magic Potion Series
A Potion to Die For

WEBSITES
www.heatherwebber.com
www.heatherblakebooks.com

FACEBOOK
www.facebook.com/heatherwebberbooks
www.facebook.com/heatherblakebooks

TWITTER
@booksbyheather

Made in the USA
Coppell, TX
20 October 2024

38960292R00204